A REVIVED
MODERN
CLASSIC

THE RAIN CAME LAST

ALSO BY NICCOLÒ TUCCI

In English

Before My Time (1962)
Unfinished Funeral (1964)
The Sun and the Moon (1977)

In Italian

Il Segreto (Viareggio Prize, 1956)
Gli Atlantici (Bagutta Prize, 1968)
Confessioni Involontarie (1975)

NICCOLÒ TUCCI

THE RAIN CAME LAST & OTHER STORIES

WITH AN INTRODUCTION BY MARY MCCARTHY

A NEW DIRECTIONS BOOK

Acknowledgments:
The following eight stories originally appeared in *The New Yorker:* "The Evolution of Knowledge," "The Assignment" (in this collection, "The News"), "Military Intelligence," "History Comes C.O.D.," "The Beautiful Blue Horse," "Terror and Grief," "The Underground Settlers," and "Death of the Professor." "The Rain Came Last," "The Schemers," and "The Siege" first appeared in *Harper's Magazine;* "Hey!" in *Twice a Year;* "This Particular Rich Lady" and "Those Long Shadows" in *Botteghe Oscure.*

Manufactured in the United States of America
New Directions Books are printed on acid-free paper.
First published clothbound and as New Directions Paperbook 688 in 1990 as part of the Revived Modern Classics series
Published simultaneously in Canada by Penguin Books Canada Limited

Library of Congress Cataloging-in-Publication Data

Tucci, Niccolò, 1908–
The rain came last & other stories / Niccolò Tucci ; with an introduction by Mary McCarthy.
p. cm. – (A Revived modern classic)
ISBN 0-8112-1124-x (alk. paper) : ISBN 0-8112-1125-8 (pbk. : alk. paper)
I. Title. II. Title: Rain came last and other stories. III. Series.
PS3570.U23R3 1990
813'.54–dc20 89-13344
CIP

New Directions Books are published for James Laughlin
by New Directions Publishing Corporation,
80 Eighth Avenue, New York 10011

Contents

Introduction

I first met Tucci as a writer in 1957—thirteen years after I had got to know him as a man. It was in Florence, on the Via Romana, and it happened this way.

Greti Ducci, a pretty Croat girl married to a man from Elba, was giving me Italian lessons. She came every afternoon to the sweltering apartment I was renting, with my husband, from Count Guglielmo Alberti (descendant of L. B. Alberti) near the Boboli Gardens, opposite the Annalena Pensione. I could already read Italian with the help of a dictionary, and Greti's idea was to teach me correct pronunciation by having me read aloud with her. For the second lesson, having explained the principle, she brought along the book that was going to be my manual. The author, said Greti, was the only current author who wrote a spoken Italian: all the others, not omitting Moravia, wrote a dead, literary language. From her shopping bag, she produced Niccolò Tucci! *Il Segreto,* a collection of stories that had won the Viareggio Prize the summer before. "But I know him!" "You *know* Niccolò Tucci?" "Yes! In New York. He's a friend." But I hadn't heard of his winning the Viareggio Prize.

Greti never got over the fact that her pupil knew the wondrous talent she had discovered—the only master in Italy of living Italian speech. Perhaps, being a foreigner herself, she had brought a fresh ear to Italian diction and heard things in a written text that born Italians missed. She had never met Tucci, though she was conscious of him as a Florentine bred, if not born, married to a Florentine, the beautiful Laura Rusconi. So it came about that I cut my teeth on "Il Segreto," the first story in that book, being carefully rehearsed by my teacher in the *raddoppiamento*—the distinct doubling of consonants in pronunciation—that is characteristic of well-spoken Italian. The stories we read aloud to each other had a strong Tuscan flavor. They were set, most of them, in the Pistoiese hills; his father, the *medico condotto* (a sort of district doctor), made his rounds in a horse-drawn buggy, always a lonely figure—he was a southerner, from Apulia—standing out on the country roads, an image of separateness like the single cypress tree of the first story. When Greti left me at the end of the summer, she took her precious book; so far as I know, she never met its author.

Meanwhile Tucci in New York was writing and publishing in English some of the stories collected in the present volume. Here, too, as the reader will see, the *medico condotto* appears though the English narratives, while evoking him, are not at all the same. Tucci has a horror of repeating himself, even though he is bound by the inescapable facts of his biography to tell the same story over and over. He is essentially, in my view, a master autobiographer, but he has never translated his Italian recollections into English or vice versa despite his perfect ease in both languages. If any text of his own falls by an evil chance into his hands before publication, he at once begins to rewrite it. This happened, I know, with *The New Yorker:* I heard from his editor there of a manuscript on which some minor changes were suggested and which was returned to the author for that purpose—a fatal mistake, for the new, "improved" manuscript bore no resemblance to the one they had wanted to buy, now rewritten beyond recovery. A practical joke, one might have thought.

In any case, I had met the English-writing Tucci at some point in 1944, probably at Dwight Macdonald's. Dwight was bringing out *politics,* an anarchist-leaning magazine, and Nika, who classed himself as an anarchist, was already writing for it. Not fiction but political commentary, very witty and unexpected. My most distinct memory is of meeting him in the reading-room of the New York Public Library and his showing me with some excitement the magazine *Cahiers du Sud* with an article in it on the *Iliad* by

Simone Weil. Simone Weil was unknown to me and possibly to Nika, too, till he had somehow come upon that text—"*L'Iliade ou le poème de la force.*" The date of the magazine must have been 1940: France had fallen, and *Cahiers du Sud* was published in Marseilles, in what was Unoccupied France. Hatred and grief were almost palpable in the text he had found—hatred of the victors and grief for the defeated. Homer's *Iliad* was offered as an allegory (description of one thing under the image of another) of 1940, yet the correspondences were not exact. "Greeks" did not translate into "Nazis" or "Trojans" into "anti-Nazis." In Simone Weil's thinking there was no place for equal signs. Her subject was force, might, power, always fearsome, always at fault, whoever wielded it, Hector or Achilles. One of the most beautiful moments in the essay is the account of the quiet meeting between Priam and Achilles—Hector's father and Hector's killer. I was used to thinking in opposites, and I can date a radical change in my mental life from the meeting with Tucci in the reading-room, which led to my translating the essay for Dwight's magazine. That was on Cape Cod, in Truro, during the Hiroshima summer; I took my typewriter to the beach and got sand in it.

Dwight was living in what was called "the fish house" in North Truro. Jim Agee came, Philip Rahv, many others. Tucci came to Truro, too, to stay with Nicola Chiaromonte in a cottage above Dyer's Hollow beach. I remember Chiaromonte in a blue ruffled apron tied around his waist sweeping out the cottage he shared with Miriam, his wife, and I remember our beach picnics at night around a fire and our discussions of Tolstoy and Dostoevsky. Thinking back on Nika, I remember how he delighted in the group of New York psychoanalysts who came to swim a dune or so down the beach, wearing Noxzema, sunglasses, boldly striped giant bath towels—he understood them when they spoke German; they reciprocated with a frank, professional interest in *him.* Another source of amusement was a heavy-drinking rich woman from Chicago who believed that George Orwell had stolen *Animal Farm* from a book she had written; when in her cups she could utter, and reiterate, a single word—"Communication!"

With Nika that summer and listening intently to our discussions were two other Florentines—Aldo Bruzzichelli, whose family ran a pastry shop on Piazza del Duomo, and Lamberto Borghi, who was in education. I think I did not realize then that Nika was half-Russian, related in fact to the family of Tolstoy's wife, Sonya Behrs, themselves of German or "Baltic" descent. He is an international man, a very unusual thing, and it is that perhaps that has put and kept him in a class by himself. As a writer of English, he has something in common with Conrad and with Nabokov—more with the latter, who, however, could not maintain a dual nationality in his literary work but ended by translating his younger self into English. Tucci has never done that.

In appearance, Nika is very Slavic. He has the broad face and high cheekbones, which at times call to mind an Eskimo, and his once black, straight shock of hair seems more Russian than Italian. As people say of him, he does resemble an actor. But also an opera singer, a conductor, a painter of the old school. In any case, a maestro, a virtuoso. This is partly a matter of costume—the use of a flowing tie. I once saw him at, of all places, Loch Lomond, alighting from the car of his German publisher with his arm in a sling that was made of an Hermès scarf belonging to Sonia Orwell, the organizer of the Edinburgh Conference we were taking part in; this suited his style very well. As he has got older he has accentuated the actorish component in his personality; his hair is worn longer than before, and the abundant neckwear is relatively new. Otherwise he has changed very little in the forty-five years of our friendship, except for his grey hair, a histrionic touch, like stage make-up. He has a fine voice, with a bubble of laughter in it, whatever language he speaks, and a great facility for mimicry. At one point, he liked to practice a simulation of handwriting such as you see in some Saul Steinberg drawings; it looked like writing but maddeningly could not be read—it was pure, florid penmanship. He has a remarkable memory and can recite whole cantos of Dante.

Many of the stories in this collection first appeared in *The New*

Yorker between 1948 and 1960. But "Terror and Grief" (1958), one of the very best and most characteristic, is far indeed from what is thought of as "a *New Yorker* story." It is a living fragment, still bleeding, of autobiography. In general, Tucci's magazine pieces divide up between the past—the author's childhood—and what, at the time of writing, was the present—the childhood of his children, e.g., "The Evolution of Knowledge" (1947). Just below the surface in nearly all is an element of barely controlled terror. "Hey!" strikes the keynote, which is a kind of strangled yell, a call (not a "bid") for attention from *somebody,* anybody. "Hey!" goes back to the author's Tuscan childhood, though the Tucci we will come to know is present only as an observer, half-unwilling, half-fascinated. The theme is death, always fascinating to children, and death here is only another name for rural poverty or vice versa. The peasant coughing in the leaky stone hut is dying of tuberculosis—the killer of the poor. The boy Tucci is brought by his father, the *medico condotto,* to stay downstairs and do his lessons in the kitchen while the doctor goes upstairs to visit the patient in the hut's one bedroom with its leaky roof—when it rains, the sick man puts up his umbrella, the green kind used by peasants, to keep the bed dry. His all-but-wordless wife, called "Gorilla"—from a neighbor family of Goris—sickens with consumption, too, and adds her cough to his in the matrimonial bed. As the parents die, the two boys, who have normally slept in a corner of the parental bedroom on a pile of old clothes and cornstalks, are sent to sleep in the stable. They already have the dry, toneless voice of t.b. patients, and their chief utterance, accompanied by whistling laughter, is the single word "Hey!" also used to horses. Nothing happens in the story, that is, nothing unusual: the parents die, each on their side of the bed, within a few hours of each other while downstairs the district nurse weaves straw hats for the American market and the two boys yell their rictus-like "Hey!" into the death-house. Tucci's father, evidently a good person, has been giving the sick peasant an education in medicine, botany, and so on, to round out his life. These terrible realities are the raw material of Tucci's fiction, which lies somewhere between excruciated memory and "happy" invention. "Raw" is the operative word, especially for "Hey!" which has an unslaked truthfulness unique, I think, to its author. There is also a wild humor ("Gorilla"!) that in the circumstances is unexpected.

I spoke of Tucci's horror of repeating himself. Can this be the ruling principle of his life and work? It is the loathing of repetition that marks him as a "modern." The modern, typically, reacts with aversion and mockery to the phenomenon of multiplication—the key process, after all, of capitalist production. The revulsion, as far as I know, was articulated first by Flaubert, who sought refuge from omnipresent banality in the Middle Ages—nobody in the Middle Ages was afraid of saying something twice. But with Tucci the horror of repetition—maybe a new form of the ancient horror of the vacuum—is sadly accompanied by the *fact* of repetition in the continuing history of his life. The reader of these confessions—more honest, I think, than Rousseau's—cannot fail to notice some recurrence. Indeed, it is one of his originalities as an author and a person that he submits to recurrence as a good Greek submitted to fate. Not only does he accept dealing over and over with the same material—essentially the history of his parents' meeting (told in the novel-length *The Sun and the Moon*), as the grotesque conjunction of two worlds that gave birth to himself, his brothers, and sister, but he also acknowledges the occasional comic reprise in his current family life—history repeating itself as domestic farce.

The crucial ordeal for him as a boy (and for the entire family) was *disorientation.* Thanks to the Bolshevik Revolution and their own lack of judgment, his parents had suddenly come down in the world. No more maids or fräuleins, no more treats or travel, these once well-to-do, highly educated people, one of them Russian, are dumped in the Tuscan back country stranger to their "soft" habits than the Wild West. The father makes his rounds in a two-wheeled buggy behind a horse on which some local dealer has cheated him. They have no friends and to the peasants they are foreigners.

Twenty years later, after a false start as a Fascist diplomat, Tucci himself, in his own career, changed language, geography, politics, carried off like his parents on what must have seemed at times a sort of malign magic carpet. He landed on Mother Cabrini Boulevard in upper Manhattan in an area populated by other displaced persons, mainly uprooted Jews from Eastern Europe ("The Evolution of Knowledge"). A fresh version of the old story: first, erratic displacement, giving rise to slight absurdity, then lack of means, like a congenital disease, leading to social embarrassment. Compare "This Particular Rich Lady" (1950), describing a parental visit to the Medici villa Artimino near Monte Albano, with "The Schemers," describing a "long weekend" with another rich lady on her Long Island estate by the author, his Florentine wife, and their two small children. At least twenty years have passed, Tucci has turned from a son into a parent, but the story is the same. Unbearable.

Such accounts wring my heart. And the truthfulness I mentioned is the source of the discomfort. One would not mind (or not in the same way) if one thought it was fiction. The truthfulness extends to what in another writer might seem "mere" factual details. Just the other day, reading "This Particular Rich Lady"—I had missed it in *Botteghe Oscure*—I gave a cry of recognition. "But that is Artimino!" Artimino, not a very well-known villa, happens to be known to me, and I was struck by how Tucci was able to make it recognizable among the hundreds of villas in Tuscany with only a few strokes—the chimneys. In the same way, I feel sure that an accurate map could be traced of the course of Dr. Tucci in his buggy along the roads around Pistoia, passing close to the "grey house" where Leonardo was born (briefly mentioned in "Hey!"), in Anchiano, I would guess from a study of the guidebook. Here is one of the marvels of these stories—the nearness of guidebook history (culture) to the painful realities lying so near it, as though the one grazed the other without really meeting. In this respect, Tucci belongs in the grotesque tradition, defined by Webster as a style "in which forms of persons and animals are intermingled with foliage, flowers, fruits, etc., in a fantastic design, hence characterized by distortions or striking incongruities. . . ." In that antic company, more Russian surely than Italian (Gogol fits), let me gently deposit this inspired writer, so hard to classify, as in reality there is only one of him, inveterately a-typical.

MARY MCCARTHY
PARIS, 1989

THE RAIN CAME LAST

TERROR AND GRIEF

They traveled all the time, those two. They were so dear to us, so afraid of not having us with them all the time—and then they left us, with the two maids and the governess, in the big apartment in Lugano, and they had no idea how much of the world they took with them. We lived in terror and in grief: they would never come back. This was true even when they went to the theater or out to tea without us. So much more so when they were gone for months, and sent us post cards of the Eiffel Tower, saying, "Be good. So many kisses to our dear little birds, will be back on the ninth." And more post cards from Venice, with the Piazza and the pigeons, and "Be good, we miss you so, will be back on the twelfth." And in the meantime the whole place was empty.

We looked for them but did not look for them; we were afraid to find them where we looked for them—behind a door, at the piano, at the desk, in their beds, in the dining room, and even in the street, passing by and forgetting to enter, as if they did not know us any more. We looked for them, in places where it would have been so horrible to find them—under a bed, in a dark corner where not even a dog would be hiding, behind the kitchen stove, in a dark chest in which one could not breathe. (We were, in fact, forbidden to play inside it, and also the resemblance to a casket was most frightening.)

When the gods of the house are away, Death takes their place. To a child, "away" *means* "death"; he gives up hope as easily as he will give up his best toy when a new one is handed to him. Whatever he remembers is already a sad thing, for this reason: he relives it in its absence. He will say, with great sorrow in his voice, "Remember when I saw that dog? Oh, where is that dog now?" And it was only yesterday.

How bravely we entered that bedroom, to make sure they were in Paris and not dead, and rejoiced in the emptiness that was the only cause of our despair! But then the bedroom door had to be closed again. The door was always closed when our parents were home, so, to remind us that they were not home, it should have been left open—like the stables when the horses are out. But no. The maids said it must stay closed. And the brass door handle hanging there a bit loosely, to the left, against the paneled oak—that it should have forgotten such an old lesson, and the soft order of the hand that lowered it and pulled it from the inside!

We tried never to look at the door handle when we sat in the living room, and yet it was always present to our minds. Every sound from anywhere in the apartment, from down below in the street, was first measured against the possibility that it was the handle of the bedroom door. Dogs understand these things; nursemaids and servant girls do not. What was there to prevent our eyes from accepting the testimony of our ears and believing that they saw what they did not see? And how could we know—how could we be sure that it would not move the tiniest fraction of an inch until they came home, our dear ones, in all their glory and splendor? How could children find peace with that door handle so still and those noises so distracting?

And then the dining room, with those two chairs empty. How can you eat when your head has been cut off? The spoon goes right to your stomach, hits it, and spills the soup on your clean suit. And you are glad, because the governess shouts at you, and that is a sufficient reason to cry.

"He is not crying because you scolded him," says the visiting friend, Mme. Kondratoff, a goddess, equal to our mother in power, beauty, and fragrance, although she favors jasmine while our mother favors a perfume called Chypre Old England. "He is sad that his parents are away," she says, and the governess, Fräulein Fischer, answers, with German logic, "If he thought of his parents at all, he would not do things that will spoil their vacation. For I will have to write and tell them. I was entrusted with the house and the children by their father—by the Doctor himself. If you wish to take over, Mme. Kondratoff, this will relieve me of a great burden. But if you are not willing to do that, then I must ask you not to side with them against me. He is crying *on purpose!*"

And even she, Mme. Kondratoff, who can scare anyone among her equals when she expresses a casual opinion, yields in front of the governess, for the sake of authority and order. "Fräulein is right. When your parents are here, you never spill soup on your clean suit. Why do it now? Fräulein is very good to you."

Fräulein was not good to us, and we knew it. And there were four of us to hold and mold and enlarge upon that knowledge: Sonia, almost twelve, and five years my elder, and the great friend of Mme. Kondratoff's daughter Tatyana; Chino, three years my elder, and officially in love with Tatyana; myself, also in love with Tatyana, although not quite (this was a matter of prestige); and Jules-Adrien, the little one, who knew nothing of love (as if we did) but said, lisping, that he, too, was in love with Tatyana. And when the rest of us denied this, he called out to the maids, "Is it true that I am in love with Tatyana?" and they said, "Yes, it is," and threatened us with punishment if we continued to tease him. So we asked him, "Jules-Adrien, is it true that you are in love with Tatyana?" And he said, very seriously, "I believe so."

Tatyana, too, had a governess, an English one, who did not like our German governess, did not like us, and did not like Tatyana when she was in our company, because our admiration and our hysterical laughter at whatever she did made her completely wild. Tatyana was not like us; she never felt unhappy. Her parents left her just as frequently as our parents left us, and she hardly seemed to notice that they were gone. She amused herself with dogs and cats, with her garden, or by nailing logs and wooden boards together, using a big hammer we were never allowed even to see her use, because hammers are dangerous. When Tatyana was with us, empty rooms lost their sacredness. Nothing existed any more but dancing and singing and violence: Cushions flew through the air; beds were jumped on; chairs became soldiers, trains, automobiles; and the most solemn portraits of dead grandparents and their own dead parents and grandparents became targets for bread pellets, for mashed potatoes. But the moment she left the house, laughter and play went with her, and the silence and the fears she had displaced came back. Not even our half brother Vladimir, twelve years my elder and the great hero of all of us, could help. Besides, much of the time he was in school. We children wandered from room to room, watched like prisoners from invisible holes and followed by the sound of our own footsteps.

There was another companion we all had in those days, who helped us a great deal—the sun. His effect was not so violent as that of the presence of Tatyana. The sadness and the longing for our parents remained but were tamed by his presence. The sun entered the living room shortly after breakfast, and at a certain moment touched the bronze frills on the handle of the door that led to our parents' bedroom. Then that handle, of which I have already spoken, lost its sinister aspect and became a source of joy, because there was a halo of light around it and a new point of brightness on the ceiling. From that handle the sun moved to the side of an inlaid buhl cabinet, and then touched the pastoral scene painted on porcelain under the face of the blue-and-bronze Sèvres clock. Also various trinkets, which reacted with blinking and signaling in rainbows on the ceiling. When this happened, the ghostly marble busts of our Russian grandparents looked less pale than usual.

In its journey around the room, the sun shone on an oil painting of Sorrento, with ruins, olive groves, pine trees, Mount Vesuvius, and the blue sea. Then on the same Russian grandparents, our mother's parents, under glass, not far from their statues—Grandmother Sophie in pastel, Grandfather Vladimir in photography, a picture of his marble bust, very close to a picture of Jupiter. Then our Italian grandparents, and our Russian great-grandparents, then Mother's elder sister Adya—proud, intelligent, beautiful (locked up against her will in an insane asylum in Potsdam by her brother). Then a sinister photograph of a huge mausoleum in the cemetery in Berlin where our Russian grandparents were buried. Other paintings, too intricate to make much sense: "The Rape of Europa," Titian's "Sacred and Profane Love." Then many smaller paintings, all with thick gilded frames and placed side by side on a background of red damask. Eventually the sun arrived at "the museum" and the piano. The museum was an eighteenth-century French cabinet, in which precious objects were displayed in casual symmetry. On the top shelf, dark medieval icons stood next to enameled Russian ashtrays, and Greek statuettes and Greek fragments next to green Pharaohs and gold bracelets from a tomb in Egypt. The lower shelves were filled with Meissen cups and saucers, Sèvres plates, and, on the bottom shelf of all, Greek and Arabic manuscripts in brown tatters and fading characters. And Chinese jades. All very depressing. But when sunshine hit the museum, revealing how much dust had settled on it, even that airless world became friendly.

Just as we always looked for our parents in the post cards they sent us, so we looked for them in the picture books on the living-room table. "Today they are in Paris. Let's try to find them." The big green book with "Vues de Paris" in gold on the cover was placed on the carpet and opened. Sonia turned the leaves with care, Chino and I prone on the floor beside her, with our elbows always too close to the book ("Get farther back or I won't turn the next page") and our hands cupped under our chins. Up and over and down went the slippery page, and a new image was before us—the Rue de Rivoli taken with a camera in full daylight, the shadows quite visible and clouds in the sky.

"Here they are, entering this car."

"No, they are *here.* See? There's Father."

"Oh, no, you are mistaken. I think they are back here, clear outside of the page. They will reach it tomorrow."

"No, they are right here in this car, and we can't see them."

This was only a game and we knew it, and yet the longing for our parents was such that to look at those crowds in the streets of Paris was like being close to *them.* If anyone had told me that a new person had come into a certain page, I would have believed it—or at least I would have looked, with an absurd hope in the back of my mind. And I did, in fact, look every morning, knowing that this was madness. Had those been drawings and not photography, I would never have thought of doing such a thing, but photography was real; that was exactly what those people *had* looked like in the Rue de Rivoli. Only one more thing was needed—that the picture go right on developing itself after it had been taken and after it had been printed in this book. And someday, by means of other inventions, such as the waves in the ether, perhaps this would be possible. Vladimir said—and also Father had said—that scientists stumbled on discoveries. Thus the frog of Galvani, Newton's apple, the lamp of Galileo in the cathedral of Pisa, and the latest discoveries of that Mme. Curie who worked with her scientist husband, as our mother was always hoping to work with hers and never did. Where normal people saw nothing, because it would have been madness to look for anything there, the scientist, possessed by impossible ambitions, had found the gift of God waiting for him, right under his eyes, as a reward for his curiosity. And would it not be wonderful if I, a child, made such a great discovery, moved by no other urge than to see my dear parents? So, all alone, on the carpet in our living room, with the book open to the picture of the corner of the Rue de Rivoli and the Place de la Concorde, I waited for Father and Mother to appear.

While Sonia practiced the piano in the morning, Chino and I sat on the carpet being "good" (that is, making no noise). Jules-Adrien stayed in the kitchen with the cook and the maids—their constant entertainment. We could hear his tiny voice only when Sonia paused, but their laughter we heard, and also their wet kisses, which tore like gunshots through the corridors and were at times followed by his crying. At times, the maids sang at the top of their voices, in their thick Bolognese dialect. "*Amore . . . amore!*" they yelled. "*Baciami ancora . . .*" Or "*Son fili d'oro i tuoi capelli biondi e al boccuccia d'oro . . .*" This was forbidden when our parents were home, and a deep sense of profanation ran through us; we turned to our ancestors, Jupiter well included, to assure them that we were no part of this invasion of their sacred silence.

But we had moments of great happiness in the living room, even with all the sadness of our derelict condition. There were so many of those huge picture books on the living-room table. Chino usually looked at two volumes on Egypt, or at some thick album of family portraits. I looked at a catalogue of the Vatican Gallery, a book on Le Roi Soleil, and a book on numismatics while Sonia did her first morning exercises; then, as soon as she began her "Gradus ad Parnassum" or her "Well-Tempered Clavichord," I put these books back on the table and took a book of mythology, leafing through it slowly but impatiently, because the thin paper covering each illustration seemed to want to stick to the plate. For me this was not a book of photographs of statues of antiquity but the house of the gods. They left it every morning to go out to their former domains, with Christ's permission; came back to it in the evening; and never left it during the night. No one had told me this; it was all my invention.

I caressed the quiet stone faces. I even kissed them lightly when I was sure no one was looking. I spoke to them, and I wished they would look at me; for they seemed so absorbed in something beyond the page and out of my reach, and I did not like it. The paper was so hard that it made a noise as I turned the pages, like fresh wood in a fireplace. And yet it was almost transparent. And the smell of that book was the smell of a very noble place, unknown to me but recognizable. And I felt that the gods were away, exactly like my parents; yet I also felt they were there and knew I was touching them with clean hands, and that even the expression on my face was one of deep respect and love. Of course, I was not unobserved; my grandparents could see me. But this was not done for them; this was done for the gods in the book. I also felt that the gods in the book were listening to the clock on the mantelpiece and to the piano. And when Sonia played Beethoven and not Czerny or Bach, I closed the book and did something else. Romantic music was neither for the morning nor for the Greeks. It was for afternoons and clouds, or else for evenings, when the gods were all back and closed in their house.

Vladimir came home from school every day when lunch was about to be served. We were as hungry for his presence as we were for food. The maid, alerted in the front hall (white gloves, white lace cap, and white apron), and the cook in the kitchen (dirty apron, red face, big wooden spoon in hand), and a third, useless maid were all just waiting for him. They had been busy with that soup (or that spaghetti sauce, that meat loaf) all morning; they had discussed whether or not to have it, bought the ingredients, washed them, cut them up, cooked them, boiled them, spiced them—always singing or gossiping or laughing—and it was now their right to serve the soup or the meat loaf "at its best," as if the masters were home. But the masters were not home, and they could not do it for us children, whom they had the right to spank and therefore could not look up to; or for Fräulein Fischer and Fräulein Thiess (who had lunch with us every day, and in the afternoon tutored Sonia and Chino), because they were Germans; so they did it for the soup. And they said so. They, too (how children know these things!), had great sadness in their hearts, and when they shouted at Vladimir for being two minutes late, it was because they were so lonely for their masters, whose approval was missing, whose chairs were empty.

When the two German women, who were without the dignity of the servant or the rights of the master—when these ruling servants praised the soup, the serving servant sneered, and commented on that praise in a way that was so insolent that the two ruling servants frowned and we children had to be careful not to burst into laughter. But when we children praised the soup, then the Kitchen was happy, and *in the soup* we met.

Fräulein Thiess insulted the maids by asking for the saltcellar, which she shook over her plate, aiming at the food from up high, as if she wished to punish it. Even the way she cut her meat or plunged her spoon into her soup was a way of refusing that food, of despising those who had prepared it with so much song. In the evening, when Fräulein Thiess was not there, Fräulein Fischer behaved like a civilized person, but at lunch she always followed Fräulein Thiess's example. And how much they ate for lunch, those two German women! We children were always afraid there wouldn't be anything left on the platter for us. Huge chunks of whatever it was, and then more, and then more, and looking carefully for the best parts while the arm of the maid shook with rage under the serving dish. "One of these days, I shall throw everything right into her face," the maid would tell the cook ominously, later, and we were so anxious to see her do it, but she never kept her promise. Fräulein Fischer and Fräulein Thiess conversed only with each other, as if they were in Germany and we were foreigners whom they were feeding out of charity. "You!" Fräulein Thiess said to Vladimir. "Get some wine. But not just one bottle—two or three. I don't like to have to repeat this every day." And Vladimir had to go and get Father's best wine. She knew how many bottles we still had, and wanted those—not just wine from the barrel. We always felt like spitting on her chair after she left the dining room, but we could not. That chair was sacred—Mother's armchair, with the two lion heads and the fringe and the gray leather cushion. After a while, the maid took it away and put it in a corner, replacing it with a straight chair. But it was awful, just the same, to see that armchair being punished in a corner.

After lunch, Vladimir retired to his room to do his Greek, Sonia and Chino had their two hours of lessons with Fräulein Thiess, and the governess put Jules-Adrien and me to bed in her room.

Chino suffered from convulsions, and very often, if he had been punished in the daytime, he would have a convulsion that night. So he slept with the governess and Jules-Adrien, like a child, although he was three years older than I, and I shared

Sonia's room. But since the lessons took place there, I had to take my afternoon nap on Chino's bed.

Jules-Adrien and the governess snored. I stayed awake and looked at their abandoned shapes under the covers, at the green lines of light filming the shutters on the ceiling, and listened to the world. If there was sunshine, I could see it, of course; the film was clearer, and shadows came and went across the whole ceiling, like the hands of a clock gone crazy. But I could also hear that there was sunshine; birds became more cheerful, and flew in higher and higher circles. If there was wind, even the voices of the children playing in the park came to me. I tried to recognize the voices, but an electric saw whining its way through wooden boards prevented this. Iron gates banged. Women down in the street spoke to each other *in my room.* If clouds arrived, not only did the film fade and lose all color and the hands of the clock become confused but birds came closer, and chirped briefly and nervously.

Noises inside the apartment were not affected by the weather. In the afternoon, table silver was thrown uncheerfully into the drawers in the dining room; the love songs of the maids became less passionate. It was no longer "Choke me, strangle me with kisses" but, rather, "Your cruelty makes me die," and other such conclusions. Fräulein Thiess asked loud questions that reached me through thick walls, but the answers could never be heard. If they were not satisfactory, the questions were repeated, in tones of mounting anger. If the answers were passable, she shouted "At long last!" and then there was a brief silence. After a while of all this, Vladimir's violin made its entry upon the scene, and the real afternoon began. The violin sobbed, uttered long lamentations, in squeaking tones, in scratching tones, in whistling tones, and always the same notes, the same mistakes, as when a nervous hand feeling a long silken robe is stopped every time by the same button. Sunshine and clouds were absorbed by that violin. It responded to sunshine with a somnolent tone that was not at all unpleasant, but when a cloud wiped all the color from the world, then the tone became offensive.

At four o'clock the governess smiled at Jules-Adrien, picked him up from his crib, and greeted him like a newcomer to a world all made for him. Speaking out of the side of her mouth, in the direction of my bed and without asking my opinion, she informed me that I was rested. Aware of the coming afternoon walk with her, I felt suddenly sleepy, and even ill. With my parents away, contact with other children in the park was frowned upon because of possible contagion; Fräulein Fischer did not want to be responsible. Also, there was a good chance that Sonia and Chino might be punished for not knowing their lessons by being made to stay home, in which case the walk was bound to be even more boring and I would rather stay home, too, listening to them discuss ways and means of murdering Fräulein Thiess.

But no. The park it must be, with or without the elder two. And the streets were full of parents who, from a distance, looked like ours. This happened also when Father and Mother were not away, but then the possibility was real: we sometimes did meet them coming home from a luncheon or going somewhere for tea. And if not, we knew we would probably find them at home, and could say, "We saw two people in the street who looked exactly like you. We ran to them and called you, but then they were not you." This mistake was now most dangerous and had to be carefully avoided; we must never forget we were unhappy, in order not to have the few seconds of mistaken happiness that would cause us in the end to suffer much more. It was all very unnatural, and like refusing to see them. Yet it had to be done. What made it harder was that the streets bore no signs of their absence. Everything was as beautiful as ever—the huge mountains surging up from the Lake of Lugano, the ancient oak trees bent over the water, the white passenger steamers full of excursionists, the canvas-covered fishing boats, the restaurants with cheerful people sitting around bright-colored tablecloths and eating pastry, the carriages waiting in line.

The return from a walk with our parents was always a pleasure. It just could not be otherwise. We would remember and go search out our toys, even those we had found boring a little while before. And then hot chocolate, and the pleasure of taking off those heavy shoes and that stiff collar and jacket and the pants we were not allowed to soil, and of putting on our dear slippers, our dear soilable pants, our grey apron with the blue ribbon all around it and the white bear embroidered on the pocket. And then dinner and bedtime, with fairy tales—always the same, for months and months—and the forbidden laugh from bed to bed in the dark before falling asleep.

But if we were returning from a walk when our parents were away, we felt a cold current of emptiness washing against us. Our chatter stopped at some distance from home, and we had a tight, choking sensation when we entered the garden. This probably explains why I so often hit my younger brother over the head just as we got home from a walk. Either he spoke about something that he knew was a secret, or he asked questions he shouldn't have asked, or he named the one thing that must forever stay unnamed. So I had to hit him.

Sonia and Chino had a way of defending themselves against misery. They formed a twindom, walked arm in arm, and said to me, "You cannot speak to us, we are twins." After that, I was forced to walk with the governess, alongside that white-and-blue baby carriage in which Jules-Adrien sat like an old lady, watching the world with tired eyes; or if he walked, then it was very slowly, and the governess spoke always to him, never to me, except to speak *of* him: He was too small to run, he was too small to understand. But I was too small to run all by myself; I was too small to understand why *he* was too small to understand. It was all very childish. I was even too small to understand why the other two were big enough to behave like small children and pretend they were twins when they were not.

In the meantime, Sonia and Chino disappeared behind a tree, then reappeared, and laughed, and disappeared behind another tree, telling each other more and more secrets from which I was excluded. And in this way they got home without feeling the current of emptiness. As we took off our coats in the front hall, the governess said to Jules-Adrien, "Go to your room. There is a big surprise for you. Your teddy bear has been waiting for you all this time!"

I was too big for such lies, and yet too small to be left—and I was left—like an orphan in the front hall. Had she said that my toys were waiting for me, too, I would have gone to keep them company. But this way I just followed my brother and took the teddy bear away from him, and threw it on top of a dusty cupboard, from which it could be got down only with the help of a ladder. To justify myself, I said, "He does not like his parents! First he cries like a fool; then he forgets them. All he likes is his teddy bear."

And in spite of my reasons I was punished: "No chocolate for you!" And again they all tried to make me understand that he was still too small to understand. "*He* loves his parents, but you don't!" the governess said. "And I will write to them tonight. This will make them very sad."

Jules-Adrien was at once reminded of his parents, and began to look for them. "Poor darling!" the maids would cry. "He was trying to reach the handle of that bedroom door! He wanted to see if his Mama and Papa had gone to bed!"

I didn't blame Sonia and Chino for not trying to defend me. Children who live in terror very quickly adapt themselves to the standards of terror. Whoever is not wrong in the eyes of the authorities has no reason to help those who are wrong. He enjoys the privilege of being right, for once, and wishes to stay right, so he does nothing, even if it is clear to him that great injustice has been done. He never knows what makes him right or wrong in the eyes of the authorities, so he just thinks he does not know why his persecuted brother is wrong. And out of curiosity, rather than hate, he wants to see his brother really in the wrong. Also, it is a relief, since that alone can put an end to his feeling that he is a witness to an injustice. The inversion of all moral standards, which causes so much trouble later in life, is present from the very beginning. "He is wrong because he has been punished," not "He is punished because he has done wrong." And the victim accepts it, too. In my brother's and sister's eyes I was wrong, and in my own eyes, too. That was what made me angry. I could find peace only if I was punished, and made to suffer more than I deserved, and then, having paid my debt and plenty more, I could make the others suffer with the sight of my suffering.

There was something religious in all this—the acceptance of fate and a repayment to the gods of ten times the price, to shame them for their cruelty. But such a system—which an adult can perceive rationally without feeling a thing, while a child feels it blindly—can work only if there are gods the child can go to. When the altars are empty, who will accept his tears and who console him? Not, certainly, the maids with their red hands and their short nails and their breath charged with garlic. And not the governess with her mentholated breath and the revolting smell of perspiration all around her. Who, then? Not other victims like himself. They have no right to comfort him; they are not gods. Perhaps a half-god, if he would: Vladimir. He sometimes let me come into his room and cry, but at other times he just did not want to be bothered with the lengthy explanations of the maids and the governess's "Don't let him tell you he was punished without reason. Do you know what he did?" and the next day Fräulein Thiess scolding him for interfering with the task of the governess. So when I opened the door, he would sometimes not lift his head from his books, or he would say, "Go away, you bad boy!"

I left, gulping down my tears, and really became bad. I did all sorts of things I was not likely to be punished for if no one saw me, and they were the worst things in the world: I insulted—not my father and mother (that I reserved for the great occasions) but my maternal grandparents, but much more my grandmother than my grandfather, because he was beyond reach of even my mother's tears (he had died when she was eleven) while my grandmother was extremely close, to us and to God. She blinked from a small star. (I still see it halfway between the center of the sky and the horizon—nearer the top, though.) And when one of us misbehaved, we were told, "Your grandmother is sad now. Her star is crying." And, of course, she saw everything. Like God. So I made faces at her marble bust, first; then at various pictures of her, but not at the picture of her tomb in Berlin, for I was superstitious. I believed that if I did anything there, it would be like touching an electric wire; God, not she, would make me die at once. And I repeated, "I don't *care!* I don't *care!* I don't *care!*" Then I went to a small table and picked up a framed ivory miniature of my Aunt Adya, the madwoman in Potsdam, and shook it until I had turned her upside down. The miniature never stayed glued to its velvet background, and it was like one of those Japanese puzzles children play with.

And finally, as I grew tired of all this I went to my book, the house of the Greek gods, and leafed through it. And the gods, walking high in the light, on soft ground, and looking sidewise, not at me, or else looking way above my head—the gods stood there in their great beauty, waiting for nothing, unwilling to judge me or to hear me, and it was they who gave me permission to live again.

This happened to me almost every day, or at least twice a week, with small variations, and yet I could never go to my Greek gods first. I first had to curse my own family gods and to upset Aunt Adya; only then did I remember where help came from, while the room grew so still that even the clock on the mantelpiece was heard again, mincing away its tiny grains of time that covered up the ruins of a bad day.

If the governess or the maids or Vladimir, surprised by that great silence, peeped in to see what I was doing, I did not turn my head, and it was not hypocrisy that made me act that way. I was finally at peace, the tears I had kept back were dry, the expression of hate was still present on my face but held, weakly, from the inside, and slowly becoming an expression of interest in outside things, no longer focused on those images of murder and destruction that my hate had produced. I was again an onlooker, and my grandmother could see that I was good.

The daylight faded on those pages until details were hardly recognizable, but I went on feeling the presence of the gods, while from the kitchen came a smell of good food that also was a form of forgiveness. Then, as the smell grew stronger and the dark thicker, lights went on in the corridor and the best moment of the day began. Vladimir interrupted his homework, Sonia and Chino interrupted theirs, Jules-Adrien joined them from the kitchen; only I was missing. They came and called me, and at first I said no, putting back into my voice some of the hate I no longer had, for reasons of dignity. But from that moment on, I waited more and more anxiously for them to come again and tell me I must not act that way, and even to pull me by the arm and force me to go with them. And if they did, because they needed me as a partner in their games, I joined them, first as a spectator, a bit held back by shame, and then as a participant, but still with a certain restraint, turning somersaults on the carpet without laughing, as if this were a funeral with a rather exceptional ritual, not just a game. And I tried to stay far from Jules-Adrien, lest I hurt him again without meaning to. Trouble seemed to emanate from me, especially in my contacts with him.

If for some reason they failed to insist enough, then I was stuck in the dark, accumulating new reason for unhappiness, hating them all, while they had a good time and I did not. And when I was called to supper, I walked into the dining room all wrapped up in my hurt dignity, with my hands behind my back, like a thinker. But the food and Vladimir usually brought me around; Vladimir was so wonderful. Also, the fact that Fräulein Thiess was not with us in the evening made things easier for him; she would never have tolerated all his stunts. "Where is Vladimir?" he would ask. And if we said "But look, he is here!" and touched his arm, his coat, his face, he would say, "No, no, this is me, this is not Vladimir. Go to his room and call him!" So we went to his room and came back and reported that he was not there. "Where has he gone?" Vladimir asked. "He must be hiding there. I'll find him." Now we all left the table; even the governess came with us. And the maids, in a procession. At his door, he turned to us, to announce what he would do to Vladimir for failing to come to supper. Then he entered quickly, closing the door behind him, and there followed a fight, with blows and groans and angry words, furniture thrown about. Finally, he emerged again, with his hair ruffled, a black eye (made with ink), marks of blows on his face, his necktie untied, his shirt torn, and a face much like mine when I was in one of my bad moods, and he marched to the dining room, followed by all of us, and sat down, his growls, as he ate, like thunder in the distance. And if we asked him "Where is Myself now?" he would tell us the most horrible stories of how Myself had been thrown out of the window and he hoped he was dead. Or he would suddenly remember that *he* was Myself, and act as if Vladimir had vanished all of a sudden. There was no end to entertainment. And though "normally" we had to be either threatened or bribed into eating, because the absence of our parents depressed us so, when Vladimir did his stunts we ate so much that the cook came into the dining room to thank us, and kissed us passionately, and called us all the most endearing names in her strange dialect. We went to bed so exhausted, yet so deliriously happy, that we still tried to laugh when our eyes had closed and the first snores came into our open mouth with the next breath.

But Vladimir was not only a clown; he was also a great scholar, a great painter, a great musician, a great toymaker, and a good and just man. No one could cut my fingernails as he did.

One day the maids, Rina and Ida, promised us that—if we were good, of course—we could go the next morning, with them, to the famous fair of San Provino, and they would buy us whistles and the Sun-and-Moon drum—a paper drum, mounted on a long stick, with the face of the sun on one side and the face of the moon on the other. I had already had one such portable Sun-Moon, but it had been punched by Chino, and I wanted very much to get another. As I got up from my theoretical nap that afternoon, I knew there was danger ahead, and to avert it I decided to be particularly nice to Jules-Adrien, and chose for my outburst of kindness the hallway next to the kitchen, where the maids could surprise me treating him just as affectionately as they did. "You are so *nice!*" I said to him. "You are the most beautiful baby in the whole world!"

I repeated this several times, because it seemed to me, from the maids' chatter in the kitchen, that they had missed this exceptional spectacle. I then tried to kiss him, but he did not want to be kissed, he wanted to go into the kitchen. I asked him whether he did not want to be carried on my shoulders, the way Vladimir carried him, making him tall enough to touch the crystal flowers of the chandelier. He did want to. So I helped him climb on a chair in the library, and I knelt down in front of it. Then I got him to put his legs around my neck, and, holding him by the hands, I slowly raised myself on my knees. But, alas, he was too heavy; I lost my balance and down we both went, flat on our faces. I cut my lip, and it bled, but he broke one of his front teeth and hit a sharp edge of a library shelf with such force that it sounded as if his skull had been split open.

At once, everyone was around us, neglecting me and taking care of him. The governess carried him, still screaming, off to her room and closed the door. After that, nothing but silence. I was aware that there would be no outing to San Provino for me now, and was resigned to that, but I wanted to know how my brother was. I was afraid I might have hurt him badly; I might even have killed him. This was my only worry. The maids saw things differently. Because this had happened to me, it was my fault, not my misfortune, and I was not to be allowed to know. I cried, "I have a right to know! I did not do it on purpose!"

"You always do these things on purpose!" Rina said.

"No!"

"Yes!"

"No!"

I went upstairs, and she followed me, and stopped me in front of the closed door.

"Get out of here or you'll be spanked!"

"I will not! I want to know!"

Rina hit me, and I hit back, with force, but missed her cheek. Instead, I scratched her eyelid, and she went wild. I ducked, she hit the doorframe with her open hand, and it hurt. "I'll get you yet," she said, nursing her hand, but in the meantime I had thrown open the door and seen that Jules-Adrien was all right. The governess held him between her knees and was searching his head with a comb, looking for traces of blood under that cloud of curls. He was playing his role again—touching his head and saying, "Bad boy. He hit me."

That took care of my fears; now I must defend myself. "I did not do it on purpose and he knows it!" I shouted into the room, ready to run away at the first sign of danger.

Rina shouted at me, "He might still become an idiot! And that will be your fault!"

This made me laugh, and she chased me downstairs and as far as the front hall, where she caught me and started cuffing me. Just then the door opened and Fräulein Thiess appeared; she had forgotten her glasses. Fräulein Thiess knew very little Italian, and Rina knew no German at all. She hated Fräulein Thiess for her habit of hitting Chino and Sonia on their fingertips with a ruler, and prided herself on the fact that she only spanked them, or, very rarely, boxed their ears.

"That boy is possessed by the Devil!" she cried now. "If he were only sorry when he has done something wrong! But you can never make him apologize. He doesn't even cry when you punish him!" This was all translated to Fräulein Thiess by Sonia and Chino, and I was enjoying it greatly. First of all, to be known as a child that never cries had always been my greatest dream, because I did cry all the time, in secret. And, second, now I was in the hands of Fräulein Thiess.

I must explain that Fräulein Thiess had always been extremely fair in her injustice. Sonia and Chino were her charges. All her cruelty, her hate, was concentrated on them. She never noticed my presence. Jules-Adrien and I were within the field of competence of the maids and the governess, and if, instead of feeding us, they had placed us on a mantelpiece and dusted us like bronze statuettes, she would not have felt called on to interfere. Not being treated cruelly by Fräulein Thiess had its disadvantages, in terms of honor. Sonia and Chino loved to tell me about her cruelty, and I knew that some of these stories were pure invention, but every time Fräulein really did something cruel to them, it was a matter of envy to me. What greater privilege, since I was going to be punished anyway, than to be punished by her? I would complain of the same enemy as my elder brother and sister. Perhaps I would become a twin forever.

When Sonia and Chino confirmed the fact of my never crying, Fräulein Thiess explained, like a teacher addressing a classroom, "But that is very simple. There are ways to make a bad boy sorry. You sit there," she said to me, almost kindly, and I sat down on one of those chairs that are fated never to be sat on, because they are placed in a corridor, where there is no reason to sit down. She asked whether I was allowed to run about the house when I was being punished. Sonia and Chino and the maid all said yes, and Fräulein Thiess shook her head disapprovingly.

"If we put him in a closet, he would break everything in it," said the maid, who did not want to see me shut up in the dark. Fräulein Thiess asked whether I played with my toys when I was being punished. They said no, and were surprised at their discovery. The fact that they were surprised made me feel superior.

"What does he do, then?"

"Nothing bad," said the maid, who was beginning to forget her anger. "He is very quiet. He becomes good again after a couple of hours."

"Where does he spend these hours?"

"Oh, in the living room."

"Doing what?"

"Looking at books."

"What books?"

"Any of those books with pictures."

"Is there one he prefers?"

No one wanted to denounce me. Sonia told me later that they would have named any book except the book of mythology. But I ruined myself by my impatience. "It's on the living-room table!" I shouted.

"All right," Fräulein Thiess said. "Now you will show me which one it is."

Acting as if under a spell, and aware of the unusual quiet, I walked into the living room, followed by everybody else. "It is *my* book," I mumbled. "My mother has left it to me in her will." Our mother had inscribed every book, every trinket in the house, to one or another of us, in order to avoid contention among the heirs.

"You seem to be hoping for your mother's death," Fräulein Thiess said.

"That is not true!"

"Remember that I am not your mother," Fräulein Thiess said. "*She* may allow you to speak that way, but I do not. Whatever I have said *is* true. Understand?"

"Yes."

"All right, now show me the book," she said gently.

I had made up my mind to resist, but her kindness again confused me and won me over.

"Forgive me for repeating my request," she said, as if I were a grown person.

"Oh," I said, and went straight to the table, touched the book, and said, "Here. It is mine. My name is in it."

She opened the book and saw my mother's inscription—"To my dear son," and so on. "Well," she said, "that can always be changed. She can inscribe it to your little brother, for example. What would you say to that? Don't you think it would be a good idea?"

"If she did that, I would burn it."

"You would? How interesting. Will you repeat that, please? What did you say you would do?"

"Scratch it."

"No, no, I heard another word before. What was it?"

Silence.

"Will you please answer my question?"

"Burn."

"Burn what?"

"That."

"That book, you mean?"

"Um."

"Very well, you may do it now." She turned to Sonia, and said, "Bring us some matches, please."

Matches, for us? That was unheard of. "*Messer, Gabel, Schere, Licht,/Sind für kleine Kinder nicht*" was our adage: No knives, no forks, no scissors, no light. Sonia hesitated. Chino, who was close to me, was pale and trembling. He kept mumbling, "You would not dare!"—because he hoped I would. And I had never been more scared. The maids were very worried, too; there was an atmosphere of madness at that moment.

"Will you bring me some matches?" said Fräulein Thiess again. "He will not do it."

And I said, "Yes, I will!"—meaning, Please believe me, and don't ask me to actually do it.

The maids protested, and Fräulein Thiess said, "Never mind. The police are going to take him to jail."

It never occurred to me that she was lying. Before Sonia could bring me the matches, I scratched the red leather binding with my nails. Chino leaned over the book, horrified and fascinated, and said, "Look! Look what he has done!"

Fräulein Thiess pushed him away roughly and said, "You shut up, if you don't want to be arrested, too." Then she looked at the scratch and said, sneering, "That's nothing. He is a coward. I knew he had no courage!"

These words went straight to the heart of every one of us. It was as if she had said that all Italians are cowards. To prove to her that Italians are not cowards, I crumpled page after page, and made a long scratch on the face of a god, after which she took the book away from me.

Now that I had proved what I was capable of, I could make any claims—in fact, I had to, for the shame was too consuming.

"All right," I said, "and I am going to break everything!" I started toward a Sèvres lamp that stood on a shaky piece of furniture next to the piano, and knew that after I had broken the lamp my next move would be to pull the bust of my grandfather down on me, so it would kill me.

Like a blessing from Heaven came a hailstorm of blows over my head, and from unknown hands, and I was happy. I only hoped I would be maimed forever, made blind or deaf, but the blows stopped too soon, and I looked up and realized it was Vladimir, who had stepped in and taken over the role of our father. "You come with me," he said, squeezing my arm so that it hurt (but not enough, never enough). Then he asked Fräulein Thiess to give him the red book, promising her that he would take care of that, too. "Leave it to me!" he said. "He will never see that book again." And he pushed me in front of him, all the way to his room.

After he had locked the door from the inside, he turned around and said, "What ugly things to do!"—but calmly, conversationally, as if he and I were talking about a third person, whose behavior had been shocking. At last, someone who agreed with me. How I cried in his hands, and how grateful I was that they were clean!

"Want to see something?" he said. He stood facing the door, and said, "Fräulein Thiess?" Then he made the most forbidden noises with his lips and his hands, then he repeated what she had said about taking me to jail, imitating her voice, and then more forbidden noises and gestures, but I was still so shaken that it took me a long time before I could begin to laugh.

I spent over two hours with him in that locked room. He pushed his homework aside and showed me all his best toys, which we were never even allowed to look at, even with our hands behind our backs, lest we feel tempted to touch them—toys he no longer played with but still kept, letting the echo of his childhood slowly die away in their metal. He showed me a toy steam engine of the most intricate make, mounted on his desk with screws, and it actually worked, but you had to use matches to light it; and his precious automobile, with tires, trumpets, handles, curtains, even the chauffeur and the people in their seats, looking aghast from pink porcelain faces; and a real Eiffel Tower he himself had put together, piece by piece, and never yet taken apart. He showed me his scientific instruments: the prism through which a ray of sunlight became colors; the large magnifying lens through which sunlight became fire if concentrated on a piece of paper, or even on a table. Then he told me that an ancient Greek scientist named Archimedes had used that lens (it seemed too new) to burn the ships of the Romans who were coming to take Syracuse. He got down his bound volumes of *Das Neue Universum,* a German magazine, with gold sunrays and planets on the covers, and showed me pictures: the skyscrapers of New York at night, with lightning hitting them;

a tornado in America; iron foundries with white-hot iron making sparks; sea shells and strange fish deep under water; icebergs and icebreakers; wildlife. Then he taught me how to hold the violin and made me play a note, and when the squeakiest sound was heard, he said that I had talent. But no matter what he said or did, I could not help yielding to my despair again. And, in a way, I did not want to be consoled, because I knew that when Father and Mother heard what I had done to my Greek gods, there would be a most terrible scene—not accompanied by blows but marked by solemn words and the sight of my mother in tears—and I preferred to suffer right away and as much as I could. I knew that two weeks from now I wouldn't care so deeply, and so, in partial payment for that debt of remorse, I was offering Vladimir the best fruits of my sorrow now, while I had the money, so to speak. It is strange how a child will calculate these things.

Vladimir set to work on the red leather binding—first with red ink, then with brown shoe polish—and when he was finished, hardly a trace of the damage could be seen. As for the pages that had been crumpled, the plate that had scratches on it, he said he would work on them the next day, with an eraser and a hot iron. He kept assuring me that everything would be all right, and he said he would tell my father that Fräulein Thiess was a bad woman and have her chased away. In the end, just before we went down to dinner, he did the most extraordinary thing; he said to me that, on condition I stop crying, he would make me his twin. But in secret, and only as long as I deserved it.

The moment I heard this, I felt infinitely tired—so tired I could hardly keep my eyes open. The honor was too great. I felt unworthy, did not know how to behave, and was so afraid he might judge me a child after all, and take it back, when he saw my embarrassment. At dinner, I did not look at him or address a word to him, so he would realize that once I had a secret, I could act as if I did not even know it. The news, as I was being put to bed, that we would all (no exception mentioned) go to San Provino the next morning at seven left me indifferent.

A letter addressed to all of us telling us of the beauty of the Hungarian forests and plains was followed by another, in which Mother described a sunrise in the woods, with the birds singing to announce the break of day, and this, in turn, by a post card addressed to Sonia, from which we learned, in a P.S., that our parents were not going to Greece after all but were coming home to be with us, and quite soon. This news made everything different. It was like Easter for us—a feast of Resurrection. Every single object in the house had to be polished, the curtains aired, the rugs beaten on the terrace. The floors shone like mirrors, and everything smelled clean and new and peaceful.

Then came the preparation of presents, each of us working in his room, either learning a poem by heart or making a drawing or preparing some object for their personal use—a folder for their letters, a ring for their napkin, an embroidered doily for their night table.

The maids were wild with joy at the thought that their masters were returning and they would no longer be under the surveillance of half-maids or of foreign spies (as they called any friend of the family who, on the excuse of paying us a visit, came to see how things were in the house).

Given the atmosphere of joy of those last days, there was no excuse for being bad, and, conversely, the threats of "writing to your parents" or "telling them on their return" no longer worked. Nothing would have been more unpleasant for the maids than to have to report that one of us had misbehaved. Chino must have felt this, or he would not have chosen that moment to act as he did. Why did he have to do it? Especially when he was always so submissive, and his revolt came when everything else had worked out for the best. One day, for various crimes and misdemeanors at the lunch table, he was slapped on his wrists by the governess, rejected by us silently as a brother, and sent to his room.

Right after this incident, as we were walking out of the dining room—Sonia to prepare for her lesson, I for my nap, and Vladimir for his homework—Fräulein Thiess said, "Now, before we start our lesson, let's put my poem on your father's desk, together with the other presents." And then, forgetting that he had just been banished from the world of good children, "Where is Chino?"

I ran to call him, and urged him to be quick, quick, or we would get there after she had already put her poem on the desk. He took such a long time buttoning his shirt and putting on his coat that I finally said, "I am not going to wait for you."

"All right, don't wait," he said. "I know the way."

"Bad boy," I said, and left the room.

They had not waited for me; they were all in the bedroom, in front of Father's desk, and Fräulein Thiess was inspecting our presents. "You cannot have the same flowers grow on trees and in the grass," she said, speaking of my portrait of Father and Mother in a forest in Hungary, in the act of caressing a deer. "And then, your parents are too small. Either make their heads smaller or their bodies much bigger."

I did not know what to say. "Must I change everything?" I asked.

"No," she said. "But next time you should remember these things. You still have a great deal to learn." She then found two mistakes in my letter; said that Chino should rewrite his because the calligraphy was too childish; praised Vladimir's drawing of an arch with columns, flower capitals, statues, and an inscription to our parents that looked as if it were written in marble; praised Sonia's embroidery, and even the embroidery attributed to Jules-Adrien but actually the work of the maids. Only then did she allow us to admire her own work—the perfect calligraphy, the elaborate Gothic initials, and the spotless paper. Chino did not seem interested at all. He stood back, looking amused, and that disturbed me. Did he know something about Fräulein Thiess we did not know? Was her work really good or should we laugh at it? I asked him in a whisper, while Fräulein Thiess occupied the whole front of the desk with her body, and Vladimir and Sonia were giving her poem the best place in the display, and he said, "I can do something much more beautiful."

"What?"

"This."

He did something I prefer not to describe. I could not even ask him not to do it; she would have heard me. But Vladimir caught a glimpse of us and pinched his arm.

"See?" Fräulein Thiess was saying. "This is the way to write. I did this all in India ink, without staining my hands."

We stood looking at the paper, deeply impressed—all except Chino.

"Well?" she asked him. "Do you like it or don't you?"

He smiled, and said nothing.

"Aha, I see. I was doing you a special favor by asking you if you liked it or not," she said. "I don't have to ask a stupid little boy if my writing is good." She took a deep breath and shouted, "Out of here, now! And get your books for the lesson!"

The next day was a Sunday. We were to go to a village called Cadro, visit a cousin of one of the maids, spend the morning there, gathering flowers to decorate the house with, and come back in the afternoon. The maids were worried lest Chino ruin all our plans and force us to stay home. They hated him already, at the mere thought of this possibility.

I listened at the door of my room and heard Fräulein Thiess say she would not give Sonia and Chino any homework, provided they did their dictation without a mistake. I ran to the kitchen to report that everything was all right. But just as I was saying this, a yell of indignation came from my room. "Is that an 'm'?" Silence. "Is that an 'm'? Answer now." And Chino still did not answer. Soon the pounding of fists on the table was heard, and then silence again. But a few seconds later, doors were flung open and banged, and Sonia appeared in the kitchen, asking for lemon. Chino had dipped his pen into his inkwell so angrily that he had disseminated stains of ink of all sizes on Fräulein Thiess, on himself, on the books, on Sonia's work and his own. And again he had laughed. Sonia was out of her wits. Now she must copy the whole page over again, and tomorrow there would be no excursion to Cadro.

Fräulein Thiess decided to give Chino a last chance, in spite of everything. If he copied that page he had spotted with ink blots a hundred times that afternoon without a single mistake, she would still let him go to Cadro with us the next day. But if he failed to do so, then he must go all the same, carrying a big sign over his forehead, on which she wrote the words "*Ich bin ein Esel.*" That would teach him a lesson.

But he was incorrigible. Instead of doing his homework and getting it over with, so he could go to Cadro in the morning, he sat there writing dirty words on the pages of his notebook, on his hands, on his shirtsleeves, on the table, even on the wall, and each time he did one of these things, my fear and horror became greater, and at the same time a sense of anguish gripping me at the throat made me a part of these crimes. I felt sorry for everybody—for him, for Fräulein Thiess, for our parents—until I needed consolation more than he did. Now for the first time I could see myself as others saw me in my bad moments. The amused smile on his face, his hateful remarks, his cold acceptance of the fact that he was a born criminal and that nothing could be done about it.

His crimes were discovered, of course, and he was punished at once: no hot chocolate for him. Sonia and I had formed an eternal twindom that was never going to be broken. And we no longer bothered to notice his presence.

We were just beginning to enjoy our chocolate with yellow corn bread, butter, and marmalade when the bell rang, and who walked in? Mme. Kondratoff. She was back from a long trip, had seen our parents weeks before, somewhere in Germany, and was wondering whether they had returned or not. We were instantly around her asking questions, and she suddenly asked why Chino continued to sit off by himself in a corner. So we began to tell on him, we and the maids, and he looked rather worried now. She listened for a while, cupping her hand around her ear (she was hard of hearing) and seeming quite indignant. Suddenly she said, "Very well, I know, I know." And without waiting for the rest of the indictment, she marched toward him, grabbed him rudely by the shoulders, and kissed him on his eyes, on his cheeks, on his hair. Then she said to him, "Come, sit down here and have a cup of hot chocolate with me."

Two cups were brought, corn bread, butter, and marmalade were given them, and they ate while we looked on, not knowing what to think.

On the last day, every vase in the apartment was filled with flowers. The accumulation of mail was placed on Father's desk, with our presents. And then we had to decide the question of who would go to the station to meet them. Would it not be much better to wait for them at home? This debate had begun the evening before, and it went on for each of us in his dreams. Go to the station and not tell them what awaited them at home, or stay home with our presents?

Chino had convulsions that night, I a nightmare (the two guilty ones who had something to hide). Sonia and Jules-Adrien had funny dreams and told them at breakfast. Fräulein Fischer, Ida, Rina, and even Fräulein Thiess had all been visited more or less openly by that mysterious thing Good Counsel, which comes only in sleep, and to all it had said, "No one at the station." As the time of our great separation wore itself to an end, we argued, but the arguments went on only on the thinnest surface of our minds—only with words—and then even the words lost all their meaning. It became difficult for us to remember their meaning. We asked questions, and when the answer came we were surprised, because we had forgotten our own question. Images of that doorbell or that noise of the carriage in the street—auditive images intruded all the time, and charged our heart with heaviness. In the end, we were ready—just ready, nothing else, and so ready that each minute seemed a delay. And yet we knew that there was still an hour, then a half hour, then twenty-five minutes, then twenty-four. Time seemed to grow tired, sick, behind the face of the clock. What was wrong with those hands? And when it turned out that they were late—first five, then ten, then thirty minutes late—we could not speak. Why were they late? What had happened? Had this anything to do with God? And therefore with our punishment? Vladimir "directed" the train traffic from the window: "I heard a whistle. That must be a freight train. It is waiting at the red signal, and behind it is the

Paris train. . . . Yes. . . . Did you hear it, too? There it goes again. . . . See the smoke? No, that smoke is coming from some freight train. But that smoke there! Wait! Hear it? Yes. That is it."

We played a similar game with the carriages that passed under our windows. "No, that is something else. I know it cannot stop. Wasn't I right?" "How about this one?" "I don't know." "But it sounds as if it were going to stop here." "One cannot tell. No, it won't stop. Besides, the train has not arrived, so why should it?" When the bell rang, neither whistles nor smoke nor carriages had been found promising, but they were there. There could be no mistake. The maids ran down the stairs, and we could hear their shrieks of joy, and then words, voices, *their* voices. And now they came upstairs, yes, they came, yes, here, right here.

The wound was closed.

"How you have grown!" they said, and we stood very erect, to exhibit every millimeter, and cheated a bit, by slightly lifting ourselves on our tiptoes. That was our first surprise—to have grown taller without knowing it. But they, too, seemed to have grown. She had a hat so huge and with so many feathers that it looked like the clouds of that oncoming thunderstorm in the pastoral scene over my father's writing desk. Grey feathers, too. And Father's neck in a stiff collar was longer than the one he had before leaving. But otherwise they surprised us by being all right there in front of us, collected in their physical presence—not in ten rooms at once and outside, too, but in one little portion of one room. And when they moved from one place, they were gone to another. This was a second surprise. And our impatience to exchange presents with them. In what suitcase would we find ours?

"Wait till you see what awaits you in that room!"

Entering their bedroom, they saw the stately display on the desk and said, "Now, what is *that?*"

"Oh, nothing, nothing!"

And now the anguish. Would they appreciate every present as it deserved? Would they know what it had cost, first in invention, then in work?

They had just begun to read the inscriptions on their presents when the sight of an envelope killed everything. They grabbed it—almost tearing it from each other's hands, like children—opened it nervously, read it together, looked at each other, making big eyes, and then whispered to each other.

"Out of here, children! Out! Out, please!" said our father. "Your mother is very tired."

"Oh, no!" she said, suddenly tired. "I am not. What nice presents! How thoughtful of you all! Really, very, very thoughtful! We will examine everything in detail tonight. And, by the way, who forwarded the mail to us while we were away?"

Exiled to our rooms, with our governess now officially in charge, we waited and waited for it to be established who had neglected the forwarding of that important letter, and then for the endless flow of self-justification from the guilty non-forwarder to be stopped. ("Enough of this now, please! It is not important! We told you now merely so you'll remember in the future. Please! We have other worries now!") The only difference between this and their absence was that then the sacred character had abandoned the house and every single object of the house. Now that the gods were back, to us human beings was given nothing but a wise instinct to stay out of their way as long as there was thunder in the high regions.

And thunder did roll down the noble peaks, like trunks on stairways. Who had told them that Chino went to Cadro wearing a sign on his forehead saying that he was a donkey we never knew. We suspected Vladimir, but were told by the highest authority in the house to stop guessing. Vladimir was no spy, they said. At the same time, whoever did not report everything to the highest authority in the house was guiltier even than he who had done wrong. There must be discipline and order in a loving family. "If your own brother has done wrong, who but his loving parents can right him again? Does he need your protection against those who love both you and him and who alone can tell what is best for you?"

Thus it could not have been Vladimir, though he was liable to be punished if he did not tell everything, and it was not the governess and not the maids. ("Do we, a loving family, need foreign spies or illiterate people to get the truth about our loving children? Is it not their first care and wish to confess everything? And don't you understand that if you hide your guilt from your own parents, the only people in the world who really love you, you remain guilty, you nurse the very seed of evil in your heart, and you declare yourself a better judge than those who, after God, are your only guides and judges in this world?")

So we confessed. I confessed that I had hit Jules-Adrien when we came home from our walk, and Chino confessed about the ink spots, and I forget what Sonia confessed but after she finished it was my turn again. At first we confessed hesitantly, and then with so much energy and enthusiasm that we confessed to things we had never done. Confession gains momentum; you become anxious to see the bottom of the well, to get there first; it is an open competition between you and your judges—the only form of liberty left to man in the presence of his gods. And this confession turns out to be an accusation (though an unwilling one) even of all those who stood by you.

Vladimir had to explain that if he had repaired the damage to the red book, it was not to instill into my soul the fear of those who loved me but to console me and to repair the book—indeed, to spare the gods one more sorrow.

In the course of the day and by these painful processes, the gods reestablished themselves on their true altars. And we felt clean and happy again.

THE BEAUTIFUL BLUE HORSE

The man who sold our blue horse to us said he was grey, and so did the rest of the people of Terra Betinga, in Tuscany, but they knew nothing about horses. They were right when they said Nello stumbled and had a few other defects, but he was blue. And what's more, he had a hunger for green. Anything green: blinds, shutters, doors, umbrellas—also grass, of course. His love of green came from the fact that he had always been kept on a diet of straw. And after we bought him, he was kept on that very same diet, in spite of Mother's protests. Grass was expensive, my father pointed out. We were surrounded by it, but all the same grass was expensive, straw was cheap; so the horse had to eat straw, like all the poorer horses in the village. As for barley, that was terribly expensive, and Nello got two measures of it every day at noon and two at night; then straw, to get used to it. So the color of grass became a real obsession with him. "Look out!" my father warned me every now and then. "The horse is chewing on a door!" Or a shutter, or whatnot. It had come to the point where damages we had to pay for chewed-up doors were higher than the price of grass, full diet, three times a day.

Nello was a monumental horse. I don't mean that he was big but that he was made for statuary purposes. His head was beautiful and always held erect, and he looked as if he were ready to believe anything, especially great and noble things such as bronze men on pedestals in public squares believe. His body was beautiful, too; so was his posture, as long as he stood still. When he walked or trotted—But as I say, monuments were his world, not the poor stable of a country doctor like my father, who cared more for his books than for his horse.

The purchase of the horse was a very important affair; he cost five thousand lire, which for the horse market of February, 1922, was quite high. We—Father and Mother, my sister Sonia, my older brother Chino, my younger brother Jules-Adrien, and I (our idol, Vladimir, Mother's son from her first marriage, had left home years before)—had barely arrived in Terra Betinga from another place in Tuscany, where we had stayed for two years at great sacrifice of pride and comfort, and where Father needed oxen more often than he needed a horse to reach his patients, who lived on the sides of mountains where there weren't any roads. But the horse dealers of Terra Betinga were not sentimental, and cared nothing at all for the sad destiny of a distinguished family ruined by the wars and the impact of distant ideologies on foreign, unknown places such as Russia. The horse dealers of Terra Betinga were tough people, and when they had a horse that looked beautiful but was slow, uncooperative (worse than a donkey in this respect), possessed of a gigantic hunger, and full of complexes, they tried to sell it for the best price they could obtain, to the first fool that came along; if that fool was surrounded and counseled by worse fools than himself, as my father was by the rest of us, it was almost too easy. We bought the horse because he was Hungarian, a foreigner in Italy, just like ourselves, more or less (though there was no Hungarian in any of us, there was a great deal of Russian, which all came from the same source—my mother), and the Hungarians we knew were charming, rich, and educated people, so the horse must have something in common with them. In fact, when my parents heard that the horse was Hungarian, they were ashamed of taking such unfair advantage of the horse dealer, because they saw the infinite horizons of the Hungarian *puszta* around the horse, like a great halo of constant poetry; they heard the music of Hungarian violins in the trot of that beautiful animal. They also liked his face. It was the face of a horse that has traveled and knows how to behave among the international set. Standing in the courtyard of the horse dealer's house, they tried German, French, Hungarian, and Russian words on the horse, to see whether he was intelligent (instead of looking under his grey wet lips to see whether his teeth were clean, and so the horse dealer knew how intelligent *they* were). And if they did not ask the horse whether he knew the people they knew, it was only because they did not want to show off in the presence of an ignorant horse dealer. Whether or not the horse could also pull a light two-wheeler was irrelevant; we could do it ourselves, as we had learned to do so many other menial things distinguished people never should have to do if the world were not what it is. The important thing was to have the horse away from that questionable environment and with us, one of the family. Only, the price was a little too high, and I remember that the best argument my father found to persuade the horse dealer that he should let him have the horse for much less was that, first of all, greed does not get you anywhere. My father said he had seen greedy people die of tuberculosis in a very short time in spite of all the money they had made, so why be so attached to money? We ourselves were not mercenary, he said. If the horse dealer had been buying the horse from us, instead of the other way around, we would have shown him how generous we could be; we would have given him the horse for nothing. We were unwilling to pay what he was asking for the horse solely because we were obliged to practice various disagreeable economies in order to reconstruct the family fortune and leave, go back where we belonged. For this was not our world; we were not at home here in this small, faraway village with no schools and no libraries and no museums.

"This horse is my companion," the horse dealer said. "I don't know what I am going to do without him." And so on. We promised that if we bought the horse we would bring him back to his former home for short visits now and then. (It sounded as if we were talking about the child in a divorce case.)

"Do you not feel," my mother said to the horse dealer, "that we are, in a manner of speaking, related? After all, we have something in common: we both love the same horse. So why bother about a few more paper bank notes? Isn't disease, isn't unhappiness, isn't death always ready to take us? We know something about that—we whose best, richest relatives have died in Russia. That's the real reason why we care nothing for money."

Neither, it turned out, did the horse dealer. He made it quite clear to us that he was not more greedy than we were. "I will explain to you," he said, "why I need that money more than you do. You have the wealth of knowledge—isn't that the correct way to say it?" But, yes, of course it was, we assured him. "You have the wealth of knowledge," he went on, "and I do not." And he swore that he needed the money and that he hated money— Did we want to hear this from someone else?

Women were called, and what they told us about the generosity of that man made him so lovable to us children that we begged our parents to be lenient with him about the money.

"Are you not here for a brief stay merely?" asked the horse dealer.

"Of course," we said.

"Well, then, this horse will take you very far," he said. (These words were made to sound symbolical, and so they were taken. Very far! How true. Yes, very far on the way back to our own world.) "Take my word for it," said the horse dealer. "You know the country where this horse comes from?" Of course we did. "And you love it?" Love it? We almost gave him a full description of it, only there was no time; the horse, he said, was waiting for a decision. "You want a horse with whom you have something in common," said the horse dealer. "This is the horse for you. Speak to him, mention the names of your Hungarian friends— Not now. Later, at home. Now he is nervous. Do it to console him. Because he is fond of me; he does not want to leave me. And, finally, you want a horse with a nice, honest face? This is your horse. I never saw such a nice face. Look at his eyes. How honest they are! And how young!"

My father asked, at last, about the horse's teeth. "Excellent teeth," said the horse dealer. "But let me tell you a story about this horse, a story that will reveal to you how generous he is. And also how young. Old horses lose their generosity, and I hope this one won't. It's up to you. This horse once tried to rescue my son from the hands of a man who was beating him, and the man hit the poor horse in the teeth and broke one. See? This one here. I always show this to my friends. It is a mark of youth—the youth of the heart. Usually—this is strange—people believe a broken tooth to be a mark of old age. And how peculiar that in this case it should be exactly the opposite. Well, such is life."

We children all looked sadly at the teeth of the horse condemned to appear old when he was young. My father was still skeptical. "What is it?" asked the horse dealer. "Don't you believe me? Then nothing doing! I don't want my horse to go to people who cast doubt on his age. Poor foreign horse, lost in this country where no one understands him or believes him! I alone can, but with me you can never speak about your country, my poor angel! Never! I know you would want to, I know. . . ."

We children had tears in our eyes. Jules-Adrien said, "Papa, I will talk to that horse every day. He won't have to feel lonely any more."

"Good child," said the horse dealer.

"I, too, will talk to him," said Mother, wiping her eyes.

"Well?" said the horse dealer. "What are you waiting for, then? Take him home, talk to him. He will like it. He needs company. I have no time to talk to horses. I must talk *about* horses all day long, going from market place to market place, and when I get home in the evening, I realize I haven't spoken a single kind word *with* my horse. Nothing but bargaining all day long. Besides, people would consider me crazy if I did. You know how people are. To most people a horse is just a means of getting from one place to the next; nothing else. To me a horse is my own brother in Christ, and even if the parish priest says a horse has no soul—Well, I answer him one thing: He may know more about souls than I do, but he does not know my horse. I alone know him, and know his soul. . . . But I must confess, I do treat him like an animal. If I were not so tired in the evening, I would talk to him for hours. I would let people say what they pleased. I never cared what people said about me anyway. But I *am* tired, and besides I am ignorant. I have rough manners, you see? My wife loves the horse, but what can she say to him in the evening? I said to her the other day, 'Talk to the poor animal while I eat my dinner. You don't have to serve me. I want you to talk to that lost soul for a moment. It will make him feel good.' Well, what do you think she said? She said no. She said, 'I don't want to be laughed at by the neighbors.' That's what she said to me. . . . Well, I say one thing: If you can talk to this poor horse in his own language, there is no telling what he might do for you. He has a heart as large as a house."

"What?" exclaimed my father. "He has an enlarged heart? But that is bad. . . ."

"Oh, no," said the horse dealer. "In actual size it is as small as the heart of your child here. I was speaking only in a figurative sense. It's full of love for the world. That's what I mean when I say big. And let me tell you another thing about this horse. The reason I didn't beat my wife for refusing to say a few kind words to this poor foreign horse is that when she says, 'The horse is scared of me,' she is right. He *is* afraid of her."

"You never told us that," said my father suspiciously.

"Give me time. I am telling you now. You hear me, I hope. Nobody is compelling me to tell you this. Admit I do it of my own free will, with no compulsion."

"All right," said my father, "but tell me one more thing. Why is he afraid of her?"

"Look, my friend," said the horse dealer. "You know poor peasant folk, ugly and deformed by birth? Well, she is one. And she spends the whole day washing bedsheets in the ditches at the side of the road. You know those big bedsheets it takes so long to rinse and wring out? And you know the ditches, of course. Well, this poor animal sees my wife beating the laundry on rocks and tossing it into the air, and he cannot explain this to himself and is scared. Very simple. But the Signora is not a poor washerwoman, and so there is no problem. You can let him carry you in your two-wheeler, or even a four-wheeler, and you will be perfectly safe. Nothing will happen. So will it be five thousand?"

"Wait a moment," said my mother. "Let's be practical. We—my husband and I—have great experience in suffering and losses. We lost everything in Russia. And also we have had an extremely hard time here. This is not the moment to tell you all about our private lives, nor do we know you well enough to do so, but as you seem a kindhearted person (the fact alone that you own such a horse and are so fond of him proves it beyond all doubt) and apparently have problems and worries (indeed, who doesn't?), I will have to step in and use my practical instinct, with which I have already solved so many difficult situations in my own family and in the families of countless other people, and tell you that perhaps you *can* find a solution to your worries without *having* to part with your horse. Don't you have anything else you might sell to meet your obligations?"

"What do you mean?" asked the horse dealer. "I do want to sell my horse. If I didn't, do you think I would have bothered to come to you? I am a busy man. Horses are my business."

"Oh," said my mother, and she seemed very surprised. "A commercial person, in other words. Pfui! And I believed you were sorry to have to sell your horse—"

"But of course I am sorry. You can ask my wife. She'll tell you I was crying as recently as last night—real tears. You should have seen them."

"Well," said my mother, with a sigh of relief, "I am glad to hear that I was right in my first impression. First impressions usually are right with me. The minute I saw you, I felt that you were a straightforward, honest man. Whether you deal in horses or in pigs makes no difference as far as the soul is concerned. We are all equals in the essence of things. The difference is moral—that's where good and evil lies."

This left everyone rather confused. "What were we saying?" asked my father after a moment.

"I had just asked you five thousand for this horse," said the horse dealer. "To me it seems a ridiculous price. The animal is worth at least six thousand. In fact, I am sorry now I said five thousand at all. I should never have said it. I am always doing the wrong thing. Five thousand for a Hungarian horse? Five thousand, I should say, for a friend, for a brother, a person with whom you can—"

"The animal seems older than you said," said my father.

"How much older?"

"I wouldn't know exactly, but older than you said."

"True. And he will be much older if we go on talking and talking, as we are doing now. Time flies. You are now buying a horse an hour older than he was when I first showed him to you."

"Now, look," said Mother. "Let's be practical once more. What is old age? A purely spiritual matter. One is as old as one feels."

My father turned to the horse and said, "And how old *do* you feel?"

The horse neighed and showed his teeth, lifting his head way up in the air.

"See?" said the horse dealer. "An old horse never behaves that way. Five thousand?"

"It is a lot of money," said Father.

"Time is money," said Mother, in his ear.

These wise words made him yield. To save money, he bought a horse.

But the last moments before we led the horse away were painful, because the horse dealer now seemed unable to part with his horse. He kept saying, "My horse, my poor little horse."

Father also seemed of two minds about the transaction, but Mother, with her sharp practical sense, found a solution at once. "Look," she said to the horse dealer. "Whatever you do in life, you must never say, 'I am a fool to be so generous.' I promise you one thing: If by a fortunate chance (and you never can tell) we should win back our money in the next few weeks, or months, or even years, I will give you five thousand more at once for the horse. But even if this is not possible (and I must ask you not to count on these vague possibilities; they are dreams, and one must never, never count on dreams), you can always find comfort in the thought that your horse is in good hands and that you can always come and see him any time you feel like doing so. Come tomorrow. Come for tea."

"For tea?" he said. "I don't need tea. I am very well."

"But tea, my friend, is not a medicine, as you Italians always seem to think. Tea is a drink one takes for conversation."

"For what?"

"For conversation."

Father left at this point, showing signs of impatience, and the horse dealer said, "I don't need tea to talk. I like wine."

"All right, then, we will give you wine. Whatever you like. But please feel free to come and tell us all your worries. I know how important that is. We all need it."

"All right," he said. "I will. What time?"

"Four. No, wait. . . . Five. Yes, five."

"At five tomorrow, then," he said. And then he added, "You understand me. You are a person one can talk with. Your husband isn't like that. He thinks everybody is dishonest."

"Oh, no. If you only knew him better, you would never say that," my mother said. "That isn't fair. He is worried, and somewhat pessimistic. All Italians are. But you must get to know him better, and then he will trust you."

"There is something I must tell you," the horse dealer said. "Something that I could not tell him, because he would not have believed me."

"Go ahead, tell me."

"You know how much that horse loves me. Now, when he realizes that I am not with him, when he feels abandoned by the only true friend he has ever had, I know what is going to happen. In his unhappiness he won't even look where he is going, and he is likely to fall on his knees."

"We will be with him," Mother said. "Don't worry."

"I wouldn't want your husband to feel alarmed if this happens," the horse dealer said. "Wait. Treat him kindly. And little by little he will get used to the idea that I am not there to console him."

"Leave it to me," Mother said. And they shook hands like two conspirators.

My older brother took hold of the bridle, and the horse was led home and triumphantly domiciled in the stable. The next afternoon, there was a bottle of white wine on the tea table for the horse dealer. Father never drank tea with us. When he was not seeing patients or out on calls, he read in his study. But we children were all there, with Mother and a Swiss friend of our parents, whom we called Aunt Sophia—a very thin and active woman, always busy with banks and the stock exchange but also interested in music and literature. Mother told her that we were expecting a very simple person for tea, and from time to time during the conversation she turned around and lifted the curtain to see whether anyone was coming toward the house from the garden. The conversation was not about money or music or literature; it was about suitable names for the horse.

Naming a horse is not an easy matter. And especially a beautiful Hungarian horse like ours. "Drug" (pronounced "droog" and meaning "friend" in Russian) was one of the names we tried on him. It did not work. So we tried "Drujok," which means "little friend"—or, in this case, "horsie"—but that, too, left him cold. He responded to "Giorgio," like most horses in Tuscany (I later learned that horses in the United States do also), and, of course, he responded to "Nello," the name he bore on a round metal ornament on his harness above his right eye. But "Nello" was not acceptable to us. The result was that for the seven years we had him the onomastic question remained pending.

Meanwhile, Mother discovered that her last emerald, which she wore on a black velvet ribbon round her neck, was missing. Suspicion fell first on Maria, the fifteen-year-old maid, whose sister had been with us practically from the day of her birth to the day of her marriage, in "the better days." Maria was asked, "Did you by any chance take that green thing with that small safety pin attached to it? Now, if you did, you must remember that in the Ten Commandments it says one should never take things—it is a sin. Do you know what a sin is? Well, there are many, and taking things that belong to other people is one of them. Besides, it is a big sin, because that green stone is very valuable, and we need it very badly right now. So if you have it, give it back, and we will give you something else."

Of course, the girl cried and said she knew perfectly well what was a sin and what wasn't; she did not have to be told. And besides she hadn't seen the emerald.

So she was given a scolding, and suspicion moved on to a second person, a blond German girl who was staying with us and helping in the household in exchange for Italian conversation. In her case, the questioning had to be more tactful. The tactful question my mother asked her was "By the way, Fräulein Frieda, while you were dusting the piano yesterday, did you throw away a green thing with a small safety pin attached to it, that someone might have placed here in this porcelain ashtray?"

"Green thing? What sort of a green thing?"

"Well, a green stone that really looked like nothing but was—just think of it—an *emerald*, and a fine one, too."

And, of course, the German girl cried and protested. Did one imply she was a thief? She was not used to having such accusations made to her; she would leave that very day.

Who had said anything about thieves, my mother wanted to know. How German of her, really! Indeed, had not that been the reason for the constant political misunderstanding between Germans and Russians in the past? The Germans always felt attacked, believed they were suspected of the worst, were insulted, while the Russians were always unsuspecting and outspoken. It had been merely a question, in this particular case, of a small, unimportant green stone, a mineral, one of the many crystals to be found in nature, but one that for stupid, unexplainable reasons was regarded as precious by a perfectly stupid humanity, and that even intelligent people like ourselves kept as a precious possession, and were now very glad to own, because it might be sold and the money was needed. That was all. And, as the emerald might have been left in an ashtray, and as ashtrays must be emptied (no one would normally search the ashes and cherry stones in ashtrays for gold or, let's say, emeralds), so it was only natural for anyone to think that if an emerald was left in an ashtray, the person in charge of cleaning that ashtray might have thrown it away. And if that was what *had* happened—why, very good. It would serve as a lesson to those who leave their emeralds in ashtrays. The thing to do in such a case was not to cry and scrutinize every word that was spoken in normal conversation about ashtrays and household work for offensive remarks against the Germans but to help search the garbage can at once to find that silly little stone, if it was not too late.

But now, the second person likely to have taken the emerald having been found innocent (and also stupid), the search for culprits became more important than the search for the emerald, because an *emerald* cannot be *lost.* Especially in a *house.* No one has ever heard of such a thing. When a precious thing is lost, it is invariably stolen. So the doors and windows were examined to see if anyone had forced his way into the house, or if they *could* be opened from the outside. It occurred to Mother that Tronco, the gardener, might have placed the ladder against the wall of her bedroom while we were downstairs at dinner, entered her room, and taken the emerald. Mother's jewels were kept in a large parchment-covered box in a chest next to the window, and the key to that chest had been lost in Baden-Baden, so it hadn't been locked for years.

Tronco, seeing Chino and me place his ladder against the house, at Mother's direction, asked us if it was something he could do, was told it was not, and stayed there looking on while Jules-Adrien was finding out that the window could be opened with no trouble at all and Mother was commenting on this fact from the foot of the ladder. When Father was informed that Jules-Adrien had succeeded in opening the bedroom window from the outside, he refused to believe that either Tronco or his sons would ever do such a thing, but, he said, there were many others who might. The world was full of thieves and Communists. There were all the factory workers in Prato. And the famous inhabitants of Campi Bisenzio, a town of thieves since the Middle Ages and probably before—how about them?

Things were at this point, and the clouds of suspicion were beginning to cover the whole neighborhood, and it looked as if Tronco and his sons were about to be questioned, first by Mother herself, in her own diplomatic way, and then by the police, and Father was insisting, in vain, that the house ought to be searched for the emerald (all he could manage was that the garbage can and the living-room floor under the carpet and under the piano were searched time and again) when the terrible truth made itself evident to Mother and she screamed, "Green! But of course! Green!"

We all thought, mistakenly, that she had just realized where the missing emerald would be found.

"Not the emerald," she said, "but the clue to the thief! We all seem to have forgotten that emeralds are green."

"What do you mean, 'we' have forgotten that emeralds are green?" asked Father. "I never did. Or do you think I have been looking for a blue emerald since yesterday?"

"Think for a moment," Mother said.

We did; nothing came of it.

"How can you all be so stupid? Don't you realize in your small minds that emeralds are green?"

"All right, the emerald is green," said Father. "And then what?"

"Think, I say, think, all of you, think!" Mother exclaimed.

A lot of thinking was squeezed out of our minds, and still nothing came.

"Well, I see you are all babies," said Mother. "We know where the emerald was last seen—on the ashtray in the living room near the piano. I remember that I sat down at the piano, and I wanted to sing, and the black ribbon round my neck bothered me, so I took it off, and rolled the ribbon up and put it on the piano, where I later found it, and the emerald I placed in that ashtray. That is a fact." The first two suspects began to look uncomfortable. "Yes, in that ashtray. I remember this so *clearly*, so definitely, that no one can persuade me it was not so. I remember there was a ray of sunlight reflected from the mirror, falling just on my emerald. Very, very beautiful. Now, think. Go on from there."

We asked to be excused from further thinking.

"Who in this household," Mother went on, "*who* is so fond of green?"

"*My* color is pink," said Frieda, and so was her face.

"And mine yellow," said Maria.

"No one has asked *you* to defend yourselves even before being accused. Wait for a formal accusation, at least. . . . But, no, they can think of nothing but themselves, themselves, themselves!" my mother went on. "Egotists! I said 'Think' and they think of themselves. All right, if that is the general attitude, I will say nothing, even though I know who has the emerald, and I know it will soon be recovered, and also know that I will never wear it again. Three things I know, but I would rather be strangled than reveal them to you now."

Apologies were made, entreaties were used and used again, until finally she preferred to speak rather than to be strangled. "I said 'Think.' Now, why did I say 'Think'? Because I wanted you to think. And to think what? To think of green, and who loves green in this family, and who was in the living room lately, all alone, yesterday morning?"

No one could think who this was.

"All right," she said. "I will tell you: the horse."

And it was true, of course. None of us could dispute it. But before I go on with this true and unique detective story in which a horse is accused of stealing an emerald, I must explain briefly how the horse came to be in the living room the morning the emerald was stolen.

The day the emerald was stolen was the third or fourth day after we bought the horse. The stable was still clean, the manger was still new, the straw a brilliant yellow; in short, the stable looked like a painting by Rosa Bonheur. A coachman was teaching our father how to drive a carriage. (He had owned horses in the past, but for riding only. This was no excuse for his clumsy behavior with the blue horse, but in a way he did feel he was driving our dream and not his animal.) And whatever the coachman said or did about the horse was memorized by us children in secret.

Mother would open the narrow door that led from the kitchen to the coach house and the stable, and call, "*Nu, drujok, miliyie sosdanyie,*" which means "*Nu,* my little friend, sweet substance," and the horse would neigh in reply. We youngsters were around the horse all the time, fighting among ourselves for the horse's attention, for the right to speak to him in whispers—secrets between us and the horse and no one else—and for the right to show the horse picture albums with photographs of all our ancestors and relatives, and post cards from all the places in Russia and in Germany and Switzerland and Italy where we had lived or visited, and, finally, pictures of horses that had preceded him in our family. We also showed him spurs and saddles and old riding boots, which we found in a trunk in the attic. Sometimes Father would stop us, saying, "Enough, now, he is tired. He doesn't want to look at anything more." And we would protest, "No, he isn't, he wants more. He is asking for company." Oh, what a thing it was to have a horse enter the family!

For the first few days, Father spared the horse as he had always spared new things, and walked. But then he discovered about the horse's love for green. To begin with, the horse got loose from his "head-apron," as we children called the halter, and ran away. He stood in a green pasture and washed his face in it instead of eating it. He plunged his head into the grass as if that pasture were a huge washbasin, and let the grass caress his cheeks—first one cheek, then the other—without listening to us. We children called to him tenderly to come back. Instead, he trotted through the village, stopped in front of a millinery shop and licked the show window, thinking he could eat the green hat that was in it, and then tried to grab the green of the national flag, flying for who remembers what festivity from the town-hall balcony. Every time people got close enough to grab him, he stood beautifully on his hind legs, scared everybody away, and galloped madly through the streets. He stopped in front of the church and tried to eat the huge green church door, freshly painted; then he made for the green tent over a potter's market stand in the square, jumped elegantly over the hedge of the pharmacist's garden, and tore two or three leaves from a magnolia tree. He lifted a green blanket off the crib of the pharmacist's child, scaring the women who were there, and ran through the whole village with that green blanket in his teeth. Then he took to the green fields and pastures once more and disappeared, while tens of people ran after him, afoot, on bicycles, shouting and hissing. Father ran, too, panting, and calling through his teeth, "Five thousand lire, you rascal! I'll teach you to ruin me!"

A few minutes later, God knows how, the horse got into the house—but first passing through the garden and ruining every one of the freshly planted flower beds. He got as far as the living room. He wasn't in there very long, or there is no telling what damage he might have done, with all the porcelains there were around here and there, on tables and the mantelpiece. He was licking a green chair when the strong hand of the coachman grabbed him tight by the lock of hair between his ears and forced the "head-apron" back around his jaw. He had green paint all over his face and a flower hanging like a cigarette butt from his lips. And the emerald had been right there in that ashtray, so of course he was the thief.

Two hours after we had been told who took the emerald, the angry voice of Mother was audible from upstairs. She was angry with Maria and the Fräulein for being so stupid, both of them, so petty, so devoid of generosity, so always on the lookout for something bad, unpleasant, while she had only meant to thank them, one of them, she still did not know which one—the one who had repented and put the emerald back in the jewel box, where she had found it *by mere chance* and where it had *not* been before.

"Anyway," said she, "none of this would ever have happened if we were not forced to live in this frightful place." She wiped her eyes with a small handkerchief, went to the kitchen and from there to the stable, and said, "Here at least is a friend." The friend neighed, scraping the floor with his hoof.

"Good horse!" she said. "Good little horse! You, too, can give me worries." She patted him on the star between his eyes, and then said reproachfully, "*When* will you learn to speak?"

The horse dealer was right. The horse *was* unhappy and did fall on his knees, and he did have an unholy fear of washerwomen, and what our father did not want to understand was that a horse also has feelings, and that it takes him some time to get used to new masters. When I said, stupidly enough, that I had known about his weak knees all along, Father was furious. "So you knew this, but you did not see fit to let me know! As if the fact that I make a bad bargain were not damaging you just as much as me! As if my money were not yours! As if I did not have a right to know what I am doing when I purchase a horse! Why you should side with my enemies against me is something I shall never understand. Never!"

"The horse dealer is not your enemy."

"He is not my friend, and neither are you."

"Why is he not your friend? He *is* your friend!" I cried.

"Nice friend, indeed, one who sells you a horse that has weak knees! Now if we want to sell that horse, no one will buy it."

I could not have been more pleased. Sell our greatest friend, one of us, to God knows what unkind people? What would his former owner think of us if we did? I said to Father that everyone in the village knew the horse had weak legs, and had known this long before we bought him. I thought that he would say, as he so often did, "Oh, well, of course. We are always the last ones to learn what we should know." Alas, his reaction was most unexpected! He jumped up in a fury and almost hit me with the handle of the whip.

For hours after that—we were riding through the countryside in the rain, in an open carriage with a large green umbrella (later eaten up by the horse) to protect us—for hours he kept sighing and looking at me sidewise with disappointed, pleading eyes that tore my heart. Poor man, his strength was all in arguments, in logic, which he never produced until it was too late. So that wet afternoon, after insulting me for what I had done—or, rather, had not done—he pleaded with me for permission to be right (which he actually was), and at such moments he not only lost all his authority but all his logic, too. And those times when he did not plead for permission to be right, he got incensed; he beat us; he pronounced absurd sentences, like a despot who does not know what to do next to impress his inferiors. I decided to go ahead and put everything in the hands of the horse dealer, ask *him* for advice, and, if necessary, get him to remind Father of his promise. This was a very Machiavellian scheme—so much so that I knew I could not mention it to anyone, not even to Chino, because I knew that no one in the family was as wicked and scheming as I. But when you want something, or when, as in this case, you must defend your dearest friend against a life of hardships and solitude, away from you who love him, you whom he loves, no scheme is too tricky, and one cannot stop to consider the morality of one's actions.

So, while scheming and holding the green umbrella over our heads in the rain and watching the rain drip off the back of the horse, I prayed: "Dear Lord, please make that horse dealer be really as good a man as we want him to be. Make it that he really loved the horse, and that it is unhappiness and not weak legs that makes the horse stumble. And also make him strong, and make the Russian Revolution stop, and make us keep this horse even if we go back to town, even if we should go to Russia. Always keep him with us and let him live a long and happy life. Thank you so much. Amen."

"How does our friend carry the rain?" asked Mother as we appeared, Father and I, in the dining room at teatime, dripping with rain.

"What a question!" said Father. "How does a horse *carry* the rain. On his back. Better than he carries us."

"Poor animal. Is he wet?"

"Of course not. First, we ran in front of him holding the green umbrella over his head, and then, seeing that this was not sufficient to protect him from the rain, we put him in the carriage and pulled him. And then waited for him to see his patients. And now we are back home. He will soon come in and have tea, and we will be tied to the manger in the stable."

"I hope that you are joking," Mother said.

"Oh, no," he said. "I am perfectly serious. Ask anybody in the village. They did not even find it strange. They had already found it much stranger that I should have bought such an animal for such a price. Weak knees he has. You, too, knew that, I imagine." And, ordering some hay for himself and for me, he left the room.

"What happened?" Mother asked, turning to me.

"The horse fell twice," I said.

"So?" she said. "This means that we must buy him those leather things you wear on your knees when you are a horse. Very simple. I know why your father is in such a tragic mood today. He does not want to buy those leather things. He thinks they will add to the cost of the horse. As if he did not still have to buy a new carriage and a few other things a horse needs. Ridiculous."

"He says he wants to sell the horse because it has weak knees."

"How *typical!* You, too, had weak knees when you were small, and did we sell you? How unfaithful they are, these Italians! What else did he say?"

"He said we sided with his enemies against him."

"Who are his enemies?"

"In this case, the horse dealer."

"*We* sided with the horse dealer? It was we—*I,* to be more precise—who had to help your father *against* the horse dealer. I forced that man to sell his horse. Without me, I would like to see the horse we might have in our stable now! He also said the horse dealer was not our friend?"

"Yes."

"I know why he said that. Because the horse dealer did not come for tea the other day. I never expected him. I saw how timid he was, and you cannot expect these low people to have manners. All you can expect of them is that they have a heart, and he does."

On days when it had rained, all the ditches were full of water, and the roads in the country were full of washerwomen, and Nello always got frightened and tried to run away. One day, he upset the carriage with us in it. He was pulled down by the carriage, the carriage shafts broke, and he fell backward, his hind legs sinking in the water of the ditch. And, of course, shrieks and commotion, whippings and more damage, and more whippings because of it, and more damage because of those retaliatory whippings. Terrible thing. The carriage we had bought to do us temporarily (and might have kept for years, still temporarily, had the horse not destroyed it in that way) was worth eight hundred lire—quite a sum, even though it was old. And now a new one would have to be bought, and they were very expensive, those new ones. But how he ran, that time! How beautiful he was when, with the carriage empty behind him, the pillows and the people still in the mud, he fled galloping through the village at such speed that it was a miracle half a dozen people were not killed.

He turned left in front of the pharmacist's house, where the sidewalk was enough higher than the street level that carriages were often overturned when a wheel ran over it, but our horse managed to pass without upsetting the carriage and continued in the direction of the cemetery. The whole village was mobilized to stop him. There is no telling where he might have gone—probably inside the cemetery itself, desecrating the tombs, devouring the green ribbon around the wreaths of recent graves, and perhaps falling into some freshly dug hole and breaking his legs—had he not been saved by a young girl. She was washing clothes beside the road and singing while she washed, so she heard nothing, not even the shrieks of other women calling to her to get up and run because a mad horse was coming down the road in her direction. Seeing that kneeling figure and those flapping wet clothes from a distance, he stopped, turned around, half upsetting the carriage, and ran back to the village square. This time, he did smash the carriage against the sidewalk in front of the pharmacist's house, and the butcher brought him home to us, with the wreckage still dragging miserably behind him.

"Now!" said Father, striking the horse in the face with his fists. "Now you will learn, you beast!"

But Mother still found words in Nello's defense. "This is what happens," she said, "when you put the cart behind the horse."

And when Nello was back in the stable, she gave him sugar and an extra measure of barley, which she took out of the bin with her own hands, and spoke Russian to him, because she did not know Hungarian.

After that, when Father had to make calls, he walked or rode Chino's bicycle. In despair, Mother declared that she would even sell the horse, provided Father stopped using the bicycle or walking all day long. "Because after all," she pointed out, "you must not forget that the horse is here to help *you!*"

But Father refused to consider the horse as his exclusive tool. No, no, the horse was a good horse, he said, only there was no way for the two of them to get together, to find a common ground of understanding, to work together for the good of the family. So a reconciliation between our father and our horse was brought about, with a great deal of talking, first to the man, then to the horse, and then back to the man again, until Father decided that the horse deserved a second chance, and also a few toys, as tokens of his friendship, such as a shining new carriage, a few head and body ornaments, and a new whip. We wanted to have a celebration for the horse on his birthday, but it seemed impossible to discover in what year and at what precise time the horse was born, so we settled on February 29th, to make sure he would never grow too old, since he would have only one birthday every four years.

Mother gave him her emerald, which in the meantime had been appraised by a jeweler in Florence and found cracked, and therefore worth infinitely less than Mother said it was worth. What she had hoped to get for the emerald no jeweler ever would have paid. Since her fortune had been lost and the good days were gone, whatever big or small objects were still left of that fortune and those days had gone up astronomically in value, beyond all possible evaluation, and in her mind this astronomical price should be paid, without hesitation—indeed, with gratitude. Which never happened. So the dear emerald went for almost nothing; it hardly paid for the new carriage, but she quickly forgot that unpleasant detail ("Why always think of the sad side of life?") and went on paying with that emerald for whatever new fancy she had. "The emerald will pay for that!" she would say. "Hay for the horse!" she would order, in February, when the price of hay was at its highest. "The emerald will pay for it."

The emerald paid for all sorts of things that were paid for

much later by going further into debt or out of Father's meager savings. Thus, and as part of the horse's birthday celebration, Maria, who had never forgotten the fact that she had been unjustly accused and was quite jealous of the horse, received a gold brooch as a present. A smaller present was given to Frieda, because her family was rich and she was German. The horse dealer, too, was on Mother's list, and received two presents—a framed etching of a horse (that was a present *from* the horse) and a cigarette holder of old Russian silver, a by no means indifferent gift, for which Mother paid nothing, because she didn't have to buy it. We had a great many silver trinkets, large and small, in good and in bad taste. We knew that the horse dealer had undoubtedly never seen such a thing in his life, but, as Mother explained, "One must be practical. We need his help to exploit the capital invested in that horse. He alone can advise us." And even the horse dealer's wife received a present—a silk shawl, quite a beautiful one, that Mother had in her collection anyway.

Chino's present to the horse was a tiny golden horn he himself had received on the day of his christening. Father was against the horse's wearing frivolous things with his equipment, so the little golden horn was kept in the box it had always been kept in. The only difference was that Chino put a note in the box stating that the golden horn belonged to his dear horse, Nello, and to avoid confusion all the other names that had ever been discussed or considered were listed on the same piece of paper.

Sonia played the piano for Nello. She played an arrangement of the Second Hungarian Rhapsody of Liszt for four hands, with Mother, but it was Sonia's, not Mother's, present to the horse, and he listened to them from the garden, with his entire head inside the window. This piano concert given for the horse audience exclusively was also a scientific experiment. We wanted to know whether it was true that horses love music. The Meyers "Konversations Lexicon," in twelve huge, heavy, green, leather-bound volumes said so, our illustrated German books of mythology said so, Homer said so, Aristotle said so, but Father said it was not so. He took the position that horses are stupid—hopelessly stupid—and that only incorrigible dreamers like us children, led by a dreamer such as Mother, could make up such idiotic fancies, taking for gospel truth the pseudoscientific statements of the ancients, as quoted by some modern lexicographer on pure, classical hearsay. Father consented to our scientific experiment only in order to prove us wrong, and we all insisted that he observe the one-animal audience from outdoors, where he could see the horse's face reflected in the mirror above the sofa opposite the window. If the horse saw Father's somber face *inside* the room, he might think the Second Hungarian Rhapsody of Liszt was part of a punishment or a lesson in good behavior. And we won, with Homer, Aristotle, and many others. We won because the horse rolled his eyeballs at the piano while the mysterious, evocative sounds were coming out of it. His ears stood erect and slightly bent toward the music. He sighed right into Sonia's neck, and she made a mistake, for which she quickly apologized. The music was interrupted while she and Mother started counting again, and then they resumed playing. And the horse resumed sniffing and sighing. Out in the road, crowds of curious people were pressing their faces against the holes in the rusty iron plate that covered the whole front gate. Word had been spread that something called a "psychological test" was being tried at the Doctor's house, and the peasant folk, who had never even heard of the word "psychological," were very much impressed. Some made the sign of the cross and said this was a devilish practice, but they came to observe it all the same. The surrounding fields were also full of people, and when Mother heard their distant chatter, hardly distinguishable from the many other noises of the country, she shouted, without looking away from the score or stopping with her hands, "Barbarians!" Seeing how much the horse was enjoying the concert, the artists played a few Russian songs, by way of an encore, and he liked them immensely.

I did not have any present to give the horse for his birthday, and Jules-Adrien almost brought about a major family quarrel by thinking he could give the horse a dog—which, first of all, did not even belong to us, even though it stayed with us all the time; it belonged to Tronco. And, secondly, we all contended that a dog cannot possibly belong to a horse, because the horse is a slave and so is the dog. My younger brother did not get the idea. "Why don't you want the horse to have a dog?" he kept asking. "A dog does not work, anyway. They can be friends."

"All right," we said. "They can be friends, but this proves nothing. The dog still cannot belong to the horse."

"And how about those other presents there?"

He was perfectly right, so we were all against him, and in the end we won, but not before we made it clear to him that a horse could not own a cat, either. Besides, the cat belonged to all of us, and we did not think that the horse should have it. We won our argument by finding something he *could* give to the horse—a leather harness with little bells, which he had received from his Hungarian godmother when he was a little boy and used to while away the sad hours of childhood by pretending to himself that he was a horse.

Every one of these episodes of silliness, while augmenting the halo around our horse, made any contact with reality, even the most innocent contact, something to be avoided at all cost. The horse dealer had been right; there was no telling how far that horse would take us.

As the crowning event in the birthday celebration, we took Nello to see the horse dealer, who felt terribly guilty in our presence and proud in the presence of everybody else, because he had sold his old horse for such a price. When the horse dealer and his wife heard of our impending visit, they must have thought that now, of course, they would have a good laugh at our expense. And I confess that for a while that afternoon we children felt extremely embarrassed. We knew that it was not very nice of us to laugh at our own mother, but we knew also that it had to be done if we were to establish a bridge between our family and the rest of the world; there was no alternative. Perhaps if *they* could laugh at her and see how graciously she took it, they might accept her—as we did, after all—because of her wit.

At first, the occasion was rather stiff. Mother spoke of the two Arab horses the Governor of Moscow had given her grandfather.

A lot the horse dealer knew where—or what—Moscow was! I explained, laughing, that Arab horses rode from right to left, like Arabic writing and like Hebrew writing, while Chinese horses went up and down. That shifted the subject of our conversation to something less connected with us and of more interest to anyone who had at least a spark of interest in what he did not know. Mother had studied Arabic during her frequent visits to Egypt, and she gave the horse dealer and his wife a lesson in that language, and this gave her a chance to exhibit the best in her, instead of the worst. And as soon as the worst began to come out again, in bragging reminiscences of her childhood in Russia, I said, "But that is nothing, what you just heard. At home, we have a picture of the horse that brings the sun to the world every morning. It is called 'Dawn,' and it is by Guido Reni." Thus the conversation became interesting again, and Mother, who could talk about mythology for hours, had a chance to exhibit her knowledge, instead of just her solitude and her resentment. She talked on and on. She showed the horse dealer and his wife some of the aquarelle drawings of horses her sister Adya had sent to her from Germany (Aunt Adya was insane, and lived in a clinic near Berlin), and when she said, "These were made by my sister, who is mentally unbalanced," the horse dealer and his fat wife did not laugh and did not have to make an effort not to laugh. Almost without knowing it, they had been converted to our side, and so our horse was accepted by those who had discarded him, and it was the horse dealer himself who later taught Nello not to fear the mysterious behavior of peasant women washing clothes in the ditches beside the road. He made his wife and other women kneel in front of his house and hold their flapping wet sheets up for the horse to examine, and in the end the horse decided that washerwomen were not really inimical to him.

Of course, new difficulties clouded the horizon and made life trying for us. Some of these difficulties were invented and some were really true. And, like all toys, our horse lost its attraction. He became one of us. The Latin words that my father would teach me—angrily, as usual—during the long drive from one peasant house to the next scared the horse just as much as they scared me. The long and pessimistic speeches that he made to me, looking intently at the trotting behind of the horse, seemed addressed to the horse as much as they were to me, and Nello and I were equally impressed or depressed by them.

Mother grew old, and we children grew young—young and resentful—and Mother resented that. We were becoming like the tough peasants of Terra Betinga. In fact, we spoke their language; we understood their narrow ways. But our childhood was still Mother's and hers alone, like the horses of Russia, the steppes of Hungary, the names and people of her past.

And the horse trotted through the bare Tuscan marshlands, ever more lazily and with weaker knees. He was sold after seven years when Father bought a car.

HEY!

The place was called Siberia: fifteen miles from Florence, smaller than the Russian Siberia and less cold, but a bad place all the same. Green and hot in the summer, almost constantly flooded in winter by one, two or all of the six torrents crossing the plain of Pistoia between high embankments. In mild winters the floods lasted only a few weeks, then for another few weeks the mud was so thick that our light two-wheeled buggy became as heavy as a cart loaded with stones. If the winter was dry, the furrows of the last carriage on the road remained imprinted like canyons in a relief-map, and whoever ventured in his carriage on that road ran the risk of breaking axle and springs and of being thrown off his seat. And once you started on the road there was no way back. Almost all roads in the plain ran between two deep irrigation canals, and if you met another carriage it was either for you or for him to pass with one wheel down the slope, very often tipping over. Even from far away you could hear those yells: "Haaaay-hooo. . . . Stop there. . . . Eee-up, eeeeee-upp!" followed by curses in the best Tuscan tradition.

I remember Tesi, who lived in Siberia, because he had built our garden and worked as a handyman for us until he became too weak from tuberculosis and knew it was time for him to go home and die. Father tried to get him to go to the hospital, but he refused. When he understood that he was going to be helped against his will, he said we had better stop interfering, because if he saw an ambulance on the road to his house, he would shoot. That is why, although there was no hope for him, Father decided to go and see him during the winter, every three or four days. He lived in a house that looked like an ancient Roman ruin, although it was only some forty years old. Haystack, plough, chicken-coop, a long, narrow cornfield in front of the house and the greyish wall of Mangoni's house beyond the vineyard: that was his view. Mangoni had a bigger house and a bigger family. He didn't own his strip of land like Tesi; it belonged to the rich bachelor Baldi, but like Tesi and everybody in every house along those dirt roads, he was visited by tuberculosis. Only his folk died more slowly, without all sorts of complications such as bronchitis or pneumonia.

I usually went with Father to see Tesi. I liked the adventure of wading, the noise of water on the wheels, the trees reflected in the water, and the solitude. While my father visited his patient, I covered up the horse with a red blanket, gave it a little hay, and read a book or studied my Latin or my botany. When it rained I sat in the kitchen beside the fire. Like all peasant kitchens, it had a smoky pot of water hanging on a black chain in the fireplace, and the rest of the room was only a little lighter than the pot and the chain. I remember a yellow leaflet nailed to the wall, dotted by millions of fly excrements. It read: "WHAT GOD THINKS OF WOMAN," and it said that God hated immodesty, adultery, bad language and laxity in religious practices. There were also a few illustrated post cards with views of towns under deep blue skies, almost completely blackened by the flies, too. In one corner there was an oil lamp in front of a post card of a Madonna, framed with a piece of paper lace.

I still don't know why the sound of Tesi's coughing upstairs had the quality of rotting wood. Perhaps because I associated it with the rotting beams that by some sort of miracle held up the ceiling, or perhaps because in that small house all voices became encased, absorbed by the holes in the wood, so that only the ghost of a voice is allowed to reach your ear.

My conversations with Tesi's wife were very difficult, because, for fear of inhaling dirty microbes, I kept my lips tightly closed. I had gone near many a wealthy t.b. patient without being afraid of anything, so it was really the dirty microbes that I minded. But even if I had been willing to talk, she never said a word, except "O my God," or "O, what a world . . ." or simply, "Ooooh." And looking at the house or listening to her husband cough, there was indeed little I could say that wouldn't have sounded silly. Her name, strangely enough, was Gorilla. She came from one of the many Gori families and there were several girls named Gorilla Gori. I recall sitting in Gorilla's company for hours, watching the rain on the three deformed stones of the steps to the house door, or the undulant floor of the kitchen itself, with here and there a brick missing and all the other bricks caved in or broken into such small pieces that they looked like the wrinkles on her face. I never saw much of her face: a large brown kerchief, with the two ends going out right and left from under her chin, left just an oval opening, a sort of window, for her face. In there she was: a ravaged forehead with furrows in all directions, two dark eyes with much white around them, and a long nose.

They had two children: Isaia and Manno, strange creatures who frightened me. Isaia was nine or ten, perhaps even twelve, they didn't know; and Manno was six. But there was hardly any difference between them in size: probably all they had to exhibit in the line of growth, all their reserves of cells or whatever it is that makes people strong, didn't reach beyond the age of six. After six they began to shrink as science teaches us normal people do at thirty-five. They both had large, shiny foreheads; the skin was tight as parchment on a drum. Their voices were hardly audible, and rattled drily, like wood, when they spoke. But their laughter was ghastly, as if it were beyond their voices: it took place in the region of sighs and coughs. Father said that was the "voce afona," the toneless voice of t.b. patients, and whenever I heard them play I hoped they wouldn't come near me, for I felt like crying out of sheer compassion. They always looked at my sad face with amused curiosity, however, then fled from me to "laugh" among themselves.

I remember that Father once told Tesi that his children should not sleep in the same bed with him, and he asked whether it would be better for them to sleep outside the window. All the peasants kept their children with them when they were ill. In Tesi's house there was only one room upstairs with a big bed in it. On that bed a child was conceived, born or "sbucciato," as they say in Tuscany, that is, peeled: shown the facts of life in a few visual lessons, then shown how one dies of the family disease, and left to do it when the time was ripe for the performance. After the big storm broke the tree outside the house and it fell on the roof, breaking the tiles, they made up a bed of clothes and sacks of corn in a corner for the children, and when it rained Tesi held an umbrella over himself in bed. The big green umbrella under which Tesi had come to our house hundreds of times in the past was very convenient: it took the few drops that leaked through the roof and splashed them in the direction of the stairway. Thus the bed remained dry.

In the spring Gorilla became ill too, and the children had to be sent to the Mangoni's where they slept in the stable. In the daytime they played in the fields as usual. They didn't even have to feed their donkey, because Mangoni had taken it into his stable. But once a day they greeted their parents, "Hey!" Just opening the door and shouting "Hey!" inside the kitchen. The two patients didn't have to reply, because every attempt to shout brought forth a violent access of coughing which usually ended in that lacerating "Gooo goo aaaht," preceding blood-spitting, or as the doctors call it, emottisis. The Billi woman from San Michele stayed with them practically all day now. She fed them and helped them defecate. The rest of the time she sat in the kitchen, knitting away at her straw hats which in those days still sold quite well in America, and every now and then she threw a strange glance at the poverty around her, as if to make sure that no one had stolen it.

We had a few beautiful days in February, so beautiful that everybody said, "This is real spring now" (and it was); and then rain and rain for two months without one single day of respite.

And Siberia was awful then. But Father went there anyway, because Tesi enjoyed talking to him. Father was funny: he hated to see patients; he had no faith in medicine anyway, but he liked Tesi because with him it was all a relationship beyond disease; if anything medical was mentioned it was only to get the conversation started or to fill a gap in it. One day I heard Tesi inquire about my brothers, my sister and myself; I heard him pronounce each name distinctly, very slowly, and my father give him the description of our "exceptional qualities" he usually reserved for guests of distinction. It was strange to hear him talk that way in the stone hut, in the midst of such desolate flooded country. It brought the light atmosphere of a drawing-room there; to me it was like a dream. Tesi tried to say something like, "I am so glad," but when he came to the word "so," he stumbled into the most desperate series of choking coughs. Gorilla never said a word, letting the men talk, but I was sure that she was listening from her side of the bed.

On May second (birthday of Leonardo da Vinci, born in the house down there on the slope of that grey hill) the rain stopped and the clouds went away. Corn, wheat, vines, and just simple grass on the edge of the fields were so green against the sunshine that it filled me with the usual despair: never could such green be told by anyone. The two patients were dying; it was hard to tell who would die first; Gorilla had made good progress in two months and was by now nearly as ill as Tesi. Father's visits lasted much longer now, because Tesi kept asking him about medicine, geography, history, botany; at home I had collected a few illustrated magazines and books for Father to show him and burn afterwards. Father was giving him an education. He enjoyed it. Once I saw him from the haystack: he was holding a white sheet of paper over Tesi's bed, describing the functioning of the heart. He had made the same drawing in my notebook only a few days before. I didn't mind those long visits; I sat in the carriage with my book open on my knees but couldn't read. I kept looking at the leaves against the sunshine. I listened to the birds, to distant church bells, I inhaled the new earth, the smell of horses, cows, flowers, and was drunk with poetry. The only thing that disturbed me was when the children came, because they seemed to like the game of yelling "Hey!" into the house. Their toneless call into that dark receptacle of death destroyed everything around me; even the sun itself seemed affected by it.

One day Father appeared at the window in his white attire and asked me to take the horse away from under the fig tree and to stand in front of the horse, holding the reins. I wondered why, but obeyed. After a few seconds I heard a shot, then another one, and I saw a branch of the fig tree fall to the ground. The barrel of a gun was still resting on the window-sill. My father explained later that for a few days Tesi had been longing to shoot. He was a good huntsman, but the season was far off. He didn't care; he just wanted to bring about a change in the view: a large fig leaf had stood right in the middle of his field of vision; he had looked at it for hours and hours and now he wanted to shoot it. It made him feel as if he had gone out and got something done. But after a second experiment Father forbade him to shoot again and taught him more about the world instead.

I had become so familiar with the idea of those two patients that now I was anxious to see whether there was an end to human resistance; it was pure scientific curiosity. On a Wednesday towards the end of May, not a clear day, not a clean sky, but just hot and unpleasant, Father said: "This is the day. We won't find them alive. I think they will die at almost the same moment. But we shall go there anyway, because from there we must go to Mangoni's. One of his daughters had a strong emottisis last night."

I would have wanted to go upstairs with my father, but I didn't dare ask him. Would they die coughing, or would they yell, or just whistle like the wind under a door? Had I been going to keep a date with a girl, I could hardly have been more impatient or more afraid of being discovered by my father. I drove the carriage beyond the fig tree so I could look into the room. I stepped on the seat, but couldn't see much: a white form, the bed, but nothing to indicate that it wasn't empty. Yes, the whistle, not so much like the wind under a door as like crickets in the first evening of summer. Such a sweet sound usually awoke in me nostalgic dreams or fiery desires: how horrible to hear it from the lips of a dying man. Why didn't I hear his wife, too? Was she dead? I saw my father pass in front of the window and bend over the bed. I blushed and jumped off the seat, but he hadn't seen me. Then I saw the Billi woman standing by the horse.

I had to explain, "I thought my father was calling me and I wondered why."

"No, he wasn't," she said and sighed, knitting away as usual at her straw braids.

The Mangoni woman came across the fields, followed by three girls. They were all knitting and all curious.

"Your father is coming to my place after this," she said.

And I said, "Yes, we are."

"The priest is due any minute," said the Billi woman. In fact, the bells of San Michele were just beginning to touch off the monotonous hammering of the occasion.

"She," said the Mangoni woman, "was dead half an hour ago."

"Oh," said the Billi woman. "So it's only he who still has to finish his suffering. Well, rich or poor . . ." and she went nearer the house to hear better.

Isaia and Manno appeared from the street, barefoot as usual, dirty, covered with dust as if they had been in a baker-shop. They were walking, each with a hand on the other's shoulder, and seemed to be having a good time.

"Shhhhh!" said the two women, and made a sign for them to go away. But they came up to the horse and began giggling stupidly. Then Isaia said something to his brother who ran like the devil to the house, jumped lightly up the three steps, pushed the door open and shouted, "Hey, hey, hey . . . !" until the Billi woman ran after him, grabbed him by his frail arm and threw him back to the middle of the yard, saying, "Shame! They are dying in there."

But Isaia laughed. In that province of laughter foreign to his voice, he emitted painful whistles from his open mouth. He sounded like his father and went on laughing that way, beating his knees with his hands, then pointing to his brother with a long, dark, bony finger, and groaning: "I fooled him! I fooled him!"

Author's note to *Twice a Year,* the magazine in which "Hey!" was first published (Fall/Winter issue, 1946):

I am sending you a story *(Hey)* which was rejected by five leading magazines devoted to Destructive Optimism (destructive of our critical faculties), on the sole ground of it's "unpleasantness." They all praised the writing, and not just perfunctorily as they do on such occasions, but telling me that they wanted it very much, but wouldn't I please try to make it a little less sad and horrifying? Tuberculosis, with which the story deals, appears to these guardians of the American Smile a little tactless, and, as we all know or should know, dying of tuberculosis *can be fun.* That was the hidden message I had failed to extract from my recollection of the two characters described in my story as (not really!) dying serenely, in an atmosphere of quiet despair. Someday I shall publish my correspondence with the guardians of the A. S. (N.T.)

HISTORY COMES C.O.D.

It wasn't easy for my father to tell his young friend Count Geppo Quaderni that the administrator of the Count's great estate in Albiano was a thief, but Father finally decided to do it, not so much because Quaderni was being cheated as because Bartoli, the administrator, had lost all respect for the forms. He stole badly and defiantly, mishandling both his victim and the things he stole from him. This, rather than the fact that Bartoli was dishonest, was what made the Count's friends furious. There is an old Tuscan proverb "*Chi dice fattore dice ladro,*" which means, "Who says administrator says thief." Everyone in Tuscany *expects* an administrator to steal, but there are ways and ways of doing it.

For example, another friend of our family, Count Tatti Atarelli, who lived in Bologna, had been so thoroughly cheated by *his* manager, Giuntoli, a former peasant, that not long after hiring him he had had to borrow money from the man, and eventually, in order to meet his obligations, had been obliged to sell him nearly everything he owned—land, buildings, and other properties. But what miracles this fellow Giuntoli had brought to pass before that! Ten years after Tatti had entrusted him with a bankrupt chicken farm, some played-out cherry orchards, and a small local cheese factory, the name of Tatti Atarelli had become synonymous with the best roasters, the biggest, sweetest cherries, and the tastiest cheese in all Italy. Even after Tatti had lost his estate and Giuntoli had moved into the Atarelli villa, Tatti liked to testify that his administrator's behavior had always been, and was still, most correct. "He keeps my house and furniture as if the place were some sort of national museum and he the curator," he once told my father, "and, what's more, he still asks my advice when he meets me on the street. Imagine how much he must think of my intelligence when he was able to steal all that godsend from under my nose without my noticing it. Yet every time we encounter each other he remembers to ask me about one thing or another. I must say I find it rather touching."

By contrast, Bartoli showed no respect for Count Quaderni. It was clear to everyone that Bartoli's ambitions were the same as those of his colleague—to steal as much as he could as quickly as he could, and eventually get his master out of the house and live in it himself. But while Giuntoli, as I have said, knew how to treat *his* count respectfully and take proper care of the family heirlooms he had appropriated, Bartoli had not the slightest appreciation of the precious things he was stealing, and, too, kept telling everyone what a fool Count Quaderni was. Once, when asked his opinion of his master, Bartoli said, "The Count? The Count is a simpleton. You could sell everything on the estate and tell him you hadn't sold it and he wouldn't know the difference."

It was this remark that led to my father's discovery that Bartoli had sold thirty of the Quaderni calves, telling the Count they had died and that he must have money to buy new ones, and naming a sum that was twice what he would have to pay. Thus, with next to no effort, he had pocketed the price of sixty calves. He cheated Quaderni in much the same way on the fruit and grain crops, the wine, and the silkworms, until finally the poor Count was beginning to borrow large sums of money from Bartoli in order to meet the expenses of running the estate. And to repay these loans, Bartoli made the Count sign away to him one piece of land after another.

For all this, no one had the right to criticize Bartoli merely for stealing with less style than Giuntoli. That was really nobody's business but his and Count Quaderni's. What incensed the people of Albiano, and especially my parents, was the way Bartoli abused and insulted the Quaderni heirlooms and objets d'art. For Bartoli simply removed every portable object from the villa and used it himself. He removed the beautiful Renaissance porcelain plates that for generations had hung on the walls of the dining room of the Quaderni villa and used them in the kitchen of his dirty little house. His dog ate out of an old French crystal bowl, a real museum piece. His wife, a peasant woman, made up her beds with the precious linen that had been part of the trousseau of Count Quaderni's grandmother, and the Quaderni silver lamps—rare specimens of Venetian baroque—were set out on her kitchen table whenever Bartoli had the parish priest for dinner. (The parish priest, shame on him, always accepted Bartoli's invitations, and then went around telling stories about him.) In the villa itself, which Count Quaderni occupied only during the three or four weeks in summer when he came to Albiano for a vacation, Bartoli often, and obviously without the Count's knowledge, housed his friends—coarse, uneducated people, like himself. It is easy to guess what they did to the furniture.

Yet for almost a year after Bartoli's misdeeds became known in the community, my father hesitated to warn Geppo Quaderni. My mother insisted that such goings on could not be tolerated, but Father's reasons for not speaking were three; I often heard him explain them to Mother. He counted the first two reasons, in typical Italian fashion, on the thumb and index finger of his left hand, grabbing each of these fingers with the thumb and index finger of his right hand and shaking them, in turn, in front of my mother as he talked. "First," he said (this was the thumb's reason), "*chi dice fattore dice ladro.* Geppo ought to know this, but he refuses to open his eyes. And, second," Father said, pouncing quickly on the index finger before it could escape, "I have discovered much of Bartoli's thievery while visiting his wife in my capacity as a physician. Now, as you know, the Hippocratic Oath demands full secrecy of a doctor. And, as Michelangelo so well wrote about his statue of Night, in the Tomb of the Medicis, '*Non veder, non sentir m'è gran ventura*—' "

"The devil with Hippocrates and Michelangelo!" answered Mother. "Geppo is our only friend in this horrible place, and we must tell him how he's being cheated."

"Third," went on my father—he never counted this third reason on any of his fingers but, instead, folded his hands under his chin and looked at the ceiling, as if he were praying—"*chi ce lo fa fare?*" ("Who compels us to do it?") This was also a current proverb, and it happened to be, of all the wise saws into which the ancient wisdom of the Italians is compressed, the one my mother, who was Russian-born, hated most.

"Who compels us to do it?" she asked indignantly. "Our honor, of course! We owe it to our friend to warn him against this Bolshevist Bartoli, who undermines the foundations of society."

I was a child when the trouble in Albiano started, but, looking back, I now realize that the truth of the matter was this: Geppo was rich and we were poor. It was a fact that he was our one friend among the landowners of the town, but only because he hadn't yet become our enemy, like everybody else. Back in the days before the Bolshevist Revolution, when my mother had not yet lost her money in Russia, we lived in Florence and had many friends. Geppo was one of them and often came to dinner parties at my parents' house. When we became poor, we retired to Albiano, and my father practiced medicine there, living like a gentleman but working like a slave. He was never willing to ask for payment from people he considered his inferiors intellectually, and since most of his patients were peasants, life became quite hard for him. Living among the poor, he had come to despise them because they hated him, and they hated him because he was a gentleman, because he read books, and because our whole family preferred the company of books and music to that of the village gossips, rich or poor. Our humble neighbors thought, as people raised in hardship and envy often do, that we acted the way we did because we had nothing better to do, and they scorned us because we were gentry who had no money and no residence in town, because we didn't spend part of the year in a summer or winter resort, and because, when we did make a journey, we traveled third class, sitting with the poor. We hadn't been in Albiano long before Father began to think of Geppo as no better than the rest of the people there. "The difference between the landowner and the peasant," he would say, "is no more than the difference between capital letters and small ones. Capital letters usually take precedence in a sentence, but they stand for the same sounds as small letters and their meaning is exactly the same. As for Geppo, he is narrow-minded, egotistical, ignorant, conceited, stupid, and lazy. His only good qualities are those we have conferred upon him because he reminds us of better days."

In this last remark, Father wasn't completely just, for Geppo did have one good quality—an almost religious devotion to the memory of his mother. He considered her superior to all other women, perhaps chiefly because she had given birth to him. Since her death, he had made it a habit to honor her memory by showing great devotion to her friends, of whom my mother had been one of the closest. And, recalling how often his poor mother had asked my father to give her son advice, he considered my father a sort of brother, ignoring both the difference in their ages and the fact that his mother had sought my father's advice only on how to make a man out of her son. The advice had been given, had been followed, and had proved worthless. Geppo read nothing, enjoyed nothing, bored himself to death most of the time, sought the company of vulgar people so that he could feel superior to them, didn't know the value of the beautiful things he possessed, and hated the people of Albiano just as much as we did. But he had decided to pretend to love them, because it made him feel that somewhere in the world he could be at home. The only way he could keep up this illusion was to stay away from Albiano and close his eyes to whatever his servants and his peasant folk were doing. Mother knew all these facts about Geppo but had decided, even so, to pretend that he was a young man of great culture and dignity, and that he consorted only with distinguished people and couldn't stay in Albiano because the people there were vulgar, ignorant, and cruel.

There existed between Mother and the people of Albiano a fierce, hidden state of war over Geppo. They watched with delight his ruin at the hands of his administrator, much as pedestrians stand spellbound on the sidewalks when they see housewreckers tearing down an old mansion. Mother linked this attitude of theirs with Communism and was quite determined to defend Geppo's property against "these Bolshevists," among whom she put not only Bartoli but the parish priest and his assistant, the chaplain, and the industrialists of the nearby town of Prato, who bought up landed properties and razed the trees and villas in order to build factories. In fact, to Mother, a Bolshevist was anyone who did anything she didn't like. And, to Mother, Geppo was like a king who had duties toward his property that were as sacred as his rights in it. The porcelain, the silver, the bed linen, the furniture, and all the other Quaderni heirlooms were not to be used by vulgar people and not to be ruined, Mother said, and she felt sure that Geppo would feel the same way if he were told what was going on. Living, as she did, closer to the villa than its owner did, she had come to have a spiritual sense of ownership of Geppo's possessions. Landed gentry everywhere recognize and respect this sort of spiritual ownership when servants feel it for their master's property. But when friends show such possessiveness, it is called interference, and not devotion.

This was the delicate situation that made Father and Mother take such violently opposing sides about Bartoli, the Quaderni administrator. Tatti Atarelli, who was also a friend of Geppo Quaderni and whom we saw every now and then, would gladly have spoken to Geppo but could not, because he had heard, from reliable sources, that Geppo had described him as a fool. "Now, it's nothing new for me to be called a fool," he once said. "That I am one is something I know, and everybody knows. But why need he say it? It isn't very nice, and, eager as I am to help Geppo, I find myself unable to."

The parish priest, too, said to Father that the situation at Count Quaderni's was a real scandal and that no one could warn Geppo as well as a trusted friend like Father. But the priest, who disliked our whole family, was playing the game both ways, and when

Father told him that he had decided to warn Geppo, the priest quickly warned Bartoli of what was about to happen, and Bartoli took his precautions. He wrote to Geppo that both Father and Mother had come to the villa frequently to spy upon him, and he told Geppo that they had criticized his, Geppo's, laxity and bad behavior. The priest's treachery was of little avail, however, for when Geppo arrived that summer, he was at first very cold to Bartoli. The sly fellow, fearing that he was going to lose his job, humiliated himself in front of his master. He cried, made protestations of honesty, but he relied so much upon his eloquence to save him that he forgot to take the most elementary precautions, like removing Geppo's Renaissance plates from his kitchen. So, while Bartoli and his wife were busily beating their chests and defending their record as good caretakers, Geppo one day saw his plates in the Bartolis' china cabinet, and blushed and looked away. His shame was so great at seeing himself so flagrantly abused that he now began to assure Bartoli he had never doubted his honesty. Bartoli went so far as to bring in as a witness in his behalf a peasant woman who worked as cook for Geppo during his stays in Albiano. This woman swore that Bartoli was honest, but late that night she went to see Geppo in his study and recanted everything, asking her master please to understand how frightened she was of Bartoli's vengeance; she had a son who was being trained in the administration of the estate, and Bartoli was his boss. But, she said, if the Count would get rid of Bartoli, everyone would be happy.

The next day, observing his usual custom, Geppo came to pay his respects to my parents. During his call, my father asked to see him alone, and when their talk was over, Geppo left looking rather pale and annoyed. Father also looked pale, and seemed unwilling to explain what had happened, but finally he did. "Geppo is a fool," said he. "He doesn't want to see. His eyes are closed, as I told you before. But I warned him that if he didn't look out, Bartoli would get not only the estate but him, too, into the bargain."

"What did Geppo say?" asked Mother rather anxiously.

"He says that Bartoli is a perfectly honest man and that he had given him permission to remove those plates from the wall. He says the people of Albiano are a very good sort, and that it's *we* who have prejudices against them. So that's the end, I guess."

"The end of what?" she asked.

"Of our friendship," Father said. "And also of Geppo, and the villa, and everything."

Geppo made only a short stay in Albiano that summer. He left three or four days later. He didn't come to see us again, and after he had left, we learned that Bartoli had moved into the top floor of the villa, supposedly to guard the place against thieves. The thought of seeing those top-floor windows open every day and lighted every night was a terrible insult to us. The Quaderni villa could be seen from our house but we no longer looked in that direction if we could help it.

Then, one day, Mother had to go to Geppo's house, to make her yearly pilgrimage to the tomb of her friend the old Countess, who, like her husband and his ancestors, was buried inside the villa itself, in the family chapel. Bartoli's wife, who was there when Mother arrived, did not say good morning, but she did say to herself, with a sneer, and loud enough for Mother to overhear her, "These good-for-nothings who find the time to bring flowers to the dead! It would be better if, instead, they didn't try to harm the living."

A day or two later, Bartoli stopped my father on the street and told him that the parish priest had warned him that Father had evil intentions. Thereupon Mother called the parish priest to the house and told him what she thought of him. "I will have you punished," she said, and that same day, although realizing that, as a Russian Orthodox Catholic, she had little influence with the Vatican, she wrote to a couple of cardinals who were family acquaintances and asked them to excommunicate the parish priest of Albiano, because he was a hypocrite and a liar, and therefore not a good Christian.

As far as I know, the cardinals did nothing to punish the priest, but the priest did something to punish us. A few days later, we began to notice that the peasant people made the sign of the cross as they passed in front of our gate, and when my father caught some of them at it and asked them why they were crossing themselves, they candidly explained that the priest had told them that an infidel lady lived there. What the priest had told them was that my mother was an *Orthodox* Catholic. The Italian word for "Orthodox" is "*Ortodosso,*" which in its feminine form, *Ortodossa,* sounds rather ominous to illiterate ears, because "*un orto d'ossa*" means a yard full of bones. This phonetic coincidence was enough to make the peasants connect my mother with some diabolical cult, and the feud dividing us from the people of Albiano became even deeper. The most distressing thing of all was that Geppo wrote to other people in Albiano, and not to us. Also, when Bartoli's daughter became ill, Bartoli did not call Father but had a doctor come all the way from Florence twice a week until she recovered. To make things worse, Bartoli's daughter soon became engaged to a prosperous rag dealer from the town of Prato, and it was rumored that this man would buy Villa Quaderni for himself. Bartoli drove around in his future son-in-law's new car, and they made it a point to drive at high speed along the road bordering our garden, so that the dust hung in the air for a long time before it settled quietly on our lawn furniture, on our magnolias, and on the furniture inside the house. There was a law forbidding any car to drive fast along that particular highway, but the policeman was a friend of Bartoli's—another Bolshevist, said Mother—and he was never to be found when Bartoli passed our house at fifty or sixty miles an hour.

This was the situation for almost a year. Then, one day, we received a visit from another landowner, also an enemy of ours, but a polite enemy, with whom we could at least exchange a few words. He came to see us because he was worried about Geppo. "It is a scandal how that administrator behaves," he said. "Did you know that Geppo needed money so badly he even sold Bartoli his mother's antique table silver? I would have bought the silver myself if I'd known he needed to sell it. I'd like to write to Geppo and scold him for not telling me, but I don't know where to reach him. Do you know where he is?" Alas, neither

Mother nor Father did. "I'll find out," said our neighbor, "and we'll urge him to come back. The whole affair is shameful. And I've just heard that Bartoli will soon buy the estate with his son-in-law."

"That fool Geppo! I refuse to write to him," said my father. "I've warned him once and that's enough. He's a good-for-nothing and deserves his fate." But Mother promised our neighbor not only to write to Geppo as soon as his address could be found but also to go and see what vandalism had been committed in the villa. "I can always go there," she said, "and in a few days, on the anniversary of Countess Quaderni's death, I shall go and take flowers to the chapel."

So she did, and the worst happened. When she got to the gate, Bartoli's wife was notified and came out to say that my mother could not go to the chapel to leave her flowers, because it was undergoing repairs. "But I am an old friend of the Countess," said Mother, "and I have every right to visit my friend's grave."

"The old Countess is dead," said Bartoli's wife, "and she has nothing to say about what happens here. Pray at home for her if you want, and give the flowers to me. I will see that she gets them."

This was the worst insult Mother had ever suffered, and she looked so angry that the Bartoli woman decided to let her in after all. She opened the gate and allowed Mother to go to the chapel by herself. What Mother saw before she reached the tomb was so sad that she spent an hour crying over the remains of her old friend. They were repainting the exterior of the villa in white, yellow, red, purple, blue, and gold, and all sorts of horrid decorations had been added, defacing the once so harmonious old Renaissance façade. Above the ground floor, all along the front of the house, a huge sign was being painted, in gold letters. It read "IRIDE PERFETTA," which means "PERFECT DYE." This was the trade name of a new commercial dye for wool, in which Bartoli had invested most of his ill-gotten money.

When Mother finally came out of the chapel, her eyes red, Bartoli himself greeted her. "How do you do?" he said. "Want to see my new place? This dye, Perfetta, is a very successful product. It will yield millions. And this sign here, once I have cut down the trees of the old cypress alley, will be visible for miles—even from the railway. Can you imagine what a boom such advertising will bring us?"

"Yes, I can," said my mother, horrified, and added, "Have you also bought the bodies in the chapel?"

"No," he said. "What use would they be to me? But they will continue to stay there."

Mother did not reply.

She came home and was sick in bed for two days. On the third day, she got up and wrote a very long letter to Geppo, a serious letter, urging him to come to Albiano at once. Then she wrote the whole letter over again, only asking him to explain to us what was going on at the villa. Then she rewrote her letter again, offering our help, for what it was worth. (It wasn't worth much, financially.) The next day, she decided to write the letter a fourth time, in a different tone, but she never finished it. I was about seventeen years old then, and I remember that it was a particularly hot summer day. We were all in the house at noon, Mother rewriting her letter, Father reading, and we children resting from a long game of hide-and-go-seek in the fields, when the doorbell rang. It was Count Tatti Atarelli. He looked worried and hot. He refused to enter the house but insisted that Father come outside with him. I followed my father out and heard Tatti say, "Geppo is here."

"Where?" asked Father.

"At the gate of his villa. We have brought his body— Oh, pardon me, you don't know—of course, you couldn't. Geppo died two days ago, in a hospital in Florence. He had been in poor health for some months. It seems that he had taken many drugs, and then—you know—well, worries, and women, and all that. To make a long story short, he caught pneumonia and died within two days, but he sent me a note when he was taken sick, asking me to come to the hospital. I was the only one there when he died. Of course, all past grudges were forgotten. He was very, very nice to me, and he asked only one favor—that he be buried in the family chapel, near his mother. He said to come here to your house and give all of you his love, and—" Poor Tatti began to sob quietly under the hot midday sun. "Let's go to Geppo, please," he said, at last. "I have a carriage."

Father jumped into the carriage and I climbed in after him, in spite of his ordering me to go back to the house. We got to the gate of the Quaderni villa and saw there a wagon with the coffin on it. Three men who looked like city people of some sort were standing near it. Tatti introduced them and explained that they were members of a Prato law firm.

"I am the executor of Geppo's will," said Tatti, "and these gentlemen here have come with me to make sure that all the expenses are paid. They arranged for the funeral, but it has to be paid for, and I have no money."

"Well," said Father, "let's see—"

"Wait a moment," said Tatti. "There's another problem. It seems that the new owner of the villa refuses to let the body in."

At this moment, the parish priest advanced toward the gate from the inside. With him were Bartoli and, at a distance, a large number of peasants, masons, painters, and the Bartoli family—wife, daughter, and future son-in-law. "What the hell!" said Bartoli. "Should *I* pay for the funeral? I'm under no obligation to receive the body here. The place was sold to me by the Count, God bless his soul, and I even had to pay off his debts, which were, I can tell you, much higher than the entire value of—"

"Just a moment," said Tatti. "Do you have a copy of the deed? There must be a clause specifying that Count Quaderni has a right to be buried in the family chapel."

"I don't have the deed here," said Bartoli, "and my lawyer lives thirty miles from here. He can't be reached before tomorrow. What will you do with the body until then? I don't want it here."

My father was about to protest, and Bartoli was already preparing for a bitter exchange of words when the priest stepped in and took Bartoli by the arm. They walked away from the gate, the priest whispering to Bartoli and making ample gestures, as if he were saying, "Be generous."

Suddenly, Bartoli stopped, turned around, and said, "All right. Have him brought in. I will take care of everything."

"How did you manage to persuade him?" Tatti asked the priest.

The priest said, "Well, first of all I appealed to his Christian feelings, and then I reminded him that Geppo was the last member of the family in direct line of descent from the original Quadernis, and said it would add value to the place to have every member of this famous family in the chapel."

"Never! Geppo shall never enter this gate!" cried Father, and rushed forward to halt the men who were preparing to lift the coffin off the wagon. But the lawyers, and even Tatti Atarelli, who understood Father's impulse, stopped him short.

"Will *you* pay for the burial somewhere else?" Tatti asked my father, and he added, "Don't forget that this was Geppo's last wish."

Father hung his head low while two young peasants opened the gate. Thus, as Father had predicted, Geppo was back at Albiano again, and now a part of the estate, purchased and paid for. His eyes were still closed.

THIS PARTICULAR RICH LADY

She was so rich, this particular lady, that she wandered all year from one of her estates and palaces to the other, like an eternal student trying to memorize a lesson. "I own this, I own that, I am this, I am that: richest landowner in Tuscany, best-known hostess in Rome, most charitable widow in Sicily, most lavish donator of hospitals in France, highest chimney in the chemical sky of Ludwigshafen on the Rhine, born in poverty, brother still serving as a clerk in a shoe store at home, never sets foot in the best houses of that town, yet none of those rich ladies dresses as well as my personal chambermaid, travels as much as my chauffeur."

An easy lesson this, to memorize, yet she learned and re-learned it and forgot it again all the time.

Now my grandmother had been richer, more generous, had traveled more extensively, and had tried not to memorize the lesson of her wealth: in fact, she had forgotten it so well that anyone who had worked for her dressed better and lived better than we did when she died. And—what is more—her fortune had not been made through financial eavesdropping behind the backs of absent-minded cabinet ministers. The Russian Revolution took away her last pennies; she believed she had lost a financial empire of her own. In this she was exactly like my father, who, because he was born in the Roman Empire and had learned Latin there, always spoke with contempt of Teutons, Britons, Slavs and other such barbarians.

A few years later we were too poor even to give the bank clerks their small pleasures. All we wanted was to move from one terrible place in the mountains, where we had lived like hermits for two years, to another terrible place in the marshlands, where my father could practice his medicine on people less barbaric than the mountain tribes, on roads less steep and stony, and on safer economic assumptions than the barter of wine, oil, venison and wool for medical assistance. Also: where we, his children, could go back to our school and learn love of the classics not through terror of him but of a teacher we could even afford to detest.

Terra Betinga was the name of that ideal place. Close to the industrial town of Prato, therefore flat and unhealthy, rich in tuberculosis and in factory workers who could pay; it was known to the medical profession as a potential gold mine. Three hundred and sixty doctors were competing for the job. They were almost all war invalids in perfect health, whose inabilities were mostly mental: they all seemed to believe that minor physical defects made up for major intellectual ones, such as knowledge of medicine.

My father won because his record was so good. In fact, his judges wondered why he had chosen to become a country doctor after having done so much in so many branches of medicine. But that was part of his romantic or rather classical idea of medicine as a discipline of life, to be taught more than practiced from above, and it is a long story anyway which belongs in a book.

But while he and we waited for the outcome of the competition, the battle for Terra Betinga was being fought, like the battles between Homeric heroes, up in the heavens. Every single one of the competitors had his gods and protectors in Rome, and the poor judges sitting in Florence had a very hard time withstanding all that pressure.

That was the occasion when my mother decided we might as well forget we had at one time snubbed this particular rich lady, and she wrote her a letter asking her for a word on behalf of our

Cause, and then waited in anguish for the effect. It came after the Cause was won. We were already living in the village of Terra Betinga and already disappointed by its ugliness, by the noise of weaving units placed in farmhouses, by the stench of greasy rags treated with chemicals and recycled into wool fabrics, and by the envy of those who had sponsored the cause of other doctors, when that famous letter came. It was a most hypocritical letter which in earlier days would have fooled no one, certainly not a person like my mother. It was obviously written in a hurry and in bad faith, absent-mindedly addressed Terra Betinga, while it said, "Let me know how things are. I spoke to the Queen Mother long ago and then again a week ago when she came for the inauguration of my new orphanage in Sicily, and she promised she would send word to the Prefect of Florence. If she has not, do let me know and I shall make it a point to remind her of her promise. She has reason to be grateful to me, let us insist while she still needs my help."

The first reaction to that letter was one of contempt and amusement. "Look at the Eternal Student, still trying to memorize her impossible lesson!" And the newspaper of that day seemed to confirm the amusing story. Three of her palaces had been transformed into orphanages, and of course the Queen Mother cut all the ribbons of the occasion and political speakers hailed the Orphan as the Thing of the Future. "You cannot ask the newly rich to do anything for you" said my mother. "They will always exploit you, because they need an audience." But then suddenly came the realization that we, too, needed an audience for our priceless piece of gossip. And not only did we need an audience; worse than this was the fact that we found one, for the rich lady, not for ourselves. No one in our environment for miles and miles of desert countryside, farmhouses, villages and villas, had the faintest idea of what it means to be rich and distinguished.

To them wealth was distinction, and the person who attained it became God the moment he laid hands on it. Besides, our letter had been read at the post office and the whole village was impressed with it. Thus Homer, Pindar and Anacreon, respectively postmaster, pharmacist and rich landowner, who had been very inimical to us until that very day, became our friends, as did Sappho, the horse dealer, his wife Sophocles, and Phydia and Leonida, the sisters of the parish priest; everyone who could read had read the letter and been pleased with it. So much so that they candidly confessed their indiscretion, expecting to be thanked for it, because the letter contained nothing against us, on the contrary, it went all to our credit. "Isn't that wonderful?" they said. "Aren't you pleased that so many have read it?" Thus an insulting letter helped us in more than one way: it helped us feel that we had friends, and it did the same thing for the rich lady. How delighted she was to have been thanked for benefits undone! How unused she was to gratitude! And our gratitude was not timid at all, it was outspoken, enthusiastic, generous, for in fact it was nothing but a present. We were allowing her to think that we owed everything to her good offices and to her influence with the Queen Mother. But the truth was that, even though she had done nothing, it had been quite a providential nothing, as things stood for us in the village. "Even if they don't give you anything," said my father, "the rich are bountiful. There is something in wealth." And it was the first time that he had praised it in our presence.

It became for the rich lady a point of honor to answer all of my mother's letters, and these were frequent, brilliant and dramatic. That my mother did not know her at all was no impediment, because those letters were addressed first of all to the whole population (and to keep everyone from knowing what she wrote she almost always wrote in French), and then to an ideal person who had interceded for us, who was besieged by envy and gossip, had no real friends, no real home and not even a face. We had not seen her yet, my mother knew her brother as a clerk in a shoe store, and had seen her but once, when one of the rich ladies of the town had said: "See that young woman there? That is the girl who married all those millions and then instantly was left a widow and the rest of his family got nothing."

But that was unimportant. She did have a face for us and it looked at us all the time, kindly and mysteriously, all day, all night, or, more than look, she watched over our lives; she knew our hopes even though her eyes were closed. She opened them only for a few days each year, when the autumn leaves fell. Then she opened her eyes and her face seemed to smile at us from a great distance. We could see her so well from every window in our house, we prayed to her in silence, even our father prayed to her although he was an atheist, for she knew everything about *his* ancient Greece, in fact, she represented all the Greek gods and goddesses in one, and all the sense of measure of the Greeks in a few lines of architecture which completed the lines of the Tuscan hills. She was a house, the least important of the rich lady's many possessions, but certainly the noblest one, a huge Medici villa called "Il Villino," but so huge that the hill on which it stood seemed some twenty miles closer than it actually was. And it was built on the same plan as our "Villa"; an entrance hall, four rooms downstairs and four upstairs and then the attic. But our villa, with orchard, garden, cornfield in front of it and farmhouse in the back, could easily have gone into her entrance hall, while the church of our village, belfry and all, could have gone into any of the four rooms without touching the ceiling. Sixty-five chimneys on her roof (this was written in a guidebook we had, but we had counted forty from a distance of twenty-five miles, with the help of field glasses), and what fantastic chimneys, especially with a plumage of smoke they looked like knights in armor: kings and queens and minor chess figures in a complex game pattern for the pleasure of giants. We had only one rusty iron pipe on top of our roof which looked like a thin priest and was a kitchen outlet. And no fireplace in our villa. "Il Villino" was for us the face of this particular rich lady, and it cast shadows that fell deep down in the valley and re-emerged beyond it, and when the sun shone on it, the dear face brightened up the forest like a reflector. In full moon it was another moon, a rectangular one: the face of real civilization, said our father: extreme simplicity with hidden elegance. How could a person owning such a place be left untouched by it, even if ignorant or vulgar when she bought it? The mere fact that this property had consented to be hers conferred upon her the hypothesis of worthiness, and rightly did the peasant folk address her as "noblewoman." Rather than flattery, that was only a reminder of the dignity that such a place exacted of its owner.

When she finally came, after almost a year since the beginning of our friendship, her presence interfered with her arrival. We were so busy noticing the effect of this event on the whole population, that we could hardly speak to her and play our part. She and her visit were two different things. We were much closer to the crowds outside our gate than to her, much closer even to our enemies who were now plotting against us in their post office, in their pharmacy, in their parish house, and we envied ourselves on their low level. This was a sad discovery. For she was better than those beasts and she did represent a world of elegance and culture that was still our own world. But how low had we stooped. In vain did we keep the gate shut, the windows shut, and try to sit as close to her as possible. We were outside. And yet she was so beautiful to look at, tall, with grey hair and blue eyes, and a voice so harmonious that it melted our hearts. And so gracious in her movements, so glad to be there, so repeatedly glad. It was not just an idle expression, for she, too, seemed embarrassed by the sight of our poverty, by the contrast between our dirty walls, our stained and humid, almost muddy floors and our old Persian rugs, our silver and our crystal. She was accompanied by a tall Roman prince who had no face at all, just two sharp profiles glued together, and by a rather youngish, bearded and ill-mannered musician. Both these gentlemen had been to my grandmother's house in Rome and in Paris, they remembered meeting my mother and they just said: "Oh yes, how are you. Nice to see you," as if nothing had happened to us. The musician even said: "What a nice house you have." Then, with a cruel smile, as he found nothing else to praise: "Solid walls. Fresh in summertime."

The lady bought our crystal: two beautiful museum pieces we were afraid to keep there, lest they break. When she asked for the price, my mother blushed and said: "Let us not mention money, please. Your house is a much better place for them than this house."

And the lady replied: "My house? I wish I had *one* house I could call mine. I am a very lonely woman, as you know."

The prince bought a large block of malachite, and comments were exchanged between the prince and the rich lady on what to do with that block. It was decided that it could either be given to the Pope with a cross surmounting it, or re-sold to make jewelry.

When our guests left their car was loaded with all sorts of things, many of them "bought" by the rich lady, and many taken into custody against thieves and humidity, such as all our eighteenth-century table linen and our best rugs. A Tanagra statuette was added to the lot at the last moment, as a token of friendship. ("Oh, I adore this piece! I wish I could afford it!" "You don't have to, it's yours. . . ." "Oh, thank you very much. I shall never forget. . . ." "We wish you would.")

The house looked rather empty after she left, but there remained a perfume hanging in the air, and I mean real French perfume, which we took in with joy, closing our eyes and thinking of her, until the acrid smell of chemicals, of poverty, of manure, crushed it out of existence. One terrible thing I did when the guests left: I kissed the hand of the prince. He withdrew it in haste and we both blushed.

"Now that we have become neighbors," wrote the lady a year later, "and I have seen your villa, you must see my villino. By the way, that was a most wonderful lunch I had at your house."

And a most wonderful lunch it had been. Never before, not even in the maddest days of my grandmother, had we spent so much for a meal. The two crystal carafes yielded one fifth of the original price as named for us by an art dealer in Florence who had tried for months to get that money from the lady and had deducted from it a high fee for himself. We had also sued the prince for payment on that malachite block which had partly been cut and re-sold to a jeweler, while the rest, with a beautiful cross surmounting it, had been sold to the Pope. The prince had paid, less than one fifth of the price, on the eve of his being raised by Mussolini to an important post.

In his case, too, the lawyer and the art dealer had further thinned that meager sum with their fat fees.

In the meantime our linen and our rugs and some of our silver had been stolen from the rich lady's country house, together with some paintings and trinkets from her private collection. We learned about the theft from the newspapers: the villino was a national monument, so the theft was historical. The thieves had worked for weeks to pierce a hole in a twenty-foot wall before they could enter the room. And now a host of experts and curators would have to supervise the restoration of the structure. "It is so sad to think," wrote the lady to us, "that my poor orphans will have to bear the brunt for this. I am told that my budget for the coming year is now thrown out of balance. I can no longer build my orphanage. Of course I have lost more than you, but we should not complain, nor lose our faith in humanity after *one* bad experience."

To which letter my mother had replied not with her usual spontaneity, but after careful consultation with a lawyer who had dictated every word of her answer, leaving only free play for a few words of friendship at the end. A long silence had followed, interrupted by a brief note from Paris, in which the lady said that her administrator, a most intelligent young man, would get in touch with us and give us all the facts we needed for our action against her. That note also seemed written by a lawyer and recopied by her with but four words of a more personal character: "How are you all?" And not even "Affectionately yours" before the signature.

The young administrator turned out to be an apprentice who was being trained for a subordinate position in the bureaucracy of her Tuscan domains. Her real administrator lived in Germany, under the chimneys of the chemical sky of Ludwigshafen on the Rhine, and to him were responsible the French, the Swiss, the North Italian, the Tuscan, the Roman and the Sicilian heads of many large offices in which a rigid hierarchy of experts counted her money and exacted her tributes. It was this young administrator who explained to us what an honor it was for him to do the best he could in the rich lady's interest. He did not even know that we were now her enemies, real or potential. And when he understood, he gave us an example of his zeal by explaining to us that the rich lady owed us nothing. Those precious objects we had given her were not marked in her books and she was therefore not responsible to us for their safety. Besides, she had so many expenses with her orphans that she could not afford to make presents to non-orphans.

When the village discovered that we were no longer protected by a person so rich and influential, we were exposed to slander and abuse. Anacreon, who was our landlord, sold our house to Sappho, who had now become the secretary of the local fascist party and the mayor of Terra Betinga, and Sappho evicted us on a week's notice, this in spite of the fact that we were ardent fascists. In vain did we plead with him to allow us to stay because there was no other decent house in the whole village. He would not be moved by anything, so we swapped houses with him. He took over the villa, we the farmhouse back of it where he had always lived, indeed where all his ancestors had lived and died.

With our books piled up ceiling high, and a whole population of armchairs and tables barricading the place, and the stench of generations exuding from the walls and raining on us in brown drops from the roof, and cockroaches and spiders running up and down the walls; with a warm hill of manure blocking our view, and chicken, geese and pigs waiting outside our door for a chance to come in, life became very difficult for us, while Sappho and his wife Sophocles entertained the rich lady's young administrator in our former living room.

The only reason for this enmity was that my father was a much greater friend of the true classics than of their modern village counterparts. He refused to spend his evenings playing cards in the pharmacy or in the parish house and leave his wife alone at home. And she refused to spend her evenings gossiping with the wives of other village notables, or with Phydia and Leonida, the sisters of the parish priest.

Our house was like an abbey in which prayer and boredom are the rule. Instead of prayer we had study of the classics, and the hours of boredom were kept secret. In the evenings, after teaching us Greek and Latin, father relaxed by reading Greek and Latin for his pleasure, and we made music. And if the village notables dropped in to see us, they were made to understand that we were not amused. Things were already bad enough for us, when Homer made the great discovery that my parents were divorced and remarried, and that their former mates were still living in Italy and still blackmailing them.

So the Classics got together and asked my father to resign from his job. He refused. The Town Council was gathered late at night, in an urgent, secret session, and my father was relieved of his duties on grounds of public immorality.

This procedure was illegal, but it was necessary at this point that an adequate number of Councillors raise the objection of principle, and ask for a new meeting. We had six months to prepare for this. The only friends we had on the Town Council were three peasants and a minor landowner: the three peasants were vassals of Anacreon and the landowner was afraid of the parish priest. Still, they were friends and they wanted to help us. But they needed support from higher quarters to persuade other members that my father was the victim of an injustice. In other words: that he had influential friends in Rome. Only thus could we hope that a new meeting of the Council would be called to reverse the decision against us.

That was the time the rich lady wrote again thanking us for that wonderful lunch and saying: "Now that we are neighbors and I have seen your villa, you must see my villino."

My mother flung the letter far from her, burst into tears and shouted: "No. This is too much!" But the letter was perfumed and the paper was blue and thick and beautiful. So the words were re-read and re-interpreted. "She is obviously ashamed of herself and trying to make up for her mistakes," she said, feeling the paper with her fingers and sniffing at it with delight.

And we of course were more than eager to accept that invitation. Little did our parents know what a horror it was to us, to have to mark off as "inimical" or "wicked" the only spot on the horizon that was dear to our hearts.

So we said: "Father, let us give her a chance."

"What do you mean, a chance? Another chance to take advantage of us? No."

And that was final. The same evening two conspirators came in from the fields and knocked on our door, waking up all the chickens and the pigs and the geese in the neighborhood. They were two of our friends on the Town Council who had secret news for us. They had heard rumors that someone very powerful was interested in us, and they knew that this fact had impressed some of our enemies. More than this they did not know. My father understood at once that the person they meant was the rich lady, whose letter had been read at the post office. "We can thank God that they have let us read it, too," he said. "But I am not going to let the rich exploit me again, in order to impress the poor."

Then Sappho built a pigsty right in front of our door, and my father went to the nearby town of Pistoia to find a lawyer and to sue him.

It was then that my mother wrote a long letter to the rich lady, thanking her for her note and telling her our troubles. And a week later came a long reply with a kind invitation to spend a day with her. She said the car would come to get us early in the morning so that she would have the joy of seeing us before her other guests arrived. "I have so little privacy," she said, "and you are such good friends. Perhaps I can advise you or help you. Please do come."

"What did I tell you a year ago?" said my mother to my father. "She is a lonely woman and she likes us. It was a great mistake to let a lawyer write our personal letters for us. Never again will I do such a thing." She accepted the invitation for very noble reasons. When the two conspirators came back and said: "The population wants to know whether you will accept," my father said: "None of their business," and our letter was posted in the town of Prato.

The car was a large "coupé" Isotta Fraschini and the chauffeur, cap in hand, looked for us in the villa and was very surprised when Sappho appeared in shirtsleeves and directed him to the farmhouse and the pigsty. We came out of our cavern dressed in our best, though very old-fashioned clothes, and crossed our former garden smiling gently to Sophocles and Sappho as we passed them, and they were very much embarrassed, for we were not on speaking terms with them and they did not quite know how to behave.

Much worse than all the humiliations we had suffered before was the change in our persons, almost in our identity, which became clear to us through the cheap pleasure we experienced at that moment. It had been bad enough a year before, but now we knew we had sunk very low. Dozens of people were assembled in the street, and they were all awe-stricken. Never before had they seen such a car. I felt the emotion in the rest of the family as I had felt it in myself. I knew this was not right, and yet I understood it, too. When my mother, who was seated already inside that wondrous china cabinet, letting the chauffeur place a plaid on her knees, cast a glance at the countryside in the direction of Anacreon's villa, I blushed, for I knew why she was doing this. She was hoping to God that he would pass and be as awe-stricken as the rest of the populace. I also knew that she would have preferred to sit there the whole day without food, than to visit our friend in her beautiful house and see civilized people and hear music. And I knew this of my father as well, and even of myself, and again was ashamed, yet powerless to make a better choice. Our excursion was finished. We simply could not leave. In fact, the moment we were out of the village, having disappeared like gods in a huge cloud of dust, we were alone, sitting between two worlds, longing to long again for a civilized world, but longing much more ardently to be back in the world of barbarians to which we finally belonged.

This was the secret we all shared but could not mention. There was one good thing in it, mixed together with that dirt, like a precious object packed and preserved in rags and rubbish: the notion, clear as sunlight, that the only way to keep my parents out of danger was to surround them with luxury, to place them, like two precious crystal carafes on a very large table, very solidly built, in a very large room, under a roof with beams so thick and held in place by walls so thick that no earthquake, no war would ever bring it down on our possessions, and this whole house owned by a person so rich that no social upheaval, no change in human fortunes, no extravagance, would ever let the ugly fear of hunger and vulgarity put an end to her enjoyment of those beautiful objects in her care.

This was the reason I felt happy as the car drove us in a matter of minutes through the familiar countryside between Terra Betinga and the industrial town of Prato: the smell of factories, of chemicals, of greasy rags, of burlap, of latrines, and the brightness of chalked walls, rows and rows of new houses representing prosperity in the gutter. We were passing ourselves all the time, on foot, on horseback, in light carriages, and giving all those wretches the dust we would get from other cars in less than twenty-four hours again.

My parents were safely in their seats, they needed no vulgarity today to cope with the vulgarity of that place and those ignorant people. As the familiar sights fled from us the two carafes, in my imagination, were unwrapped, freed of their protective coverings, and in that villa they would find their right place, they would shine in their beauty, and be once more, an addition to all who came near them. For these reasons that car became immensely dear to me, even the chauffeur symbolized something noble and worthy of worship. No matter who would be the lady's other guests, they were sure to be kind and civilized, and that was like a clean bed for a very sick person. I already felt rested at the mere thought of that company: no pigsty to hide the view and poison the air, and no sneers from illiterate enemies. When we finally arrived I was on the point of crying with emotion. Yes, of course, this was only a day; in a few hours we would have to go back to our pigsty, but let us not think of the ugly afternoon, let us live now and take in some of this beauty and this peace for future reference.

The arrival was symbolic, too. A sudden hill at the end of the marshlands (still our marshlands, but so far from our village, so much more beautiful, not at all industrialized), and a road so steep that the front of the car stood erect in the air, like a scared horse. We were pulled back by the force of gravity. The chauffeur's cap fell on my face. I gave it back to him, and in grabbing it from my hand he lost control of the car. At that very moment a carriage with a grey horse, like ours, and an elderly gentleman, somewhat like my father, accompanied by a boy, somewhat like me, appeared at a turn of the road. There was a sudden stop; too sudden, in fact, and our big car began to slide on gravel, backward toward the torrent, while the grey horse was sliding on its front legs and befogging the crystal of our left window with its breath. The poor animal was frothing at the mouth, his eyes were terrorized, and the old gentleman was pulling him with all the strength of his arms, while the boy next to him was frantically turning the small handle of the brakes. We were all terror-stricken; the chauffeur pressed the accelerator with such strength that there was a bombardment of gravel on the horse. Also on the car; it sounded like a rainstorm, and we were still sliding. Suddenly there was such a start forward that we all bumped into one another. The nose of the horse was bruised, there were terrible cries outside the car, then the screeching of metal against metal, the rocks bumping against us on the right side and horse and carriage disappeared beyond the precipice, while we came to a sudden stop against the mountain, with pine-tree branches in our faces and on the windshield, and a void right in front of us. A boiling yellow cloud, with dust and noise of gravel, began to rise from the front of the car and also from the road. It took us a few seconds to realize that these were sheep. Loud cries from the shepherd, barking of dogs, and distant cries of distress behind us. "Don't move!" shouted the chauffeur to us as he jumped out of the car and ran downhill, where the carriage had disappeared. We looked at him, saw three men on the curve down there. Thank God the men were safe. Too bad for the poor horse. After a brief discussion between the chauffeur and the two men (of which discussion we saw only the gestures, and they seemed rather friendly, though excited), the chauffeur ran back to us and said: "Everything is all right. Carriage undamaged, only a bruise on the nose of the animal."

He then inspected the wheels while the sheep were continuing their descent with cheerful tinkling of their bells, and the shepherd bent very low to greet us. A strange perfume of pine needles, dry leaves, and mountain flowers, thyme, and warm earth kept reminding us pleasantly of the difference between this air and the polluted air of our own countryside. "All's well that ends well," said the chauffeur, as he sat back in his seat and put on his luxurious white gloves again.

"Their fault entirely," said my older brother Chino.

"Yes," said my father. "You have saved our lives."

"Magnificent," said mother. "Heroic."

"Not at all," he replied in a tone of equality we did not like. "And don't you mention this to Madame if she asks you about the trip. I am going to tell her that it was all my fault, so she will give that fool a little money. He needs it."

"You should not be too generous and take the blame for other people's foolishness," said my mother with authority. "He had no right to come down on us like that without blowing the horn."

"He has no horn. Horse carriages carry no horns!" he said now firmly and my father pressed his elbow into her arm to express his disapproval.

"But I hate to see you take all the blame!" she said.

"That won't hurt me. I can do what I please, she will never get angry with me. She knows I am the best chauffeur in Tuscany. This car, without me, would be worthless to her. She might as well throw it away. We have two more cars like this. Then we have a Hispano-Suiza in Rome, a Rolls Royce in Paris, and a Daimler in Milan. And she has other chauffeurs, too, but she knows she can trust me. I was given her by the Archduke of Bourbon, who did not dare take even a short trip without me. But he bored me, because he liked to drive too slowly. Then he is no lover of travel, so I left him. No, no, I can do anything, take any blame, she will say nothing. But if I tell her that this road is being used again by horses, after we spent two million lire to widen it for the use of our cars only, and built a new road back of the hill for all the services, she will get mad and put all the blame on him."

"Still," mother said, "I think you are very generous."

"I protect him, you see? He is our country doctor. He does not know much medicine, but he is a good devil, he plays cards with my father, he is just one of us. And if I tell my lady a good sob story, she is so kind, she will give him a few thousand lire for damages and that's not to be thrown away, you know?"

At that moment the doctor himself appeared again, asked the chauffeur a few things, almost in whispers, then greeted us most ceremoniously, taking off his hat and bowing to us all. From the height of our temporary dignity we greeted him, trying to make him feel by gestures that we were with him, very much with him. He did not seem to understand, was baffled by so much cordiality, bowed even lower and then disappeared, not knowing how much we envied him for his few thousand lire, just the money we needed so badly.

When we arrived and were received by our rich friend, we were already inferior to her chauffeur. Another thing our solitude had done to us: we had lost our independence at an age when children usually begin to find it. I noticed the change in myself as well as in my brothers. We were more timid than the previous year, and we all marched in a unit behind our father. It was he who had grown stricter, true, but that was also the effect of our having grown taller, stronger, louder, more difficult to handle. He was afraid that he might have to use in public the same threats and reminders he was now forced to use at home (which he had not been forced to use the year before). Thus the same natural development produced two disadvantages, or rather, three: our own clumsiness, having grown taller and more critical in solitude; our father's fear of us on that account; and our own clothes, which had not grown with us, and did look rather funny in comparison to the more adult, new and comfortable clothes of two young boys who were there with their parents. They seemed so much at ease, those boys; they seemed to have always lived in such a place. They praised the view, the furniture, the paintings with those loud words of enthusiasm that are the very symptoms of indifference, while we, who were unable to detach our eyes from every single thing we saw, could say nothing at all, and that was noticed by the lady, by those young boys, by their parents, and by our parents, too. "Don't you think this is beautiful?" We were asked that same question several times in a tone of hurt surprise, which culminated in our father's remark: "Look at this house, this is like a museum."

Scowls on our part.

"What is the matter with you?"

"Nothing."

Improvised trial on the side, in the presence of all, and in whispers, as if they could not see what was going on: "Tell me what is the matter with you, right away."

"Nothing, I said."

"I don't believe you. Here we are giving you a wonderful vacation, taking you with us to see the most beautiful villa in Tuscany and this is how you show your appreciation?"

"Who said I did not like it?"

"You show it. Everyone is looking at you, wondering why you seem bored . . ."

"I am not bored and leave me alone."

"All right, but this is not finished. Tonight at home you'll render account for these words."

After which the rich lady intervened. "Youngsters have their problems. I have no children of my own, I have only nephews and nieces, who are exceptional, like you," she said, "because they, too, had a difficult time. It is funny how poverty turns out to be a blessing, while abundance is nothing but a burden that may crush your soul completely!"

"Oh, not yours!" said my mother, squeezing her arm.

"At times I wonder," she said. "Only a few days ago a very dear and trusted friend, one whose word I have reason to believe, said to me that I don't know how to give!"

She had tears in her beautiful grey eyes, and we all felt a passion for her at that moment.

"What nonsense!" said my father, while my mother was shaking her head in sign of disapproval and beginning to sob.

"Thank you, my friend!" she said. "You have almost convinced me, because I know that you would never say such a thing unless you meant it!"

"Well," said my father, "you should know me to be a man of principle, perhaps too much so at times for my own good."

"How true!" Then she said to us: "Children, you are exceptional!"

At this point my father squeezed her hand. "I so envy you at times," she said. "Yes, I do. If people praise you, you know this is meant, this is true, this is a feather in your hat, not a knife in your flank, not a bandage over your eyes, not a subtle poison in your food. Except for friends like you, I have no one. I am a very lonely woman. I never can trust anybody, except when they say unpleasant things. But how am I to change, to live simply?"

"Oh, but you do!" said my mother, "you do!"

"Thank you, my dear. *You* understand it! This is a little cotton dress I am wearing. It was bought ready-made at La Belle Jardinière in Paris, and these shoes come from the Bon Marché, where I buy all my clothes."

"Don't I know it!" said my mother. "That's where I still buy mine!"

"Well, you see? We are sisters in taste. I always knew it. Besides, I wear no jewels. I hate jewels. Yet my brother reproaches me that I live in great splendor, that I have too many guests, that a host of worthless noblemen sponge on me all the time, and this is partly true, but how can I avoid it? My brother is more fortunate than I. He still keeps his modest job, even though he advises me in whatever I do. He, too, could live in splendor if he only so wished, but he prefers to be my employee at a very, but very low salary, I must say. My butler costs me far more. Yet there is one thing my brother cannot see, and that is all the burden of wealth, the social obligations that go with it. If I tried to live as modestly as I dress, you know what would happen. I would be called a miser. In Rome, I am already. You know what evil tongues the Romans have, you have lived there yourself long enough to remember it. And it is your good luck that you no longer do, I tell you. But believe me, I am not doing it to appease the evil tongues in Rome or elsewhere. I must do it because, strange though this may seem to you, the poor are forcing me to do it. They would be disappointed if I did not appear to them as some sort of a Fairy Queen riding a gold carriage through the skies, with white horses and everything."

"*Panem et circenses,*" said my father sententiously. "*Vulgus vult decipi.* And they are right. Man is a born spectator, and it is not for him to have, rather to wonder at the riches of this world. If man were to transform the light of the stars into fuel for his kitchenstove, and the blue of the sky into garments for his children, would he be happier that way? Would he not rather freeze under icy blue skies, and pray in vain for warmth from merciless stars? The myth of Midas . . ."

But he could not go on. She kissed him on both cheeks and said: "You must teach me a little mythology. I so need it at times when people ask me about those figures in the paintings I own, in the statues that decorate my garden, and in the frescoes right here in this villa. And, by the way, I am supposed to make a little speech at the dedication of the archaeological museum of Pallalta donated by me with the school of archaeology to that town. I cannot ask anyone else but you to help me, or the rumor would spread that I know nothing of these matters!"

"Anytime," said my father, "anytime. And you can count on my discretion."

"I know I can. You no longer circulate in society. You are lucky that way."

We were still standing in the entrance hall as she was saying this. "Let's make a tour of the house, or do you know it already?" she asked.

We took a walk through those few rooms, for a walk it was, the distance from one window to the next was so great that the same countryside was seen in a different perspective already, and we stopped to admire every single member of the Medici family: men, women, children, in muffs, in décolleté, in armor, feathers, caps, cardinal hats, papal costume; all of them stern and stupid on a background as black as the night, the effect of their presences being one of immense cruelty against which there is no defense and no redress. They excited me, I saw that countryside, the city of Florence, Rome invisibly distant from there, and all the mountain passes, all the roads, all the forests, dominated by fear of exactly those feathers, those velvet caps, those furs, those pearls on bulging bosoms and those moronic babies with a poor bird in one hand, and a sword in the other. That indeed was the symbol, that bird, and no one (typical, the fact that governesses could not be portrayed: in our day governesses could not be left out of a family picture with babies) no one anywhere with enough power to tell that child not to hold that little bird that way. But soon came the equivalent of modern governesses: somber faces of tubercular peasants I well recognized. They seemed to have preceded us on our excursion, leaving the plough, the manure fork or the shovel in the fields beyond the pigsty that was home to us, and taking up their ecclesiastic dignity and their place in those oval, gold, worm-eaten frames, to play a dirty trick on us. Portraits indeed! Those were our enemies, and we all recognized them. And we knew why they scowled, why they fixed their eyes on points beyond the upper left side of the frame: Heaven indeed! that was a comedy to scare those bastard Medicis who could do anything they wished because they were so rich! And how some of those saintly figures exhibited the crucifix as a weapon, ready to hit the offender, and how well they peddled their starvation and their tuberculosis for true saintliness! I was aflame with a violent historical curiosity, not to retrace traditions, institutions, the whole framework of society, as a serious historian instinctively will, even if he be only fifteen years of age, but to evoke the living persons in their passions and crimes, in their fears and their helplessness, the rich ones and the poor ones, all in their helplessness. Because these were people I knew: the Medicis looked like many of our landowners, some even like the peasants, and those friars and clerics and saints were the scum of the countryside, we could name them one by one. "Look at Sappho! Look at Sophocles! Look at Anacreon. And his wife! And his daughter! . . . Look, look, There goes Pindar . . . Here is Homer . . ." There they all were, all with their backs to the wall of four centuries, and the silence of those halls, deeper and cooler than the silence outside (which slid lightly on a gravel of crickets and cicadas) wanted to be re-filled again with cries, with whispers and with words of love, with historical references to powers now long emptied of all danger, with orders to betray, assassinate, proclaim and excite. How knowingly we looked inside those portraits, deep under the paint, in fact, almost turning our heads to see the living models as they sat for those portraits. And how we knew that the rich lady had not the faintest notion of those tragedies, those lives, those times. She had been poor, but in a different world, in a world less soaked with history. We instead who were plunged now into a poverty much worse than the one she had known, because it was so sudden, so unrelated to our habits and minds, knew all the archaeology of decay, understood all the reasons for the cruelty of the Tuscans in general, for their mixture of critical awareness and unmitigated coarseness, which makes for a much greater ignorance than the coarseness of a people with no history in back of them. I knew then, we all knew, we were plunged into something like the opposite of "history in the making," namely history in decomposition, the pre-fossil stadium of a decaying forest. That was the reason we could "smell the corpse" in those portraits, those games and those trinkets. For (that was the most fascinating complement to those portraits) there was a whole museum of children's toys, games for adults, musical instruments and household utensils, all assembled there to prove that something had been going on every day in that house, even though the historical climate was different, and it had been destroyed by the dripping of minutes more than by enemies or tyrants. The only elements not subject to that change in shapes, in ways, in feelings, were the crickets, the smells of falling leaves, of new wine and old barrels, and the colors of autumn in its last summer sun dress. That indeed was antiquity to me, not the antiquity of Greece or Rome, all stiff in monumental attitudes, in exemplary virtues, cold perfection, colorless centuries illustrated by marble. What link of accents, habits, facial resemblance, bodily decay could there exist between classical antiquity and our time? That was still called antiquity for purely logical reasons: because one knew it had all taken place before the Middle Ages or the Renaissance, but for no other reason.

We were those people of whom Dante had said: "*Che questo tempo chiameranno antico*" (who will call this time ancient), and we could not make an exception and be with him in calling classical antiquity ancient, too. The problem of how ancient it seemed to a Renaissance man or a man from the high Middle Ages in comparison to us was already a second problem, one to be studied after the construction of both Renaissance and Middle Ages, not before and not together with that study.

These intuitions came like those golden sunrays in paintings representing a saint, face-up, palms-up under some spiritual sunlamp. I was exposing myself to inspiration, and my younger brother, the only one who could really understand me, was careful to say nothing at all, but I knew he had that same experience, in fact, he was almost in a trance. The party went on to the dining room as the butler came toward our group and whispered to the lady that lunch was served.

She turned to my parents and said: "Let's accept the suggestion. Perhaps it is not a bad idea to nourish the body, too."

My father bowed, almost in imitation of the butler, and that disturbed me, but I tried not to be distracted, for I knew I had only a few more seconds to live in the Renaissance. Hungry as I was, good food would bring me down to earth and make me a much more vulgar person than I was at that moment. On a full stomach I would crave all those riches without having them, while now I had them without craving them.

"We better shut that door down there," said the lady, obviously speaking to the butler, and using such indirect terms to avoid giving orders. She was extremely sensitive that way, and I could only agree with her. But my father did not grasp the finesse of the touch, and told Chino, "Go, you shut that door."

Chino shrugged his shoulder, saying "Tell *him*, he is closer to it."

"You," called my father to me, "Shut that door!"

I knew this was all wrong, it was a gross indelicacy, like usurping the authority of the lady of the house, but I obeyed, perhaps because I was so hurt, and ran straight into the butler, who was going to shut the door because that was his job. He looked at me, said, "Pardon me," and with a gesture of his left arm slowly pushed me aside as a policeman pushes away the curious crowds from the coach of a king, then slowly, professorially, a bit annoyed, approached the door, closed it with dignity and passed by me again giving me such a look of contempt that I said, "I am so sorry." When he heard these words, he turned around, stopping for a brief moment, to register the grave infraction of the rule that a guest should know better than to interfere with such things, then resumed his slow walk toward the dining room. We all waited for him, then marched behind him like a flock of sheep.

The food was excellent, but again, my father's fear of our indiscipline, and even more so, his timidity, made him behave like a warden who accompanies a gang of prisoners to a penitentiary. He watched our every move, reproaching us with severe glances, when not with loud whispers that amused our hostess and her other guests. And my mother was irritated with him, because she had regained some of her lost composure and she knew that the best thing to do with us was to trust our good manners. What vexed her was the fact that he had lost all social ease in a year's time. The other guests, who had been in their rooms until then, were a retired general with a red face and a fiery white moustache that made him look like an exaggerated version of John Bull, his wife, whose face was not only so coated with powder that it seemed made of velvet, but was all hidden in the shadow of a white hat that came down on her neck and then over her ears like an Easter egg cut open with a surprise inside it. These two spoke only of money. They declared themselves poor, asked the rich lady how much she had paid for this, that and the other, and abandoned this subject, so painful to us for we knew so much more about it than they, to say they were resolved, but definitely resolved for good, to enjoy their estates more than they had until then. "It is a shame," said the retired general to my mother, "when you have such a beautiful villa as we have here in Tuscany, and another one, equally beautiful near Rome, that we should spend our time in Monte Carlo, in Bordighera, in Paris and in Rome." And the lady of the house scolded them many, many times, and they always admitted she was right and promised to behave the next time, but then said, "You, too, should set us the example by staying here a bit longer than you do every year." But then they added that of course she never never went to Monte Carlo or other such frivolous places, she only traveled to look after her hospitals, her schools, her reformatories for vagrant girls, so who were they to reproach her for not enjoying her estates more than she did?

Another guest who was mentioned a great deal but who sent word that he would not come down from his room in order not to be tempted into eating too much was the pianist A., of whom it was said that the way he played Mozart on the harpsichord was unequaled by anyone, and the lady of the house hoped very much that he would play for us before we left, if, of course, he was in the mood.

The prince said very little, listening a great deal to my mother's description of our maturity, will-power and erudition; we could tell from stray words what she was saying, and even more from his glances, full of faked admiration, and his frowning (which made him look like a hunting dog listening to a speech), and we knew she was letting herself be carried away by his good manners. She was boring him stiff, he became more and more polite all the time and we wished she would stop. But she did not. When we heard the word *Odyssey* we knew it was too late. He made big eyes and looked like a comedian on stage. He must have thought that this was his best chance to take revenge on her and exhibit himself with a *bon mot.*

"But the *Odyssey,*" he said, in an unusually loud voice, still pretending to speak only to her, "is the story of Ulysses who went home to his wife and his family, if I am not mistaken. And he must have enjoyed it, for he took all his time to get there. You say your husband went on an Odyssey *with his whole family.*" My father flashed danger signals to her.

But she was not in the least disturbed. "Then Ulysses was wrong," she said. "He *should* have taken wife and children along. A family must stay united, especially on an Odyssey."

"I see, I see," he said. "I understand your point, and I can only admire your husband for his courage."

"Oh, he is an exceptional person. We all are, to tell you the truth, or in such a terrible situation as the present one, we would have lost our minds."

The lady of the house came to her rescue. "The bravery of this family is worthy of an epic," she said. "I have never heard anything like it before. Compared to it, the *Odyssey* is a silly old tale."

Everyone looked at us with a pointed indifference that slowly changed to amusement as they began to discover details of our clothing they had probably overlooked before.

But my mother was beaming. "These are my treasures," she said of us, then added, "as that woman in ancient Rome said, what was her name?"

"Cornelia, mother of the Gracchis," said the lady of the house. "Am I not good in history?"

"Excellent," said my father, frowning in my mother's direction.

But the Roman Prince was determined to punish her. "Tell me," he said, "and does your Odyssey take you cruising along the coasts of the Mediterranean, or is it the Adriatic you are cruising?"

"Cruising?" she asked, in a shrill voice, "don't be a fool! I am speaking symbolically! We are not traveling *at all,* that is the tragedy of our Odyssey! Mediterranean? Adriatic? Ach, don't mention these names, so dear to my heart! *Inland* we are, down in the marshlands, with a view over chicken coops and pigstys!"

"Oh, oh, I see! A land-Odyssey is what you mean, and not a moving one at that! Must be quite an achievement!"

"It is! And without these young sailors of the great ship of Life, even I could not manage it! Imagine, they have built a pigsty right under the windows of our living room! When we play the piano, we have an accompaniment of pigs!"

"How interesting! Did your children build the pigsty?"

"My children? How would they dare! *Our enemies* have built it, to *spite* us! Communists! Heathens! From the parish priest down to the whole population! But I am going to get him excommunicated by Monseigneur de Samper, you will see!"

"Oh, my good friend Monseigneur de Samper?"

"Do you know him?"

"Why I should say so! We all do at this table! He is such an amusing old devil!"

Now indeed everyone was interested in us. The prince was proud. His cheeks were slightly colored as he spoke. "And you say he will excommunicate your local parish priest?"

"If he is a friend, he will. He *owes* it to me, or he will *never* be admitted to my house again!"

"Oh, but I think he would be greatly flattered by the high esteem in which you seem to hold him! And I am sure he would wish nothing better than to be in a position to excommunicate anyone! But I fear, and I am sorry to disappoint you, that he will never get there! We just had a new Pope a year ago, and Samper is not young. Besides, his chances in the Vatican are not half as good as they are in your house! Where else would he enjoy such a reputation of power! And of virtue! I personally think, if he avoids being excommunicated himself, that is as far as he can go!"

My father was so humiliated he could hardly speak a word, but she was only worried. "Then *who* will excommunicate that hypocrite?" she asked. The prince sighed, and the lady of the house seemed to have abandoned his victim to him. "I am afraid," he said, with deliberate pathos, "no one, Madame."

"What? Will he stay unpunished? But that is a scandal!"

"Building a pigsty does not seem to me such an offense against religion. Don't forget that Our Lord was practically born in one, or very near one, I suppose."

"But the priest did not build the pigsty himself! You understand? That is the dirty trick! He inspired others to do it! It was all his idea!"

"Still, Madame, inspiring others to build a pigsty is not a crime against religion, either. I know very little of religion myself, but I have an idea I am on safe ground here."

At this point my father intervened. "This whole idea is nonsensical," he said. "But it is true that he . . ."

"Wait a moment!" she said. "I was forgetting! He neglects all his duties, he is not at all spiritually inclined, all he can think of is duck-hunting!"

"Alas, Madame, duck-hunting also will be found missing on

the list of major theological offenses. I love to do it myself. Of course I am a sinner, as everybody knows, but I am still in the graces of the Church despite my hunting habits."

"You are joking, I know, because you don't have to live with those beasts! He wants to starve us, to ruin us completely, only because I am divorced and so is my husband!"

"Ah, ah, ah, ah, Madame! There lies the secret of his enmity! You know how biased the church is in matters of dogma!"

"Dogma, my foot! His first duty as a Christian is to be a human being, to have a bit of charity and to leave people alone when they live honestly and mind their business!"

"I can only agree with you, Madame, but priests will be priests. You were lucky to get a divorce, I never did."

At that moment the wife of the retired general seemed to feel rather uncomfortable, and the lady of the house noticed it and said, in a hurry: "There are so many sad and intricate situations in life that an ignorant parish priest is unable to grasp. It takes a great deal of humanity to be a priest. Our parish priest up here is a saint; if my friends lived up here they would have found in him a man of exceptional understanding."

"By the way," said the general, "do you know where Nino is right this minute?"

They all wondered where Nino was and he said: "On his way to South America."

"To South America?"

"What? To South America, you said?"

"Did he say South America?"

"Tell us."

"Yes, tell us."

He was beaming with joy. It was his turn to be the center of attention.

"I'll let you guess."

"No."

"No, please not."

"Come on, we are impatient."

"Three guesses."

"A woman!"

"Two more guesses."

"What? Is it not a woman?"

"No."

"What could it be?"

"Two more guesses, I said."

"Oh, please!"

"Two more guesses!"

"You are being cruel!"

"Yes, we are suffering!"

"I don't care. Two more guesses. Come on, have you no imagination?"

"It is Nino who has none," said the prince.

"Right! *How* right! Come on, General, don't keep us waiting. This is sheer torture!"

"I have it!" said the prince.

"You do?" asked the general. "Then someone must have told you. That is unfair."

"Oh no, I guessed it all by myself."

"Impossible. Don't tell them if you did."

"How will you know?"

"Whisper it to me."

The others were against it, they all shouted: "Unfair! Unfair!"

"The majority rules that I must speak!" said the prince.

"You, with your name and tradition!" said the general, becoming all excited, "you, accepting the principles of the French Revolution, shame and curse of the world! I am surprised!"

"Times have changed, my dear friend, times have changed. I bow my head, as my French ancestors bowed theirs to have it cut. And I shall speak. You know what my two guesses are?" And with a glow of triumphant stupidity in his eyes, he said: "Two more women!"

Even the lady of the house shrieked with delight, and the prince, with princely modesty, tried to belittle his wit. "What have I said, I ask, that makes you laugh so much? I really meant it; what else could be expected of Nino?"

And, while my mother and my father were exchanging mournful glances, he said to her: "You, Madame, be the judge, with your Russian approach, tell us in all sincerity, was that so funny?"

She looked at him, trying to smile.

"Why," he said, by way of conclusion to the words she had not spoken, "you, too, have been made speechless by my words. I am confused. I did not mean to make a joke, I am not a born wit, as so many are. I am the dullest person in Italy, I am always told."

These words provoked more and more laughter, which he kept kindled with an expression of faked innocence, almost of fear. "What is the matter with them all?" Then he turned to my father. "You alone, Doctor, seem to have kept a strong grip on your clarity of mind. But all the others . . . look at them, please!"

Now the laughter was touching on vulgarity, with yelping sounds and faked sounds of discomfort. "Coco, stop looking so funny! Please stop, I don't want to lose my dinner!" shouted the wife of the general. "I cannot look at him! Please make him stop!"

The general was the first to regain his composure. He had been laughing out of politeness, but it was clear that he felt cheated. "Enough!" he shouted several times. "Enough! Let's not be childish! This is serious. You still have not guessed!"

"You see, dear general" said the lady of the house, "we are all too stupid. Please tell us what Nino is going to South America for."

"To inherit a slaughterhouse," he said.

"A slaughterhouse? Not true. You are joking."

"A slaughterhouse, and he will stay there and become the director of the whole industry. Thousands of pigs a day made into sausages."

"My God," said the prince, "we must rescue him at once, or he will get himself made into sausages by mistake!"

Again the conversation was brought to a halt by the success of this remark. "Now, stop laughing," said the prince, "or you will make me think that I am really a clown. This is more serious than our friend himself has said. How did poor Nino get himself into this mess? *Que faisait-il dans cette galère?*" he added, delighted to be able to quote from Molière.

"He just inherited the whole thing."

"From whom? He is poorer than even I am."

"From a rich lady who just died in Paris."

"Cheater! You lied to us! There *was* a woman in all this!"

"Oh no, she was extremely old."

"She must have had a daughter, a niece, someone, or perhaps it was she herself Nino was chasing."

"I believe she has a niece . . ."

"Ah, you see? I was right!"

"Poor Nino," said the lady of the house. "He was already a bigamist, and now he'll get himself into a still greater mess!"

"No," said the prince. "You don't understand how these things work. When you are a bigamist, get a third wife and let the other two unite against her. If she is rich enough, they will settle in a body with her, and Nino will be reduced to one wife like the rest of mankind."

"Poor Nino! But he is not the man to get married, ever. Why, General, you knew this and you did not tell us before? When did it all happen?"

"A month ago. I was in Rome and saw him as he received the telegram and left for Paris, and I remember he said he was sailing from Cherbourg in four weeks exactly, which would have been yesterday."

"And you mean to say you have known this for a month and haven't told anyone?"

"You know me, my friend. My memory has never been my greatest quality. I confess; it completely disappeared from my mind, as if I had not even seen him."

"And you," said the prince to the general's wife. "You, too, forgot such an important piece of gossip? I can hardly believe it."

"I knew nothing about it until this very moment," she said. "You can trust me not to let anything as good as that stay with me for more than one minute!" Everyone laughed.

"I am really ashamed of myself," said the general, who seemed as proud as possible. "And I remember now that I went home thinking how this would amuse you, darling," he said to his wife. "But then I don't know how it slipped my mind, until I heard that story about pigstys a few minutes ago, and it rang some sort of bell, but I still did not remember what it was. You must have noticed that I looked rather pensive. That was it: I was thinking. Then I overheard the word divorce. Am I correct? Didn't someone mention a divorce?"

"Why certainly," said the prince, "we all did. I mentioned it, too."

"You see? I was right. I heard that word, and suddenly, connecting that with the word *pigs,* and then *slaughterhouse,* the name of Nino flashed into my mind by sudden intuition, I saw this name in front of me (funny, how the mental processes always seem to develop, isn't it?) and . . . well, I told you. That's all."

"Interesting," said the prince.

"That's right," said the general, in a new burst of mental processes, "that's right. It was you, Madame, who told us about pigstys and who also spoke about a divorce. Or *two.* Wasn't it *two* divorces you mentioned? See how attentive I am? I *do* hear everything, even if I don't seem to."

"My husband is not a great thinker, let's leave it at that," said his wife, turning her head to a forty-five degree angle, so she could see my mother from the depth of her hat. "If you only knew Nino, you would realize what a service you have rendered him by making my husband remember this story. And someone at this table will make this an excuse to sail for Buenos Aires at once."

There was a knowing giggle from the lady of the house, then the prince said: "That someone is my humble person. You could have said so from the beginning, since everybody knew it anyway. Yes, my friends, I *am* going to sail. And Nino will have to pay for my passage. Because I *am* going to rescue him. The fact that I have someone there myself is an *entirely different matter.*"

There were shrieks of "No, no, it is not!"

But he lifted his finger and said: "She is not rich enough to make me slaughter pigs!"

On this note the meal was finished, and the lady of the house, taking my mother by the arm said, in a whisper: "Don't let this shock you. These frivolous people are incorrigible. But the prince is lots of fun, is he not?"

"Oh yes, yes" said my mother, gulping her tears. "So, this window here overlooks the valley of Empoli."

"Exactly."

They walked to the window together, then the lady of the house said: "Shall we all go to the village now? I mean you and your family and myself?"

"With great pleasure," said my mother, and went back to the group to drink her coffee in perfect ease.

The other guests went to their rooms for an afternoon nap, and we walked to the village in the warm autumn sunshine: the lady of the house holding my mother by one hand and my father by the other, and the two looking like children. We, who were walking right behind them, in fact, *their* parents and guardians, had our first consolation as grownups.

The village, a microcosmic medieval town with walls and towers, everything being in strange contrast to the Renaissance villa, which was so much quieter in line but fiercer in proportions, was on top of a small hill at the end of a road that went down and then up, making the distance seem much greater than it was in reality.

There, too, one felt the antiquity of antiquity. That Medici villa laughed at the Middle Ages: it was modern and civilized and feared no knights in armor and no dragons, and for us to be caught in the spell of those towers and ramparts and laughed at by that villa, which stood *in their future,* was a very strange experience. Yet the whole Renaissance was full of wars and condottieri, all still in armor, still with plumage and draperies and banners that would have fit a medieval background more than that villa. I understood that day why Don Quixote had looked back with nostalgia on the lost days of chivalry, at an epoch when highway robbery was the main occupation of most noblemen. Now these two epochs, the Middle Ages and the Renaissance, stood both equally silent in front of us "moderns." The distance between us and both of them seemed on first sight the same, like peaks on the same mountain range at the end of a plain, and it was only by approaching them that what had seemed a bluish wall began to melt into green hills, with roads and villages and larger towns, and more green hills beyond them, with more towns and more villages, and finally, the mountain range, exactly as we had seen it from the plain, a bluish wall, still infinitely distant. Those were the Middle Ages. And these hills, and this villa, this whole epoch we had extracted from that wall by trying to reach for it, was not much closer to it than we were. What had happened to those people that made them suddenly build villas and not ramparts, faked drawbridges and not real ones? Where was all their antiquity, if they still looked upon the Middle Ages as something long surpassed, something pretty and quaint? And where stood we with all our proud "modernity?" Were we, with our telegraph poles, automobiles and factories, still only the last echo of modern times that had begun so long ago? And how could we feel that nostalgia for the dear Middle Ages and mistake it for an interest in history, when it had been a distant dream already to people who had *us* in their own future, more than five centuries ago?

Oh, how I wished I could sit on those ramparts forever and be laughed at by that villa, then run back to that villa and look with modern eyes at that medieval town, and back and forth, walk my dream every day from end to end until a great poetic reconstruction *made by me* allowed the dead of both those distant epochs to come back and tell me all their secrets. And to think that the lady in front of me had the keys to that world, and never used them. I would have sold my soul that day to be able to live there as her servant and listen to the voices of history.

That afternoon we visited the orphanage, the nunnery, the local chapter of her nationwide school of Renaissance and Medieval embroideries, the local grammar school and a few other charitable works, and everywhere there was a little scene of gratitude which the Good Patroness acknowledged and tried to fight off, as a Hindu believer in the rights of flies would try to fight off flies. I saw through all this very clearly; what tied me to the train of her comedy was the calculation that if she could use my own parents as her toys, this would allow me to use her town, her house, her library, her oxygen as my toy, and my toy was my greatest ambition, my true love. I did not therefore have to fake an interest in history. In fact, what made it difficult for me to flatter her into letting us stay a little longer, or letting me at least come back to study, was that my love paralyzed me completely. Had my interest been false, I knew I could have found the words to flatter her.

This way, in spite of my seeing through her comedy, I was the victim of my passion. I hoped she would be noble enough to understand me and I was wrong. Every time I realized it I felt hurt. We were touring the ramparts and watching the horizon. As we faced the hazy marshlands where we lived, she said, "That must be the direction of Terra Bentinga."

"Terra Be . . . tinga," said my father.

"Oh, isn't that too bad?" she said, as if ten other guests of the worst kind had been present to hear that. "I so prefer to say Terra Bentinga. It is much more amusing than Terra Betinga. Listen to it: Bentinga. Doesn't it sound more amusing to you?"

Why all that comedy? Why that misuse of the adjective "amusing"? At that time, the word "amusing" had not yet been dragged down from its place in the dictionary to mean anything boring but officially accepted as elegant. "Amusing hat!" a lady in Rome would say back in those days, and the expression sounded so new. No lady would say that in Florence as yet, let alone in the country. They began a few years later in Florence, and much, much later in the province of Florence. It was the equivalent, in the early twenties, of the use of the word "divine." As an extremely sensitive philologist, my father could not understand any departure from correct usage. So he tried to correct her. "You cannot mean *amusing*," he said. "Quite aside from the fact that to us the mere name of Terra Betinga sounds ominous, I don't see what can be so amusing in a name. What you probably mean is 'ridiculous' or 'barbaric,' meaning 'unusual,' and there you are right. '*Betinga*' is, I understand, a Longobard word, and '*Terra*' means, in fact, a Longobard fortification, the same as '*Castrum*' in classical Latin. 'Terra' for 'Castrum' is already a medieval corruption, and the marshlands where we live are full of Longobard reminiscences. There is a farmhouse in the middle of the marshlands, in fact, which must be the last building of a town that has probably been eaten up by the earth in the early Middle Ages. And that region bears the name of Carbolinga, no one knows for what reason. The name probably survived because of that one miserable hut, and it is certainly indicative of the presence of a large town in that place, for we find, only a few miles from there, the name Betinga for our village, and further up toward the hills other names with that barbaric ending. And to your ear, so used to Italian harmony, the version Bent*in*ga sounds a little less ludicrous, and that is what you call, incorrectly however, *amusing.*"

"Oh, no," she said, "I find it amusing because it *is* amusing. That is correct Italian. I bought this hat for example, because it was amusing, too, and for no other reason."

"A *hat* amusing?" he asked.

"The King said that to me the other day. What an amusing hat you have, he said. So don't take away my amusement and let me say B*en*tinga. Will you?"

"As you please," he said, a bit annoyed.

We were all saddened by that incident, as if she were amused by what was tragic for us.

But the next moment we were drawn to her again by sheer necessity.

As the tour of the towers turned west, the flank of Monte Albano was in front of us, and the sun in our faces, not far from the setting line. A valley of oak trees and that dark shape of the mountain beyond it made it the most idyllic place on earth. A view over two valleys made it grandiose. "What a beautiful little house down there!" said my mother. "Oh, how I love it! That is the size of house that I feel is now within reach of my dreams. It is still a great dream, but very, very far from the wealth of the past. What a beautiful house that is!"

"That house," said the lady. "Oh, that is hardly more than a farmhouse. I had it remodeled by my architect to suit the needs of our local country doctor."

"Oh!" said my father. "We saw him."

"You did? Where?"

"On the way up. Your chauffeur said to us, 'That is our country doctor.' "

"I hope it was not on the new road, which is only for the use of my cars. Too dangerous for mixed traffic."

"Oh no, it was not. It was up here."

"Good. Yes, my chauffeur protects him. He tells me (he is so touching, you know!), 'Excellency, he is not a great doctor, does not know too much medicine, but he's all right!' I trust my chauffeur's understanding. And he speaks for the whole village, I know that, too."

"Your doctor is quite fortunate to have you as a neighbor and landlady," he said.

"Do you think so? I never see him, I do not interfere. And you know, the doctor's sons play tennis in my garden at times and they have permission to use the library."

"Fortunate boys!" I said, with burning envy.

The tour continued and now we faced the villa again. A historical landscape was in front of us. Beyond the villa, in a pink haze, the city of Florence with the Cupola and the white tower of Giotto. Further out, the white church of San Miniato, rolling country with cypresses, medieval towns, very little that was modern, a few roads, smoke from a chimney, oxen in the fields, yellow leaves in the wind, like distant birds, a smell of fresh wine-cellars and warm grapes in fermentation, cries of children, voices of men, snapping of pruning shears on the trees, a churchbell, a brown roof. And the voice of my father, close to my ear but voided of proximity by an evening breeze, the voice of my father explaining where Dante fought, where Boccaccio was born, which road the armies used to take to fight the great enemy nation of Siena, and how important all that was.

Suddenly the whole countryside became infinitely poetic, as if it were singing. It took me a few minutes to realize the reason for this: that distant notes of a harpsichord were coming from the villa. Never, never before had music passed through nature so completely and spoken for all things so well. A joy too great to be kept free of tears began to swell my breath. I tried hard not to cry. I was able to kill it for a moment (and what pain that is!) by taking part in the general comment on the sonority of the air at sunset. "That is my guest," said the lady. "He is practicing Mozart. Let us hope we will still find him at it as we go back to the house."

Then they all fell for the enchantment. They all opened their souls to receive the music, as it ran like a brook under the leaves of trees, the blades of grass, the spots of sunshine. And again tears of joy came to me in such quantity that I felt them in my shoulders, in my fingertips, not only in my throat and my nose.

How could I keep them from my eyes?

To hide my face and yet to go on looking, I leaned over the ramparts, as if trying to identify something in the valley. "What is it?" asked Chino.

"Look," I said, stretching out my arm.

"What?"

"There."

"*What* 'there'?"

"A bird."

"Where?"

"Down there."

"Cannot see it."

"Gone."

He left me alone. I went on looking, the whole countryside blurred now, and that music so ancient and so pure. Suddenly a hand passed lightly over my cheek. I could not turn without showing my tears, but I guessed from the perfume that it must be the lady of the house who was trying to console me. I withdrew, still with my eyes fixed on nothing, my head turned away, and found another place of observation further down to the north.

I heard her ask my father: "What is it? First pangs of love?"

And his answer: "If so, he better be cured quickly and think of other loves, such as his books and his exams!"

"Oh, don't be cruel," she said.

"I am not being cruel," he said. And as they walked away from me, I heard, then guessed, that my father was telling her about my "acting stupidly" with peasant girls. And again the word: "study" came to me and killed my joy, stopping my tears.

We were hurried back to the house to be able to hear her guest in the music room. But he stopped as we came in, to come and greet us, and did not want to play again. He could never be asked, and we had asked him. What a mistake! And not even the fact that we were leaving, that we would hardly ever have a chance to hear him play in Rome or elsewhere, made him do us the favor.

"Later, perhaps. After dinner," he said.

We were speechless with joy. So we were going to stay!

An urgent family meeting took place. We flocked together, and decided we could stay also for the night. The only problem would have been my father's patients, and he stopped briefly to review the situation in his mind. "That one . . . can wait. The other one . . . can also wait. The third one . . . well, why not? Let him wait, too. Ambulatory tomorrow morning? Er . . . let's see. Hm . . . A loss, yes, a loss. Of how much? . . . Could write it off as price for this vacation. After all we don't often go out, all of us . . . Had we all gone to Florence by train for the day, had whipped-cream with biscuit, then of course a meal . . . makes so and so much, multiplied by six . . . Well, I believe I can write it all off, thinking of the two meals today, breakfast, probably lunch tomorrow . . . tea . . . Why not?"

We were so happy and so grateful to him, even though he said mournfully, "Nothing can be had for nothing." So, for a few more minutes, we kept thinking of the many more things we should have counted in the imaginary price of the day. "A Mozart concert, in such a setting . . . a visit to such a museum . . . etc. Think how much these things would cost, if you had to pay for them as such . . ."

"Yes, children, that will do. They are looking at us. Please!" The lady of the house was in fact looking at us and smiling as she spoke to her butler. While he waited, she gave him orders, his face, although they were both the same size, looking up at hers, and his huge back protruding in a tentative bow. It seemed, at a certain point, that they were speaking of us, counting us, first the lady then the butler, and then nodding to each other and thinking.

"I'll leave it all to you," she said, aloud, dismissing him, and then came to us to explain: "When I have unexpected guests, this man is wonderful. He knows exactly what I want to do, even before I myself realize it! It is so comforting to have such a person around!"

This asked for an acknowledgment, which my mother could find only by digging deep into her past and mentioning Bernhardt, Grandmother's faithful butler, and Monsieur Morin, her cook. Then the butler came back carrying a small silver plate with biscuits. The whole plate was not even as large as the two hands that carried it, and the biscuits rested on a white napkin, and those white gloves of his and the starched shirt and the beautiful black evening suit into which he had changed since lunchtime made me feel as if someone important had suddenly been taken ill, so ill in fact that he or she, whoever it was, could not even carry that plate. For a moment I felt like laughing, but then I realized that everything had changed, as if the day in that house were divided into seasons, and this was a new season: tea-time, like an autumn of drawing rooms, for which new clothes were needed. Warmer ones perhaps, or at least darker ones, more solemn ones, not the ones we had worn until then, but everything should change, even thoughts, even friends. And it occurred to me that another season yet might come at dinnertime.

"That very nice family with the two boys is coming to hear the concert," said the lady of the house, as if that were good news for us. "And we have three more guests, who just dropped in on their way to Venice. They are spending the night."

We were somewhat perplexed, and when my father nodded for all of us and said, "That's all right," we were ready to say that we had never known him and she could have him crucified if she so pleased.

"We still have time for a tour of the house," she said. "You have not seen the upper floors, the guest rooms, or the carpentry shops and the cellars downstairs. And the torture room. That should interest you," she said to me. "It is of historical interest."

We visited the upper floor, the guest rooms; they were much more beautiful than the huge halls downstairs. Then we visited the servant quarters in the attic, and found them still more beautiful than the guest rooms. The view was more dramatic, one could see not only way beyond the ramparts of the medieval town but one saw the green lawn in front of the villa as if it stood erect in front of the window, and one had the brown beams of the roof covering parts of the sky like an awning outside the window. Also the furniture was simpler and as such more within the reach of our present-day dreams. Then we visited the carpentry shops down in the basement, where she had room for another new orphanage to be organized (where did she find so many orphans? I wondered), and then the theatre for the orphans, and their dormitory, and then the huge wine cellar, and the torture room. My father said, touching the walls of the torture room: "Not at all humid, like our house," and mother sighed, and Sonia said to Chino, "Would you live here?" And both Chino and I answered, "For the rest of my life, starting tonight!" In fact, the window, huge, with iron bars, was in itself a picture. Oak trees outside and a bit of blue sky allowed the mind to construct any historical fantasy. The lady of the house overheard us, and smiled, obviously pleased.

"It is a most romantic place," she said. "Of all the estates I own, this is the one I love most. More even than the castle of Sua Maestà I so would want to show you. If you ever come that way, southeast, you must stay with me. Promise? But write to me first, for I am rarely there. In fact, I may transform the place into an orphanage, but before I do that, I want you all to see it."

We went back upstairs for tea, and the other guests, fresh from their nap, were waiting for their hostess.

"You should have come with us," said the lady of the house.

"Oh," said the general, "I am no longer mobilized. Only in war time do I display all my energies. Otherwise I am lazy."

His wife was wearing a new dress and a new hat, and everyone discussed the hats of women; how they all hated the *cloche* hats at first but how bewitched they were after a while by any change in fashions. "I am now horrified by last year's hats," said the general, and the prince nodded. No one seemed to notice that my mother's hat was old. Then the maestro came and spoke at length about medieval music that had come to light in archives in Turin that year, and promised he would play some of it after dinner. At that point, I began to have a feeling that these promises excluded us, despite the fact that he came over to my sister and said, "Do you like ancient music?"

The lady of the house was next to Sonia and seemed displeased when she heard him ask that question. She looked at Sonia as if she had done something wrong. Then, suddenly, her expression changed, she smiled, and asked. "One more cup?"

"No, thank you," said Sonia, who had tears in her eyes, and moved away from her.

I found her in front of a china cabinet, looking at a collection of medieval dolls.

"Sonia," I said, "what is it?"

"Nothing. Why?"

"You are crying."

"I want to go home."

"Go home? You fool, we are going to stay for dinner, for the concert, and perhaps even for the night."

"No, we are not."

"Who told you?"

"I just know and I don't care. Look at Mother's hat."

"What's wrong with it?"

"Look at your suit, and my dress, and father's suit, and then look at those people, and the butler . . . I don't want to be laughed at."

"What will you do?"

"Tell mother that I want to go home."

At that moment Jules-Adrien came to us and said, "Do you think we could play with those dolls?"

"Are you crazy? Those are museum pieces. And besides, at your age, to even think of playing with dolls . . ."

"What else is there for me to do? Smoke a cigar? Drive an automobile? Am I not the child of the family?"

"Don't start with that nonsense again."

The lady of the house came toward us, running like a good angel. "I see that you are tired," she said. "Perhaps you want to go home. Shall I send for the car?"

"Oh no, no, thank you," we all said in a hurry. But she had gone to tell our parents, who were drinking their tea all by themselves and talking to each other like two guests who had just met. They both blushed, as if caught doing something wrong, my father bowed in front of her as she spoke, exactly as the butler had been bowing before. Then the three of them came in our direction.

"Are you tired?" asked my mother, with a suggestion of tears in her eyes, and we said, "No, not at all."

"Well, I hope not," she said. Then, to her hostess, "How could anyone be tired of this beauty and this place? They love music, you know? We all do. It is, in fact . . ."

Her voice dropped as she noticed the face of her friend. The muscles of the mouth were smiling and the eyes asking: "Tell me, am I good at imitating a kind hostess?"

"I was hoping so much the butler could think of some sort of a solution, so that I could keep you all here for the night," she said, "but he tells me the house is too small, and he is right."

"Oh yes, of course" said my father, looking intently at the walls and the ceiling of that "cozy music room" in which all of our house, with garden, pigsty, chicken coop, and stables could have been contained.

"As for sending you home, late, after the concert, in the heart of the night," she continued, "I don't dare suggest anything so cruel. My chauffeur kindly said he would not mind at all, and I know he means it, although, as a rule, I don't want him to work so hard, but it is I who would not want to impose upon you such an ordeal."

"As far as we are concerned," said my father, "it would not be an ordeal at all."

"I am thinking of your children," she said. "The little one looks pale already."

"Oh, that's nothing. He always looks pale."

"So, when would you prefer to go? Now, or . . . in an hour, two hours . . . You tell me when. We won't dine before eight-thirty; there is still plenty of time. Although I imagine that getting home too late would not be too convenient, either."

"Any time that suits you," said my father.

"Oh, no, don't think of me," she said. "The chauffeur is your chauffeur today. You just give him your orders. I will send him to you promptly, And don't hesitate to tell him exactly what you want. If you want to drive by any other route, say so. If you want to stop at the house of a patient before reaching Terra Bentinga . . . pardon me, Be . . . *tinga,* right? You just say so and he will be glad to obey you." And she took leave of us, almost for good. It was a dress rehearsal of leave-taking. "We *will* say good-bye later. I *refuse* to say it now! Just enjoy yourselves, and *do* have some more tea, please. There is, I believe, a most wonderful cake circulating around. I caught a glimpse of it, but then it disappeared behind the general. Don't let him eat it all, children! He is a *most dangerous* glutton!"

In a few moments the chauffeur came and said in a loud voice to my father, "Is it you I must drive back now?"

"No . . . oh, er . . . I don't know," said my father.

"Well, I wish I were told more precisely then."

He went to the lady of the house, who was surprised to see him. He bowed and came right back to us, while she looked at him sternly and nodded two or three times.

"I am sorry," he said, in a very subdued tone. "I understand you wish to have the car now."

"Yes," said my father. "Now or later, whenever it is convenient for you."

"Just a moment," said my mother, and stopped him. "We would really prefer to go by train. If you could drive us to the station."

"There is no train from here," he said. "*She* did not want it. If

I were to drive you to the next station, it would be the same waste of time as driving you home, and you would never get there before tomorrow morning."

"But we really don't mind . . ."

"Come on," he said, rudely but kindly, so that we all felt attracted to him at that moment. "I'm not a beast. I have kids, too. I would not let you drag them through the countryside all night by train. I'll drive you home safely, and it won't take more than an hour. All right?"

This, in a way, marked our final return to a safer haven of humanity than we had seen and known that day. That chauffeur was in our class, sad though this may seem, and even his resentment was understandable to us, while all those sudden shifts of humor in the lady of the house had been too much for us. There we huddled together in a corner without speaking to anyone, feeling hurt at the same time that this should not attract attention. The same people we had encountered in the morning came back, still in their tennis clothes, and carrying with them not only their rackets, but also the whole fun and the movements of their game. What the tennis ball had done seemed almost as important as the trip of their friend Nino to Buenos Aires, or any gossip of society people. "And then the ball went this way . . . and then it came back . . . and then I . . . and then he . . . but the ball passed him by, and the server . . ." How cheerful they all seemed, what good results were expected by all from that innocent game!

The lady of the house caught a glimpse of us and said to the general's wife, "You sit here and serve tea for a moment, will you?" After which she ran to us and said: "Did you speak to the chauffeur? Is everything all right?"

"Yes, perfect," said my mother, nodding a bit too much.

"You are not leaving right away, I hope?"

"If you don't mind, he said . . ."

"Mind? What a word to use! Why should I mind? I am delighted. This is good news! How long do I still have of your dear company?"

"Forty minutes or so, he said."

"Oh, that is disappointing! I was counting on two hours at least! But let me take you to the garden, I want to pick flowers for you."

"Oh, thank you, that is very kind! But we don't want to deprive you of your flowers!"

"Deprive me of my flowers? What an unkind thing to say! It is a joy for me to give my friends some of these flowers I so rarely have a chance to enjoy myself. Come, let's go."

She preceded us running, with movements that were really so gracious that we felt well rewarded for our sufferings, as if she were doing this only to ingratiate herself with us again. And in a way she was.

We walked the whole length of the villa to the south, and reached a very large rose garden, which seemed small in proportion to the house, but became larger and larger as we walked from one rose to the next, from one flowerbed to another. She picked every single rose that was neither too open nor too young, as if she recognized in it some secret link with us. "This one will do. This is really the flower for you. And this one, too, and I see one down there which is just asking to be sent to Terra Bentinga (oh, pardon me! Be . . . *tinga,* I meant), where it will speak to you of this abandoned garden where no one ever looks at the flowers . . ."

Her charms worked. My mother followed her, clapping her hands with joy every time a new flower was added to the bunch; it was embarrassing for us, and yet there was no comedy in her gestures, for she looked like a child: there was light in her eyes.

When we went back inside the house, the stars were beginning to pierce through the evening light, and the shapes of the hills, the towers of the village, the large roof of the house itself made the place look more beautiful.

The thought of leaving it became unbearable. Church bells from invisible belfries in the valley, a bitter smell of burning leaves and cooling earth made us feel hungry at once, and we moved back to the music room where tea was still being served.

The two boys and their parents had changed clothes. How

elegant they looked. We could not speak to them. And neither did they care to notice us, except to say, "Still here? We thought we had seen you leave!"

Then they resumed their conversation with new people who had not been there before. I caught a phrase from one of the boys: "Paris is overrated. I think Berlin is the only great city today."

The last half hour was the worst. There we stood against the wall, next to chairs that are always placed against a wall between tapestries or china cabinets: purely decorative chairs. And so were we, each one of us with roses in his arms and sadness in his eyes.

The lady of the house pointed to the last slice of a chocolate cake, and winked to me. "Go get it," she said. "No, thank you," I said. But she went over to the table and came back with the plate. "I know you like it," she said, "and you will not refuse it from my hands." So I had to take it and thank her. "Say thank you!" "Take it!" "Eat it!" I did as told, with shame, like a poor beggar in the house of the rich, and crumbs kept falling on my roses.

THE SIEGE

For three full years, from 1915 to 1918, at nine o'clock every morning, we had waited for the postman, right before breakfast; or, if he was late, during breakfast. At times, my sister Sonia, my brother Chino, and I went all the way to the gate to look for him on the big road, but then, if he was not in sight, we preferred to wait in the garden for him to "ripen" from around the corner of the gardener's house. This idea of his ripening was our invention; we had coined the word and it described the situation very well. He brought news of the war, or rather of our brother Vladimir, our "Kostia," who was in it.

When the newspaper he delivered was spread open, we glanced rapidly, all of us, and in secret, and sideways, at the casualty list. There was no reason why Kostia's name should have appeared there before the next of kin had been informed, but that casualty list was like a precipice into which all our hopes might fall in one, two, three or God knows how many days. We hoped that his life would continue after that precipice was closed, that there would be peace and him again with us after that peace. But nine o'clock was an hour from another life: in fact, one could be seen idling around the house at that hour, which in itself was a crime, and even doing such terrible things as scratching one's head or putting one's finger in one's nose, and rarely a word of reproach would be spoken. If then there was a letter from Kostia we had another half-hour of joy and vacation before going up to the library, but if nothing arrived, then all the irregular things one had done right before nine were remembered and loudly criticized, often with sanctions, too.

One day in November 1918, almost together with the news of the armistice, came a short letter which said: "Any day from Tuesday week you may begin to wait for me. Should my plans change, I shall get in touch with you again." Just dry and short like that. No mention of the great event, the hard-won victory, none of the vivid tales of what had happened to him; it was almost a letter from a stranger. But of course this meant that the written word was abandoned for good as a means of conveyance. Words were now free again to go where they were needed: we had no use for them; we would soon see him, touch him, know that he was there. The postman too was no longer the sovereign of the day. This letter was his abdication.

And that was how we graduated from the calendar to the clock. Two weeks, just waiting for the right to wait. The big clock in the dark corner of the dining room, hidden by the heavy curtains between the two windows, would have a lot of work to do now, mincing away slices of time until two weeks were filled. But what is it for a strong clock to do a little extra work when it has remained idle for three years, marking fictitious hours that no one filled?

Our father was the first one to break up the joyful meeting. He had nodded to his good luck, smiled, touched his little white beard with two nervous fingers, and that seemed enough to him. "No sense in waiting now," he said. "This is just another day of work. Go to the library and do your lessons, all of you." He put on his shapeless old hat and we saw him walking angrily as usual down the main path of the park, to go and find out how much damage had been done him by the peasants, the administrator, and the wind.

When his staggering form, his hat, and his white hair had disappeared behind the last tree, Mother smiled at us, we smiled at her, we did not leave, she did not tell us to leave, and we knew it was all right. She wanted to talk to someone, and for that reason we were made grown-ups by her royal decree, just as a chair is "made" an airplane by a child. And we knew that we would hear the secret story of what had happened to us these three years.

"You know," she said, "the only thing one must be careful to avoid is dreams. There are little devils, microbes of dreams, around us all the time. They know our hopes and feed on them. They always come and offer us the things we want, and we are always fooled by them. We say, for instance, this is a dream, but *he* is not, because I *see* him. Kostia is here. So then we start leaving the dream with him, and then . . . (she smiled) I have a word for it. I call it landing on the deserted shores of the morning." She was crying now. Jules-Adrien, our younger brother, who was six, wanted to tell his own ideas about dreams, sensing that this was a moment for great revelations, but he was stopped by Clorinda, the white-haired maid who had exercised spanking powers on our father when he was a child, and now retained, nominally at least, the same privileges on us. She was carrying the *scaldino,* a clay fire-basket which mother held in her hands all day.

"All of you: out of here," she said. "And you," she said to Mother, "don't sit there and cry like that. Do something instead. You are a fine lady who knows so many things: read, keep busy, fill this time with something else but your impatience."

"I promise," said Mother, who in normal times would not have allowed Clorinda to address her that way.

We went upstairs, and of course did not do our lessons at all, and we could hear that Mother was not doing anything either. We knew it from the noise of her rings on the clay handle of the fire-basket.

Lunch was unpleasant that day. Father sat with his head bent over his dish as if he were reading. His bald head, surrounded by white hair, looked like a wooden model for a face as it protruded against us. And when Chino began to talk about dreams again, he said, "Don't you have anything more intelligent to talk about? Dreams are dreams and reality is reality. It has always been that way." This seemed very stupid to us, but his voice had the right of way, no matter what he said. He had taken his option in the conversation and now he did not know what to do with it. So, without lifting his head, he fixed his small blue eyes on us through the white curtain of his eyelashes and coughed his ill-humor into the napkin until he became red as a lobster. Then he ate his soup until he saw the blue pattern of the arms in the middle of the dish, cleaned it carefully with bread and gave the dish to the maid, saying: "Away. The bread is for the cat. Don't forget."

The slow, heavy afternoon was again working its way up the naked hills of Spazzavento, and dragging the old house with the peasant houses around it toward another night. At Spazzavento the sun went down at two-thirty in November, but even in June it never stayed on the horizon later than four, because the villa was built on the north slope of the stony Calvana, facing the Bisenzio valley and the northwester that always came down that way. Only from the big window on top of the stairs one had a glimpse of the distant hills around Florence and of the railroad some three miles away and the wide, dusty new road that had been built quite recently, only forty-five years before, to link the station with the village.

Mother had not yet inaugurated her watch but she gave orders that very day to have a chair placed near the window on top of the stairs. For the next few days the maids were forever stumbling into that chair when they came down from their quarters at five o'clock in the morning, but they did not seem to mind. That chair had a meaning, like the wooden platforms they used to build in the village square a week before the procession of the patron saint. And the maids knew that the chair would stay there until after Kostia had had a chance to see it and to understand how much his mother loved him.

The house was always silent in the afternoon, or rather, the family quarters were silent. Nobody raised his voice in the corridors, in the bedrooms, in the library, or anywhere else. If Father was at home, he either snored for an hour in some dark corner, under a portrait of someone who had snored there before him (I still see his white beard defiantly facing the opposite wall); or he was in the small office near the oil-mill down in the basement, where his administrator used to receive the peasants and tell them day in day out that they were thieves.

The silence of the big house, which we called the Main Silence or the Master Silence, was cut out of the eternal silence of death to which it belonged, and lifted on a pedestal made up of the various sounds that came from the kitchen, the pantry, or the fields. The sad linear song of a maid surged from the cellar and went all around that silence; out in the fields, the scissors of the peasants binding and cutting the vines for the winter broke the air like distant gunshots, and often this noise too was underlined by stripes of shapeless chanting. But when the wind moaned through the valley (indeed the name "Windswept" was appropriate for the place), then the Main Silence became so high, so monumental, that it scared everyone in the house.

Today the wind had suddenly awakened from the air and was in one of its moods. We all felt depressed. Little Jules-Adrien, who took orders from everybody and passed them on to his toys or to chairs or imaginary people, had finished his daily battle against the Germans in the living room, and probably had found nobody in the kitchen to talk to (dreary place that kitchen, with the huge smoky pot hanging from a black chain in the fireplace and simmering all day). So he must have decided to go and see whether his beloved hero and brother, Kostia, was coming home, as he had heard in the morning, because he climbed all the stairs, stood in front of the rattling window and looked and looked. And as he saw a carriage, without thinking what he was doing, he shouted joyfully: "Kostia is coming . . ."

Doors were flung open, the maids appeared from nowhere, we came from the library, and mother advanced on the stairs, pale, and with wide open eyes. He saw us all come toward him and began to cry: "It wasn't Kostia, no, no, it wasn't."

"To scare me like that," shouted Mother, trembling.

"You have no business standing here," shouted Clorinda, shaking him with anger. "Go downstairs and do some work, you idle child, you."

We all gave him our part of the general indignation, and

Mother ordered that no one should start waiting like that until two full weeks had passed. But another wall had been broken down: the fact that someone had begun to look at the street had a strange effect on her. She went downstairs, "to prepare everything." Then twice she climbed a few steps and compelled herself to go back to the dining room. But the third time she had another reason. She wanted to see whether the servant quarters were in good order; a thing she had not done for years because she knew that Clorinda would have resented this lack of confidence in her. As she reached the window, accompanied by Sonia, she said that after all it was unnecessary because Clorinda knew better than anyone else, and besides, three flights of stairs were already too much for her; she was no longer young. "Let me test this chair," she said. "What does one see from here?" She sat down and she looked. Just for one second. And the siege of the road began.

Sonia tried to protest, but she said, "What difference does it make, whether I wait here or downstairs? Bring me my needlework and the green book from the mantelpiece in my room."

When Clorinda called to her not to be unwise, she answered that she was not used to carrying on a conversation from one floor to the next. It was sheer good luck that she was able to restrain herself and not add "especially with a maid." She would have been sorry, because Clorinda came right upstairs and took her kindly by the arm like a child, saying, "Now you come with me." Mother answered that she was used to doing as she pleased in her own house, but could not help laughing because she felt weak in front of this determined old woman. Finally she broke into tears and said she would go downstairs in a little while.

But the next day she was again seated up there, this time with all her ancient pride burning in her eyes, and Clorinda must have understood from the rhythm of her rings on the handle of the *scaldino* that this was not the day to speak a word. Sonia began to pay her long visits up there, but she did not want us boys near her because we startled her with tactless questions, such as: "Do you see that man coming down from there? Who could it be?" Or we said: "There, a carriage slows down on the curve. It will certainly stop here." "Barbarians," she used to tell us in an angry voice, just as she did when she was playing the piano and someone dared talk aloud in the room. But Sonia knew how to behave; she let Mother do the waiting, the guessing, everything. She saw, of course, trains and carriages and people on foot, but she went on with what she was saying, and after they had passed and nobody had agreed to bring him or to be him, she found something interesting to say, so that Mother would not have to feel ashamed of the "defeat." Then also Clorinda began to accept the siege. At times she stopped near Mother for a second and threw a glance into the street as one throws a glance at a canvas, trying not to disturb the painter at his work.

We spent our mornings in the library as usual, then, every other day, we went to the nearby town of Prato with the carriage for our Latin and arithmetic lessons, and every time we crossed the hall we walked on tiptoes and tried to hear whether any carriages were rolling on the road. That dark figure against the glaring light of the window up there made us feel better. It was the only sign that a new era would begin. It was an assertion of our right to hope, a right that everything in that old house seemed to deny. Also the absurd idea that the road was being walked upon, that people were in the habit of coming along that road, seemed a hopeful sign: they were all part of *his* return; they kept the stream running.

Thus at the end of the two weeks, when the real expectation began, we were already a little too impatient, all of us. The first disappointment was that he did not appear in the first hour of light the first morning, a Tuesday it was, I remember so well. And then the second hour and then the third, and fourth, and then a whole morning full of hours, and then lunch-time too. The conversation stopped, as if by common understanding, every time the noise of a wheel was heard. It no longer passed on the road, it passed through the dining room, through the table, through all of us, and we resumed our talk in a state of weakness, as if we had been tramped upon by a real carriage.

How the entire third week managed to pass that way I can hardly recall. The fixity of our anguish, geared to such a high note, was the only true thing; the house, the people in it, our own actions and bodies, were all way behind. The only thing that took place in *our* world was Mother walking up the stairs, determinedly, stepping on each step as if *that* obstacle had been subdued, and then sitting majestically on her throne, fixing both eyes on the top of the horizon from where the road flowed down to her like a dry stream. The road was hers, she was besieging it; it must produce her son.

Nothing could happen in that empty space that did not fall into her eyes. When people crossed the road, it bothered her, and if they stood on it for any length of time, she made impatient gestures with her hand. Because *he* was to appear from there like a small point and ripen slowly into the dear figure we knew. And once he had adopted every form we had guarded so jealously in our hearts, as a last thing he would receive his voice, and we would all be free. No more stopping to ask ourselves: What is he really like? How does he act? Have we forgotten him? Oh, to be able to say: "These lines, this voice you take back now, for they are yours, and see whether we kept them well." We knew we must have kept them much too well, for time brings change, and time was dead in us. Our time flew all around that point: his face, as we remembered it; that was our watch. For us it was just then and always then, and it continued to be then all day. On the night he had left, three years before, Mother had put a photograph of him into the wooden frame of her small desk-watch. Now that the clock downstairs had done its work, this was the new impediment: nothing had really happened since that image had been put there. But he would come and set us free, we knew.

Oh, but too few of those small points came down the road in the afternoon. They always seemed to accept the gifts at first: Kostia's stature and way of walking; then, half-way or so, they would begin to shake them off and show that they had nothing about them even to start pretending they were Kostia: such people as old men, even women, all sorts of trespassers. Every single time we felt like shouting at them, "We are going to extract him from the unknown, even without your help!"

After eight more days of this Mother began to feel that we were all abandoning her. She was alone now on the rampart. All the doors were closed, all the hearts were closed, too: the old Nothing (another of our familiar images to describe the atmosphere of the house) was taking hold of us again like a bad winter. Now it was as if *she* were trying to conjure a dream in the midst of reality and plant it there. She had unfurled the canvas of her lively imagination with a new world painted on it, which was to cover everything—the stony countryside, the trees, the people. If there could only be a conspiracy of hope, if people helped, if they began to hold the canvas down with their feet, it would perhaps stick to the ground. If they could only fasten it under the houses, she could finish her work. If only the postman would bring that decree, empowering her with the exercise of rights she had already taken days ago, she might manage to win, but this way, all alone, it was too difficult.

We continued to work as usual in the library, and although we were too oppressed by the silence to open our hearts to any hope again, we felt defended by her faith. God, or Whoever or Whatever there was, that stood behind the curtains of the world, would find his, its, their match in the aspect of this mother who had the dignity of a queen and could want things like a queen. However, we did not communicate with one another during those days. It was all right to be crushed inside, but the air should not vibrate with dangerous words of doubt, or really the happiness it was so hard to evoke would feel offended and not come at all. Saying anything sad was like opening the doors to the old Nothing. So we all waited in *her* shadow and somewhat also in the shadow of the house door. Every time the big hand-bell rang, there was such a sinking of hearts, and the familiar faces that appeared were so disliked! We felt like saying: "Did you *have* to come? Only one person has the right to come these days and you are not that one."

Then an incident occurred which, although we understood that it meant nothing, made it even harder for us to interrupt our anguish. One day I saw my father come home with a face that was not only angrier than usual, but which said clearly: stay away, everybody. I was so afraid that I ran to the library and waited there to be called downstairs for tea. I heard him go through all the rooms. He was obviously looking for something and I knew what: something wrong, something on which to hook his anger. He found it. A chair had been displaced. He called Clorinda three times in a voice that was almost desperate with anger, and in the silence that followed, Sonia asked me stupidly: "Is there any news?" (Why oblige people to answer "No," when they would give anything in the world to answer "Yes"? There is a code of mutual respect in such situations.) "You fool," I said, "if there were any news, do you think I would wait to tell it until you asked me?"

Again Father called Clorinda, and again his steps were heard, and they changed from the heavy hammering of stairs being mounted to the lighter scuffling on the same surface. He must be in the hall now. Why didn't he say "Good evening" to Mother up there? And then, to call Clorinda that way, Clorinda, who had brought him up, spanked him, used strong words with him until he was fifteen! The fourth time he called, one note pierced the volume of his voice, and came out in a falsetto tone. Finally she arrived; and it was as if she had been guilty of everything that had ever happened in the world, when he asked: "Have *you* pushed this big chair against the frame of that picture again? Can't you see that it has left a mark? . . . I . . . this precious painting . . . my orders disobeyed . . ." etc.

It was so awful that Clorinda cried, and they both went downstairs together and way to the end of the corridor, and then a door was banged and their voices died down like thunder in the hills.

And Mother continued to sit there at the window, away from all this, indifferent to the loudest expressions of reality, as if these were the threatening waters in which she did not want to drown.

Then, for three days, Father was ill, and Clorinda was ill, too, and Mother hardly asked about Clorinda or why she was staying at the house of her brother, the gardener, instead of in her own room upstairs. And we hardly asked about our father's health, and everybody was alone in his anguish, like a dog. Then Father recovered, that is, he got up and looked so old, so terribly old, that Sonia cried one day for hours on her books, while my brother and I insulted her by way of consolation.

Then another incident, meaningless of course, utterly meaningless but there are moments in which everything creates an atmosphere of tragedy, even though there is no reason for it. Father went up to Mother's ramparts, and at first it seemed as if he, too, were interested in the road. He dragged a newspaper behind him as a child would drag a piece of cloth or a toy; and he said:

"I see here in the paper that there is going to be a League of Nations to keep the world at peace. The President of the United States of America is coming to Europe." Strange for him, with his cynicism, to make such a remark. Mother nodded without looking at him, then he said (his voice was very quivery after his illness): "Peace. Yes, peace for a great many years to come. At least our sacrifices will be rewarded, all of them."

And this must have seemed strange to Mother, because she screamed: "What do you mean?" And then she was out of breath and screamed again: "What sacrifices? *We* are beyond that and we have forgotten. *Our* sacrifices *are* being rewarded."

He was pale and trembling and said nothing.

"But what is it?" she said. "Why do you look so disturbed?" He did not answer, and Mother rose from her chair, and asked in a terrible tone: "Tell me, tell me right away! Why do you tremble so?"

And he said: "Why . . . I only thought I saw someone there, on the road."

And she sank back in the chair, crying: "Oh, I know. I know that. It happens to me all the time."

That evening I spoke to Sonia at length. Especially now that Clorinda was ill and no one dared scold our parents, it was necessary that we do something, because it was no longer human. Waiting had become a malady, a family epidemic, a strange fever. And we talked and talked and reached no conclusion, and the next morning she told me that she had had a dream: the wind had been so strong against the house all night that in her dream she had seen the house sailing toward non-existent shores; and it was Mother's fault, because her eyes had melted down the mountains and the road, and everything had been made into a sea, and we were drifting away on it. She was trembling as she told me that dream. She said: "You see? Even I am all upset by these silly ideas now. Kostia will laugh at this when he comes."

"I think that he will not have the time to laugh," I said, "because in this state of affairs they will start quarreling with him because he did not get here on time."

"You are right," she said. "And it's so silly. Let's do something. This spell must be broken."

And I said, "Yes, it must be broken."

The trouble was, however, that the house held our anguish so well, just as it held the silence, and then (it was about three o'clock in the afternoon), while I was having another conversation with Sonia about it, one of the maids came and said, gasping: "The Signora is talking."

We couldn't help smiling at such a silly statement. "What do you mean?" we asked.

"She is talking," she said at last, "alone, by herself."

Sonia began to tremble; she was afraid for Mother's health, and I felt my heart bang against my ribs so that I almost resounded from it; but Sonia, who was always courageous, said: "That's nothing," and began to go upstairs. She found Jules-Adrien who was climbing step by step, slowly, in the hope that nobody would notice him, and she had a quarrel with him. He called Mother to his defense: "Mamma, may I come upstairs?"

And Mother shouted with a voice full of hate: "Quiet there. Go away."

We all left. Doors were closed again, one in the face of the other, all along the hall, and there was silence, a high silence, the highest silence that ever was in Spazzavento: silence mounted on a monument of roars, moans, and cries that the wind brought from somewhere with it. Then, suddenly, we heard the voice of Mother and we slowly opened the door to the library, and she was saying, as if she had a fever:

"Go away, go away. It is not true." And then she said: "If you are true, then I must be your dream. You reflect my desire. . . ." And then she said: "Thank you. You are offering it back to me, for it must ache up in the air alone, detached and naked; it must suffer up there as it does here."

And we all walked to the middle of the hall and I had to lean against the wall so as not to faint. Then we began to walk downstairs, away from her, and stepped along the stairs and saw in the middle of the hall Father with his red bald head, standing, as one stands at Mass during Elevation. And then Mother again spoke: "Who makes this wind of light?" (This was one of her expressions to describe the beginning of dreams.) "Who detaches the paper from the faces, the mountains, and the houses?"

"Oh, my God," murmured Sonia, "she is ill."

"Who puts that cup there, on a hill?" said Mother again. "Go away!" she shouted. "Go away. I know you, devils of dream. *These* things don't happen here. . . . I know I am waiting. You don't have to tell me." Then, in a tired tone: "I know I have waited much too long." And she cried quietly, like a sick child.

Sonia walked up the stairs, knelt beside her, and said: "You are right, Mother." She said it so gently, so well, sneaking into the unreality of the situation, feigning herself unreal too; and Mother looked at her and said:

"The dreams were coming again. But don't be afraid. Let me alone."

Sonia came downstairs, and this time it was as if all of a sudden Mother had lost her battle, because she greeted Kostia with so much strength in her voice:

"Oh, here you are," she said. "And tell me now: how are you?" Then she whispered: "Did you come from downstairs? Tell me," she repeated, "did you? Through the garden? . . . Did you batter the ground with your own feet? You are expected to do that, you know. . . . And did you see the maid? She must have let you in." After a silence, she said, a little louder: "No, go downstairs first and ring the bell before we sit and talk."

Then she seemed scared by something and asked with great anguish: "Oh, but you have forgotten! How could you just be here, without a trip behind you? Kostia," she said, "my darling!

How did you manage to avoid that? The trainman must have seen you! You must have waited, sitting in the train, to get here slowly, with permission from them all."

Here she laughed, and then spoke again, in a weak voice: "That's right; you are coming to see your mother. But we mothers are the last ones to see you. First must your soldiers see you leave for home, then many other people . . . oh, so many, so many, you can never count them all."

At this point, luckily, the dream seemed to be over, for she coughed a little, then spoke cheerfully although still in a dreamy voice: "Because you see, my dear," she said, "between you and us there is this road. Yes, this road. Then that mountain. Oh yes, a high mountain. Your mountain. Then . . . other mountains." She stopped to listen, as we were all crying aloud. But she went on. "Then," she said, "then . . . the plain of Bologna. Then, Venice. . . . And then . . . mountains again. That's right. Mountains again. And then . . . and then . . . ?" (We could hear her breathe with difficulty.)

And then she screamed, oh, how she screamed: "I know! I know! . . ." and ran downstairs ranting so terribly that we all fled as if a wild, wounded beast were after us.

THE RAIN CAME LAST

I was riding a bicycle that afternoon. My friend Giovannino was with me. We held each other by the shoulder at arm's length and rode lazily along, making plans for a trip to the mountains. When we turned left to a smaller country road, we saw that one part of the sky was black with rain. "Here," I said, "if we don't run fast the rain will get there before us."

Others felt that way too: women were quickly unpinning laundry from the lines and rolling big bedsheets toward themselves; children were being called home; chairs removed from the front of the houses on the highway; dogs, ruffled by the wind, came out and sniffed the air. Only the crickets were still going "z-z-z-z-z-z," but the wheat in the fields was already in a strange motion of fear. Up in the sky, the line dividing clear from cloudy, with its geography all marked in sungold, was still mounting and mounting and had almost passed us. But the world was still dry. Still, all that came from the storm was dust—a dust that blinded us and whipped our faces like the needles of pine trees in the woods.

"Car coming," I said, and we parted, to clear the middle of the road. It had seemed thunder for a moment, but the horn, bidding for space, warned us it was not in the sky but here, right on this narrow road and right behind us.

It was a truck, loaded with sand, three men sitting on top of it, huddled together under a huge canvas which kept fluttering noisily in the wind. They too were out to beat the rain. We sped head-down into their dust and were still in it when another car passed us, and it was a miracle that we were not run over. It was an open car with veils, scarfs, sunglasses, tennis caps, and naked arms—we saw it all in the split second we had to look away from the stones on the road. We even saw the license number: there was an eight, a nine, but then the dust went up behind it and we stopped to let it settle. And that was when we heard the shrieking whistle of the brakes, those awful screams, and the motor being started again with frantic roars. We rushed to see what had happened and right near the narrow stone bridge on the curve we saw it. A man with his head off. The body here and the head there. A line of blood across the road. Two peasants who had been working in the field nearby ran madly after the cloud of dust, but as the wind curled it up and the road appeared empty again, they came back and did instinctively the least they could: they put the head back in its place, face-down, just as the body was. I recognized them only at that moment: Gino and Emo, and the dead man too I recognized: Elia, Angelina's husband.

We began to shout: "Murderers! Damn murderers!" and our voices were trembling. The four of us were horrified and grieved, ready to cry, but for some reason, and it wasn't shame, we didn't. Angelina must cry. That was her job. The air was hers, hers was the loss, so the next thing now was to call her. Emo looked at his bloodstained hands shaking in front of him, then said: "And now, who will tell Angelina? Three kids at home and a fourth one coming any day. . . ."

We tried hard to think of something else to do, but there was nothing else to do. We had let the murderers escape, so, having failed our job as avengers, we were accomplices. Now we must go and finish up their job for them—find Angelina, tell her, and come back with her grief.

"Damn you too, rain," shouted Emo, and began to tell what

had happened, only to prove that it was not for him to go, as he was busy telling us. "I was right here," he began, "right near that tree, when Elia called: 'Wait for me, boys, I just want to put the silkworms inside before it rains, then I'll be back.' And, *Dio Madonna,* he had just finished saying this, and just jumped over the ditch and reached the road, when . . . there you see him." And he looked embarrassed that his story was finished so soon.

"Come on, boys," I said; "this is no time for words. It's going to rain any moment. Let's find a pushcart and carry him to his house."

"I can find the pushcart for you," said Emo, "but I won't go there."

"Who will, then?" I asked. "Someone must. I am ready to go, but not alone. Who is coming with me, boys?"

"Bringing a gift like *that?* Not me," said Emo.

And the two others made no with their heads.

Two shrill bicycle bells now. Laborers back from work, trying to beat the rain. They had to jump off their seats not to run over poor Elia's body.

"My God," they said. "Look at him . . . Elia. And where is Angelina?"

"I saw her this morning," said Giovannino. "She was picking the leaves on the mulberry tree down near the highway."

"She can't be there now," said Gino. "She was through with that tree by noon."

"Over by the house, then."

"No," said the two laborers. "We just passed it now. Nobody on that tree and it was all clean of leaves."

"She must be on some other tree, then," I said, and we all hoped ardently she would be, for this meant that until she was called she was not likely to descend on us. Perhaps we wouldn't have to call. She might learn it the way all things are learned in the open country. Whatever happens there is soon known. It is almost already known by the time it happens. Why this is I have never understood. But for example, right while we were talking there, we saw the faces of women peeping from amid the thick foliage of the vine-trees half an acre away. They wanted to make sure, before coming, that it was important. They had heard our voices, but also seen the clouds. One of them was sent as an advance scout. She crossed two fields, looked at the body, ran back, called the others. In two minutes six women with their yellow straw-knitting in their hands were with us. From the road came small boys: first one, then three, then twelve, barefoot, dusty, half-naked. They formed a circle around Elia's body and looked down intently as into a deep hole. The women pitying him with whining words, in the same tone that would be Angelina's in three weeks or so, the time it takes to have the fate accepted and the sorrow nursed.

Suddenly one of the women, fat Gigia, untied a black kerchief from her neck and covered up Elia's head with it, saying: "Pity for the dead, Goddamn it. Shame on you, men, not to have thought of this before."

The children were quite disappointed. "Oooh," they said, "now we can't even see."

"And you," said Gigia with her big hand almost in Emo's face, "go call that unfortunate creature now. Call her before it rains."

Emo departed slowly, looking into the distance everywhere. "Call her," said Gigia again.

"Angelina!" he called, but as his feet were unwilling to go, so his voice seemed to retreat from those few sounds.

"And you," she said to Gino, "go find a pushcart, quick."

Before Gino could leave, Tonino arrived. Tonino was a supervisor on the Tanti estate. He was half-peasant and half-public accountant. He had served with Elia in the army. He knew many things. In fact, although he too was grieved, he soon understood what must be done next.

"Women and kids, away," he shouted. "No pushcart. Call the carabineers."

"But the rain?" asked Gino.

"The rain has nothing to do with this. You can't touch a dead man when there has been a mishap or an accident, because he's a *victim.*"

There was a murmur of surprise as if this were a secret about Elia nobody had known until then.

"No. You can't," said Tonino again, although no one had said a word. "And not even in other occurrences of death. Not before the competent authorities arrive." Then, becoming suspicious, he asked: "Why, have you touched him already?"

"We had to," whispered Gino.

"What? You displaced him from the position into which the traffic accident had left him?"

"No, no, not that," said Gino promptly. "We just put the head back near the body."

"That was against the law," shouted Tonino. "You will have to respond to the police for that. Go now, find the carabineers and don't come back until you've found them."

I gave Gino my bicycle and he went down the road in a hurry.

"Women and kids, away," shouted Tonino again. "Break it up. . . . Break it up. . . ."

"I have a right to stay here," shouted Gigia angrily. "That is my kerchief on his head. I put it there. It takes a woman to command respect for the dead. . . ."

The wind lifted one corner of the kerchief and uncovered part of the head while dust was being blown on it. "Did anyone call the doctor?" asked Tonino in a defiant voice. "What do I know about doctors?" answered Gigia. "Doctors can't even help us when we are well, what d'you think they could do here?"

"I didn't ask you," said Tonino to her. Then, seeing me in the crowd, he took off his hat and asked politely: "Did anyone call the doctor, sir?"

"I don't think so," I said, "but I will go myself."

"If you don't mind," he said, "we will send someone else. You may be more useful here."

Giovannino was sent. Now Gigia placed herself between the storm and the dead body so as to keep that kerchief from being lifted again. The wind played with the black skirt on her immense behind, and every now and then she turned around quite angrily as if someone had tried to pinch her. Then she looked at the clouds.

From the far corner of the plain the black was coming in like smoke blown into a bottle. All the rest of the air was green. The mountain range was gone from sight.

"The doctor," she kept saying. "Even the doctor . . . May the Lord blind me if the rain won't come first." Then, turning to the women and children around her she asked: "Can't we see that he's dead? Can't *you* see it?" she asked me from a distance.

"Yes," I said, and was embarrassed, so I tried to explain: "The doctor is the only one who can pronounce him dead," I said.

"What do you mean?" she asked, and the children drew away from the corpse to gather around me as if from me now they were going to learn something very important about death itself.

Tonino nodded to my words and sneered, which meant that he and I, of course, the only two civilized persons in the crowd, knew what it meant. "Haven't you ever heard, you ignorant woman," he said, "that if the doctor were allowed to issue a death certificate without seeing the deceased, he could give false reasons for the death, and then claim that he had not seen the case?"

"Hm," she said. "And the police? What business have they to come here now? Why don't they run after those murderers instead of coming here?"

"One can't explain these things to an ignorant woman like you," he said.

"Is that so?" she said. "And if a good Christian puts a head back where it belongs, they may throw him into jail? Why that?"

"Shut up," ordered Tonino and she went back to her guard against the wind. "I only hope," said Tonino, "that Angelina won't get here before the doctor and the police."

But she did. First we heard Emo's voice: "Angelinaaaaa."

Then hers: "Yeaaaa-oo. What do you want?"

Silence. Then, again: "Angelinaaa."

"What is it?"

"Come here. Something."

"But what is it? Can't you tell me?"

"Come here. . . ."

"It better be something important or you'll hear me, for disturbing me when I'm working on the trees."

Now we could see him. He was running away from her, in our direction. She was running after him, and still talking to him: "To disturb me when I am working . . . It will rain any minute . . . And you, damn it . . . Can't you stop, you fool?"

A short pause, then a first shriek of terror. She had seen the crowd. She was beginning to understand. A more important job than picking leaves. Her fate, what remained of her life and her hopes, that must be lying there.

Emo ran past us, and many in the crowd began to flee with him.

The same wind which had pushed Angelina's voice ahead of her, now blew the kerchief from Elia's head again. With contempt. Like the unveiling of a frightful gift. But no matter where the Fates were hiding now, her voice was sent way up and reached them.

And here came the police. The blue uniform of the carabineers with the red stripes along their pants. The brigadier was on my bicycle, with Gino running afoot behind him and holding clumsily in his arms the brigadier's sword, symbol of justice.

From the other road, the doctor, on his light two-wheeler, with his new Panama hat and his grey horse. They both came to pronounce, in the appropriate terms of law and science what no one here seemed able to pronounce correctly. Gigia and Tonino, aided by the other women, were now trying to hold Angelina from touching the body. She seemed possessed by one desire alone: to undo at least *that,* the posture in which death had delivered her destiny to her. . "Let me take him away from the middle of the road," she cried. "Let me turn him face-up . . . I must see his face. . . ." Doctor and brigadier greeted each other silently and acknowledged the passage of the Fates.

Then they looked at the clouds and the doctor took off his hat, employed one of his sighs of compassion to blow away a bit of dust from its black ribbon, and placed the hat carefully in the carriage, from which he extracted a red blanket and threw it over the horse. "The horse is perspiring," he said to those around him. "It may catch pneumonia in the rain."

Now the approach to the body was clear. Angelina was being held back by five people, and she cried as if the doctor were going to do her Elia some harm. "What are they going to do to him?" she yelled. "Murderers, murderers, isn't it enough that they have killed him? Must they write it down too?"

"It's for your good," said Tonino, who knew, among so many other things, also this one . . . "It's for the good of your children, Angelina. Have patience, it will soon be over and you'll be able to cry over him as much as you like." While the doctor was taking out his pad and fountain pen, the brigadier was beginning to gather information for his own pronouncement. What was the number of the car? The color? And the speed? The exact hour of the accident? He nodded and marked down these symptoms of the relapse suffered by Justice on that day. Temperature, pulse, the various functions, everything.

"Is the head detached from the body?" asked the doctor, to avoid lifting the kerchief. "Yes," said Gino. "We picked it up and put it back ourselves. Was that against the law?"

"Take it up with the brigadier," said the doctor, and the brigadier, who had heard him, said: "Yes it was. That was the worst mistake. . . ."

"One thing at a time," said the doctor. "I am almost through, I am in a hurry."

"My pencil is in a very bad condition," said the brigadier. "May I borrow your pen, Doctor?"

The doctor looked at the clouds with his clinical eye and diagnosed: "It will rain soon, but if you can do it quickly. . . ." He gave him the pen.

Now the brigadier took over and began to describe everything in detail: position of the body, of the head, removal of same by so and so (name of father, mother, mother's maiden name, living at . . . age . . . occupation . . .). How long after the accident had the head been removed? How many yards approximately had it *first* been from the body? He wrote slowly, poor brigadier, and with those peasants breathing down his neck, and others with their noses almost over his pen, he couldn't see.

"Please, stay clear. . . ." He was embarrassed. Even the clouds were gathering around that sheet of paper and looking intently, and perhaps with intentions. . . . Then a certain word didn't want to come . . . he closed his eyes. It was important, it was all about the description of the driver's wickedness. . . . "Thereafter . . . deserting the scene of their murderous. . . . No, not murderous. There is a better word. . . . Of their . . . of their. . . ."

"Murderous is all right," said the doctor, playing impatiently with his pad.

"Thank you, thank you so much. Then . . . murderous act, without stopping to . . . without stopping to. . . ."

"Without stopping," suggested the doctor in a conclusive tone.

"Thank you again. That's it. Without stopping. I hope this will do. Here is your pen, Doctor. Do you have room for me in your carriage?"

"Yes, please get in."

Before leaving, the doctor tried to put the Panama hat under the seat, but the brigadier said: "It is unsafe there, it may fly away."

So with an anguished look at the sky the doctor put it on his head again. Now they both went as if they had a very important prey; they left with their certificate; they disappeared into the very mouth of the storm to tell the greasy records of the old medieval town hall that this rain, without falling, had already made a victim.

Quick, quick, Doctor, quick, beat your horse so it may beat the rain; quick, trot, quick, go right into the clouds, or it will make another victim yet—your new Panama hat. . . .

Now it may come! Now the Fates are appeased: the winds are all unchained. I hear a savage scream of birds somewhere. But the pushcart is here. In time, in time! The victim of the rain may stay dry to the end. The sad procession leaves: Angelina and her gift, fresh from the Fates. Oh, if she only could undo their will as she is now undoing the doctor's work, pronouncing him alive, alive, alive. . . . "You are not dead!" she screams. "You are not dead. . . ." Inside of her he is not, her heavy body tells, but here, who will obey her here? Even the records in the town hall, protected by five towers and three lines of century-old walls, defended by the shining sword of the brigadier, and endorsed by the knowledge of the doctor, even the records have him dead by now.

The birds, the birds again! The rain must be quite near. But no, those too are on the road, not in the sky. I see them now: a group of women, panting, running, losing on their way some of the cries they are to unload on *him: his* mother and his sisters, five in number, and two of his kids. And here they stop. "Oooh." They look at the blood. "Oooh, they have taken him away. . . ."

"Out there," I say. "This way . . . No . . . *This* way . . . to the cemetery. . . ."

They go straight, toward the house.

"The cemetery," I shout.

They curve, like birds, in a long line, and out they go, losing more cries. As if to mock them, in the sky, a similar procession of wild ducks flees in the same direction, crying too.

But who's calling my name? Yes, that's my name, clearly, in the very center of the wind. . . . "Oh Sabina, oh little peasant girl from home: what are you doing here with that umbrella that is bigger than you?"

"Your mother saw the storm," she says, "and she worried. And I knew you were here, so I took the umbrella and ran to meet you . . . Elia has been killed . . . Oh, but where is he?"

"Who?"

"Elia. May I see him?"

"No."

"Where is he?"

"I won't tell you."

"Did they take him home?"

"I won't tell you."

"To the cemetery? . . . Yes, to the cemetery, I know, I can see you are smiling. I guessed right . . . Please, give me the bicycle, I *promise* I'll get there before the rain."

And as I watch her ride away, one drop falls on my hand. One on my face. One on the stain of blood still fresh across the road. The rain too has arrived. No one else is expected.

MILITARY INTELLIGENCE

In the early thirties, when I was a student at the University of Florence, the government announced that a required course in "military culture" would be a part of the curriculum in all Italian universities. What was meant by military culture, no one knew. It had nothing to do with drilling—that, at least, seemed clear—because there were going to be lectures about it and examinations at the end of the term. What also seemed clear, and alarming, too, was that if we did not pass our examination in military culture, we would not be considered fit to get a degree in any subject, whether mathematics, paleontology, medicine, or canon law. Apparently, the military minds in the immediate environment of the dictator felt that the country needed a warlike youth with a natural love of discipline—habits of mind and character that the Italians, thank God, never have had and never will have.

From the way in which the ambitious program was announced in the papers, one would have expected every university to be transformed into an armed camp for the training of killers. For a few days after the publication of the news, foreign ambassadors were busy underlining in red pencil all the boastful comments in the various organs of the government-controlled press and drafting comments of their own for the enlightenment of their various Foreign Offices or State Departments throughout the world. The foreign press commented upon the plan, it was discussed in all the legislative bodies of the European countries, and Mussolini, in his childish way, was happy. People had spoken about his idea; the militarization of Italian youth had worried foreign governments. This was all he needed to make him believe that what had been launched solely as a program was already an accomplished fact.

Foreign diplomats and foreign governments were not the only ones to worry. Italian university professors did not like the idea, either, and at that time it meant something far more ominous for them than for the world at large. As if it were not bad enough that they had had to swear loyalty to the Fascist government, they were now going to have the Army spying on their work, day by day. They could not avoid the humiliation of the loyalty oath, for to refuse to take it meant banishing themselves from the teaching profession in Italy, but many of them had managed to avoid mentioning Fascism in their courses. One professor of political science at Florence took to lecturing on the folklore of Sardinia, and the more social reforms the Fascists came out with, the more he found to say about Sardinian costumes and folk dances. When reproached for this by some Fascist official, he lectured on the educational value of mountain climbing. Another professor, who taught contemporary civics and government, spoke only about ancient Greece and, if he mentioned modern times at all, never seemed to notice that the world had existed after 1919. But once the Army was in control, the professors would be compelled to teach what they so disliked.

The students, too, did not take to the idea of military culture. They were harassed enough with Party duties (for all students were under pressure to join the Party) or with inventing tricks to avoid them. A few professors and students held protest meetings, but nothing helped.

The only ones who really did something to sabotage the project were the people entrusted with carrying it out. These were the poor devils of career officers, who had, for the most part, no use for culture of any sort and were strangely in awe of anyone who taught or even respected it. They felt ridiculous in the presence of university professors, and they almost apologized to their newly acquired colleagues for the absurd situation that put them, ignorant men, on the same footing with so many learned minds.

Naturally, there were some Fascists among the professors, and they, of course, hastened to voice their unconditional approval of the militarization plan. But the officers seemed even more afraid of them than of the other members of the faculty, as if an inner decency made the military men prefer the silent scorn of the anti-Fascists to the loud flattery of the Fascists.

The first of these officers we had at the University of Florence was a tiny colonel who blushed frequently and allowed all sorts of infractions of discipline in his classrooms. He did not quite tell us that we would not have to take his course in military culture seriously and that we would never run the risk of flunking his exams—that, indeed, would have been a little too much to expect of him—but he did make it clear to us from the start that with him in charge we had nothing to worry about. For the first half hour of his class, he would read aloud to us from a booklet of Army regulations, droning off article after article in a monotonous voice. During this performance, we would reread our notes on other subjects or prepare for an exam in some other course. Then he would throw aside his booklets and tell us about his experiences in the first World War. Apparently, he had been a brave soldier; twice he had been separated from his unit and had gone on fighting alone; he had lost his health on account of poison gas, and also, it seemed, his faith in the wisdom and usefulness of wars. But he did not harp for long on tales of his own bravery. After a few lessons, he began to tell us the story of how he had been forced by his financial circumstances to enter the Army. He said he envied us, who could get ourselves an education, and began to urge us, in true fatherly fashion, not to waste our time with women or in playing around but to try to make the most of this blessed opportunity and of our youth. "Youth is short," he would often say at the end of a lesson, "and it never comes back."

After a month of military culture with him, we were all less warlike and less eager to join the Army than we had been at the beginning of the course, and we felt a sincere pity for the man. But he could not keep up his harmless little military preachments for long, because the War Department soon issued to professors of military culture a long list of regulations and suggestions to assist them in the militarization of the Italian mind. One of the new rules was that the professor must inspire his pupils by reading to them examples of great military eloquence taken from addresses made by Italian generals to their troops before sending them into battle.

Our colonel consulted a few manuals of military history, but nothing he found there seemed to satisfy him. Finally, he decided to rely on his memory and told us that in his opinion the most moving and courageous of all war addresses was the one made by the last Bourbon King of Naples to his troops before sending them to fight against the hero of Italian independence, Garibaldi. This is how the colonel told us the story: "'My boys,' said the King to his troops assembled in front of the palace, 'how many blows you are going to take now!' After which, shaking his head in sign of sheer compassion, he withdrew. He was a great, courageous king. There must be other war speeches that are interesting," the colonel added. "Find some in the library and read them."

Eventually, we were all to take a test on our knowledge of military affairs. So again he read to us from this or that manual, interrupting himself to point to one after another of us in the class and ask, "Right?" "Right" was our answer, to which he would echo "Right!" and enter good marks for us in his classbook.

Shortly before the exam, our colonel was removed from his post and assigned to a regiment in a small town up north. It was almost with tears in his eyes that he took leave of us. His last lesson was entirely devoted to a talk on the difficulty of finding good schools for one's children if one was a career officer. In Florence, the schools were good, he told us, and children learned to speak the best Italian, and also, in Florence, his wife had an aunt who owned a house and they had occupied an apartment there at a very convenient price. But now all those advantages were gone. We paid little attention to his talk that day. What we wanted to know was who would be our next militarizer.

Well, we soon found out. The next militarizer, another colonel, was an active Fascist; that is, a man who had ambitions and would stop at nothing to secure his chances of advancement. I was very much in doubt whether to take the exam at the end of that term or wait and repeat the course, so that I could acquire more thoroughly the kind of military culture that this new man favored. I tossed a coin, and it came out heads, which meant that I should take the risk.

The examination in military culture was oral and began at nine-thirty in the morning. One by one, we filed in before the examining commission. I was not called until noon. Six or seven professors of our law faculty who had examined me the day before in their own courses and had given me marks just above failure sat there and looked at me with tired eyes as the colonel asked me to name at least three battles participated in by the House of Savoy. Here he leaned forward and half rose from his chair, standing for a moment at half attention out of deference to the Royal Family. I sat there and said nothing. I had forgotten everything. The colonel waited, then modified the question. "Name at least one," he said. I mentioned one, and he frowned. The professor of civil law, who was neither a Fascist nor a Monarchist, seemed pleased.

"What happened in that battle?" asked the colonel, and, forgetting that it was one of the blackest pages in the history of our Royal House, I said, "The House of Savoy won it."

"Tut, tut," said the professor of civil law, who knew his history. Then, pretending to tip me off, he whispered to me in a voice that everyone could hear, "They lost it."

The colonel blushed and said to me in a loud tone, "Very good. They won it."

"Pardon me," said the professor of civil law to the colonel, looking very much amazed. "Pardon me, but as far as I can recall, that battle was *lost* by the Savoy." As soon as the words were out, he seemed to feel uncomfortable. He was probably thinking of his job; he, too, might be transferred upon short notice, and his children, too, might have to go to cheaper schools than the ones to be found in Florence. It is always a tactless thing to be right in the presence of a military man. In Italy at that time, it might have been a bad mistake.

The colonel said in a sharp voice, "For the standards and purposes of civilian history, which history is often written and taught in a destructive, critical spirit, the House of Savoy"—again he rose slightly and stood for an instant at half attention—"lost that battle, but this young man here has the right approach to history. He said they won it. For your information, the House of Savoy"—up and down again he went—"does not lose battles!"

The other members of the commission were intensely, though noncommittally, interested in the argument. The professor of civil law had a gleam of satanic joy in his eyes, as if he were about to ignite a bomb under the colonel's chair, and said in a quiet, slow, almost a sleepy, tone, "They may never lose a battle, but *that* one they lost."

"Well," said the colonel, panting, "what does that mean? What, indeed, *can* that mean when you think of the unfavorable meterological conditions, the high winds, the fury of the elements ominously and most unfairly unleashed against the brave Prince on that tragic occasion? And, I may add, *what* do we know about the number of men he had under him there? Nothing. Or, rather, there seems to be every reason to believe that the forces at the disposal of the Prince were ill equipped and scant in number, from which we may logically conclude that what civilian history refers to as defeat was in reality nothing but victory, and rightly does this young man here describe it as such. *This* is the history we want."

Then, turning to me, he said, "Very good. *Cum laude.*" And he shook my hand.

There was a painful silence. I wanted to apologize to the professor of civil law for my ignorance but could not do this without gravely offending the colonel—and, who knows, perhaps even the Fatherland—and condemning myself to learn that kind of history for another full term. The professor of civil law was pale. His hands trembling slightly, he looked up at the ceiling, as if trying to find his calm up there. He must have thought hard again about his job and his family, for he quieted down. But as I pushed my chair back, ready to leave, a spirit of revenge went through him. He looked at the colonel without saying a word and then looked at me and, stretching out his hand, said in the quietest of tones, "Allow me to be the first to congratulate you on your knowledge of history."

THOSE LONG SHADOWS

In the summer of 1938, having attended to some business of mine in Rome, it suddenly occurred to me that, before going back to America forever, I might as well go back to Tuscany for a few days and take leave of my parents.

I had seen them but twice in the space of two years: once before leaving Italy in 1936 on a sinecure Government mission to New York (and then only for a few days because the boat was sailing), and once on my way back from New York, a year later (and then also in a hurry, because my desk at the office in Rome was waiting for me).

Yet Rome, by train, was less than three hours from Florence; Florence itself less than an hour from home. I had gone back to Florence frequently during that year, but had always most carefully avoided going near home.

Home meant long arguments, old nonsense, things I knew and disliked only too well. Home meant a trip backwards in time, to places nonexistent anywhere, to the world of my parents, who had stopped living back in 1917 (with Mother losing all her money in Russia) and were waiting for History to correct that "mistake." Any contact with them involved a careful choice of lies, implied a serious mental preparation, also a serious stunt, to lift the sadness of that terrible place.

This time however the situation was different. I was leaving for good, and it was only fair, I thought, that I should make this last act of submission, see my parents again, listen to all their warnings without laughing, and, above all, without impatience.

Their ideas were old, but they themselves were aging, and their children had left them, each had gone his way, only their daughter had remained, she was already thirty-four, not married, full of imaginary ailments, deeply melancholic, so everything was just the opposite of what it should have been.

I went alone. I told my wife that I did not want witnesses to our family comedy. She was not coming to America with me, she was supposed to join me after the birth of our first child, in five more months, so she had plenty of time to see my parents later.

I took an early morning train from Rome, and on that train I felt suddenly and strangely important. Why? Because I had attended to some business of mine in Rome. I kept telling myself these very words, as if they were a line in some imaginary play, and I should memorize it now. I felt exactly like those lawyers, prefects, mayors and party secretaries from all over Italy who, going back from Rome to their provincial universe, used just that phrase to appear important to their friends and scare their enemies. And it soon became evident that the trip had been fruitful: they had obtained all sorts of secret favors and settled their affairs in a convenient manner.

But I, what had I done? How had I settled my affairs? I had resigned from my small job at the Press Ministry, insulting, without any good reason, some influential people who had always been kind to me; had wrecked my best connections, refused two more jobs, "jobs with a future," as these things are called when your future is known in advance and tied behind you like a sack of food to be used as you go; and finally I had made debts, astronomical debts, to leave the country and go back to America, where nothing and no one awaited me but hunger and despair. This at a time when many refugees were forced to leave, and I had no claim on such a title. No one was persecuting me.

Nice business indeed, with a child coming in five months and not a penny to my name. How lucky I was that my father ignored what I had done. The mere thought of his comments made me laugh with amusement. But then the spell came back, the words kept hissing through the window, scanning the rails, galloping with me on the red velvet seat: "Some business . . . some business . . . some business of mine, important-personal, important-personal, personal . . . personal . . . important business of mine . . . business . . . business . . . business. . ."

That, the crickets, the wind and the telegraph wires, up-and-down in waves between quick, varnished poles, stood between me and the Sabine mountains, then the hilltowns of Umbria, then the black, priestlike, fingerlike cypresses of Tuscany. With the help of that view, I understood the reasons for my sudden importance. Never before in my life had I done anything of any importance, anything *of my own,* involving *my* opinions and *my* future, as I alone could shape them. Even my wedding, two years previously, had been first duly approved by responsible persons in two families, after due consultation with responsible persons in the Government, who had "approved" my future like perishable merchandise. Whether at home or away, in Italy or abroad, my life had either been a silly game or a kind of employment, and quite a useless one at that. And now this *invention* of mine, that I was free, that I could go to hell or heaven in my own, personal way, that I, too, was in history, an obscure history, a ridiculous history, but mine, not national, not Roman, not trumpeted, not Mussolinian, had put me in direct contact with the forces of destiny. This was indeed my own business, a stepping stone in my career, and *because* it might ruin me completely, it meant more than advancement in bureaucracy and an increase in salary.

But as the train left the more cheerful countryside to enter the dark Arno Valley, with purple mountains on one side and industrial poverty on the other, I began to feel guilty. Not a speck of self-importance left in me, now that I needed it to impress my parents. That seemed unreasonable, more so than my pride of a minute before. It was the first time in my life that I was doing the right thing, so why should I feel guilty?

And yet it seemed to me (and was) a privilege, that they, at home, no longer had: to be acting on principles, to revolt against everything and leave. They would never have wanted it? True, but irrelevant. Relevant was their fate, and their fate tied them to that hated place and to the prejudices that cast shadows on it, like the big poplar trees and cypresses at sunset. Nothing is worse than doing the right thing; one acts in the first person, driving the horses right through other people's lives, willingly, coldly, rightfully and frightfully (which is so much the same), and not like one who finds himself on a strange vehicle of which he is not himself the driver, and does not like, and *fears* what the horses may do to the crowd.

Therefore this was to be regarded as a dangerous subject with the family. I was closing the door on them and going out alone, treating them with the same contempt (to all practical purposes no doubt the same) as I was treating the paternal government. Once I had left the country, there was no such thing as going back to *them* for a personal visit and not back to the Fatherland in case of war. Desertion, or exile, whatever one may call it, was complete. "Careful now," I thought, "avoid the horrors of leave-taking." The thing to do was make them good and angry. A little of the old family dust, a little of the loud, pointless discussions, a little of my nonsense and a little of theirs was most likely to give them the certainty that this would be repeated soon and many times again, as part of an eternal thing like boredom.

As for nonsense, at home, there was a wealth of it. Mother's nonsense had something of a divine nature about it. When the world was too petty for her (and that means every single day God sent on earth) she told herself a story and then, if it was good, she began to rejoice, and the whole house was filled with her joy; if it was bad, she suffered in the most terrible, heart-breaking manner. So frightful was her sadness that, before we could tell her this was all her invention, we just *had* to console her, or to suffer with her, and this whole comedy was far more true than the truth we were able to offer her with our clear logic. Thus there remained in all of us a resentment, much like her own, against reality, for not being more sincere, more passionate, more *real.*

Indeed reality was not up to our standards. She had suspended time. "This is no life," she said, and would refuse on certain days to put the correct date on letters. She spurned geography. "This is no *place,*" she said of Tuscany, and never looked out of the window, never took a walk, never even smelled a flower. She spent months at her small desk, behind closed shutters, writing long letters to her lawyers. She had five or six of them posted at strategic points all over Europe (she spent more money on postage stamps and telegrams than on all other items combined in the family budget), and from her hiding place she sued—the Soviet Government, three or four banks in Finland, France, Germany and Switzerland, some of her former lawyers, some members of her family and a few other minor evil creatures who had refused to play the role assigned them in her plans. People were terrorized by her "inventions" of them, for no one, not even those who lived far away from us, could cope with those great shadows of generosity, intelligence and kindness.

I, for example, was assigned the role of "pure aesthete, living in splendor"; was allowed to develop into a second Napoleon and lead a great crusade against the Soviets, with better luck than Napoleon.

All noblemen were noble, all the rich lavish, Mussolini was God, his word the Gospel. He always spoke of Order, Discipline, Authority, he ran the country like a family, admitted no free speech: what could be greater?

Sabina, the small peasant girl who had been living with us ever since her father died of starvation, was a "jesting philosopher." Mother would quote Democritus to her, then laugh because Sabina had said things she could never have said because she simply did not know them. Sabina's mother, an itinerant beggar, was an "invented" Grande Dame, lunched with us twice and, when she failed to play her role, Mother was very hurt and said terrible things to her, in French and Russian.

Father's nonsense was much less colorful and more didactic. It came in Latin, Greek, Italian, French and German, and then was historical, botanical, etymological and medical. To get it going one just had to exist, and that had never been too hard for me.

At the station of Florence I got off the Rome Express and took the twelve-five local mountain train: there it was, in the sunshine, the black train. Nothing had changed: the varnish of the third class seats stuck to my trousers as usual. Familiar faces filled it: the local pharmacist, the brother of our parish priest, the sister of our gardner and even two landowners who explained to everybody that, on exceptionally hot days, they actually preferred to go third class, because the first class cushions were a little too warm. And by making this clear their dignity was saved: everyone knew that they were rich.

I answered all the festive words with festive smiles, as if I had last seen those people that same morning and not years before, then sat down in a corner and closed my eyes to rehearse all my nonsense for the coming reunion.

But I had to look out of the window, for the mountains came home, they all began to turn on their underground pivots and go back to that place *from which the world was far.*

Just looking at those peaks, some of which I had never climbed, and avoiding the sight of what was closer to the train, I could guess where I was and tell exactly when the white station building would conceal the horizon. Here the trip was finished. One mountain looked like a sharp face snoring up the sky, one was all put away behind another, one was rounder, one taller, with a small tower born to it, right on top. This was the view *from* home and now came home.

Swinging his whip, the coachman offered me a ride. How often had I not refused and he had mumbled angry words against the stingy children of the rich. Now I must pay him an exhorbitant price and take the entire stagecoach to myself.

"Let's go," I said, "let's not wait for other passengers."

"Very well," he said. "And I won't charge you extra. You are coming from Rome. Important place. What do they say in Rome? Is it hot there? How have you been? You were expected weeks ago."

"Was I expected? Really? Did they tell you so at home?"

"No, but everyone knew it in the village."

I began to apologize then and there.

"You are quite right," I said. "I should have come much earlier, and I intended to come much earlier, too. But you know how it is in Rome . . ."

"Don't I know it?" he said. "Important business to attend to. Rome is Rome. Here in the province nothing ever happens."

As we turned from the highway to the poplar-lined road that led down to the village and went by our house, I saw a group of people in the distance right in front of our gate. I recognized my mother (even from far away pride was her sign of recognition). She was wrapped up in a large shawl. "Strange on a day like this," I thought. Next to her was Sabina, holding an open parasol way up with outstretched arm, to protect Mother's head, and Mother was now scolding her because the parasol was not in the right place (yet Sabina was short and Mother tall and never quiet for a moment). Then there was Father, with his huge Panama hat of 1908, his 1908 sunglasses (a proud relic of our 1908 car), then Sonia with no parasol and no hat, and Father telling her about the dangers of the midday sun. I could hear everything despite the distance and the noise of the carriage and the million cicadas on the trees; even Sonia's reply I understood, although it was in whispers, because that was all part of The Pattern, and patterns can be heard thousands of miles away without the help of radio sets.

And now they were just a few steps away from me; only the coachman stood between us, hiding me from them with his whole body, as if he were doing it on purpose. In reality he was taking the luggage down from his seat, and I was opening my wallet, taking out the money and still speaking only to him. I paid him ten times the fare, enjoyed his surprise and his words of eternal gratitude, and only then took notice of those other people behind him and prepared to hug and kiss them one by one, as of tradition and regardless of the heat.

But when I saw my mother, I decided to take all my time and made many useless movements to collect my hat and briefcase. Because she was no longer the same person. That was somebody else, a very old, sick, feeble woman, wrapped up in a woolen shawl and shivering. So, even after I was ready, the pain was too great; I had to turn my head back to the carriage and went on fumbling in it: I was looking for something, that is, nothing, a breath of wind to justify my tears.

But as there was no wind, I had to face her finally, and really I thought that I would never make it. Nothing remained of her; pride, beauty, everything was gone. Even her hair, her beautiful blond hair was flat, gray, dead. What I had seen from the top of the road was The Pattern alone and the past. Time had been working here; there had been changes and these corrected my eyesight in the most violent manner.

"You look quite well," she said. According to The Pattern, she should have said:

"And how long will you honor us?"

"Yes," I said, "I am doing all right." I didn't say, as I usually said and had planned to repeat this time, too, that she was looking well, and then add a remark about those poor lawyers of hers. I could not bring myself to do so. The Pattern had been broken; the traditional nonsense had lost meaning. This new nonsense was much too strange: here it was hot, one could not breathe, and she, there, trembling in the heat, with that shawl on her shoulders, was so foreign to everything; to that picture, that season or that family. Had I not known that it was daytime, I would really have felt the dread of night. Never before had there been such an absence of lies in the first minute of a family gathering. The worst ones usually were out by then.

"Mother was sick," Father said. This, too, was unusual. *She* should have been the one to say it. According to The Pattern, she should have said that she had been terribly sick with an attack of symptoms accompanied by heartbeats and Father should have looked at all the treetops while waiting for an end of that lie.

"I am much better now," she said. It sounded like a promise to come and see us soon, but spoken from a very great distance.

Thank God my father came to my rescue.

"A new suitcase," he said. Then he noticed that something was missing. "Where is your wife?" he asked.

"In Rome," I said, "she will be here next time."

"Next time when?"

"In a couple of weeks, when I come back, before sailing."

"But you *are* back," he said.

"I still have business to attend to in Rome . . ."

"You never stay put anywhere," said Sonia, and that, too, was in the best tradition. The farmer came, greeted me cheerfully, took my suitcase inside. We walked behind him. Mother could hardly walk, Father and I were helping her, and I of course pretended that it was all my fault, that every step arrested my attention.

"It is really discouraging," Father said. "We have so many suitcases up in the attic, and you must go and buy yourself another one. And it looks very expensive, too."

"It is," I said, in a discouraged tone. "I am so angry with myself I didn't ask you."

"You might have asked," he said. "Parents are there for that, to give advice, to help. But now don't think of it; don't ruin your happiness and ours on this day with your pointless regrets. Think rather of the future. Put a sackcloth protection on your suitcase. There must be one upstairs, I'll gladly give it to you."

"Thank you so much," I said. "That will be helpful."

I ran up to my room, sat on my bed and tried to breathe.

"Dinner is served," they called.

"I'll wash my hands and face and come," I said. And I went to the bathroom, submerged my face in cold water, and went back downstairs rubbing my eyes with my fingers and cursing a mosquito in the vilest terms I knew.

"Is that the official language of the Capital?" Father asked, smiling from the nose down, while the rest of his face remained serious.

Then he began to fill the dishes with a steaming concoction.

"Too much for me," I said.

"This is a soup," he began to recite, "a soup your sister has prepared for you, for her dear brother, working almost all night, a thing she should never have done in her precarious state of health."

"Sonia," the dear brother said now, "you should never have done it."

"It was nothing," she said, implying that it was really too much.

Mother lifted her spoon. Her hand was trembling. I began to cough.

"Caught a chill on that train," Father said. "I could have told you. Summer is the best season for pneumonia. Everyone thinks it's warm in summer. At least in winter no one thinks it's warm. Sabina, shut the door."

The door was shut, now we were in a glass house. Windows closed, a green light through the shutters, and the steaming cicadas all around the house.

"Now eat," he said. "Here in the country we must eat. The fine air of the country could awaken the dead and make them eat."

"I haven't had a chance to breathe it," I said.

"Take your time, take your time," he said, "and take this, too." He poured another spoon of soup into my dish. "With the best wishes of the family. And that napkin . . . like this, tie it behind your neck, as I do. Or you might soil that new silk shirt you have. Beautiful shirt. Expensive."

I looked at *her.* She seemed herself again: younger, prouder, she held the spoon defiantly. If only she would speak in the old tone.

"And precisely how much did you give to the coachman?" Father now asked.

"Two or three times the fare."

"Ten times," he corrected. "I saw it. Once and a half would have been more than plenty. That man is rich."

"He doesn't look it."

"The dirtier, the richer. He has millions, I tell you. And you are ruining the market."

"Sorry," I said.

"Now don't be sorry," he said. "No regrets on this day. When, as I hope and trust, you will come here to live with wife and child, first of all you won't need him; we have our own car. But if you ever did, I would go with you every time. From me he would never exact such exhorbitant prices."

"But I tell you, it was I . . ."

"Or accept them. He should not have accepted. He should have known better, if you didn't. Now let's talk about something more cheerful. Where would you like to have us build an addition to the house for your family? In my opinion the best place is on top of the garage. This afternoon we will look at the place together and decide, so I can tell the architect to draw the blueprints."

"The blueprints?" I said. "But I am leaving. I have been writing this to you, I've told you. I am going to America."

"Again?" he asked. "What for? Is the Government sending you?"

"No," I said. "But I told you that, too. I have an offer there . . ."

"And your job here?"

"I resigned from it."

"Did you consult with your superiors before doing so?"

"Consult? But . . . how do you imagine these things? I *told* them."

"Told them what?"

"That I was leaving."

"Did you strike a good bargain at least?"

"Bargain? But I resigned."

"When you *resign* that's what you do. No one ever *resigns* without getting a pension or a much better job."

"Some people do," I said, looking at Mother. She said nothing, but looked on quite intently.

"*Some people* . . . who?" Father said. "Idealists, Tolstoyans, fools? Look what Tolstoy has given us: the Russian Revolution. And besides, *you* are not made to live like an idealist. You need silk shirts and luxury."

"Poverty is also a luxury," I said.

"Can you feed on ideals?" he said.

"Now look," I said, "Mussolini, too, calls himself an idealist, and is called one by others. And he also calls me an idealist, as long as my ideals coincide with his will. But if I disobey him in the name of my own ideals, then I become a traitor, or a fool. Is that right?"

Mother looked at me quietly and said nothing.

"Mussolini makes history," Father said. "He knows a great many things that are unknown to us."

"All right," I said, "but we want to know them, too. So why doesn't he tell us?"

"Tell *you?* And who are *you?* You will know everything by the results. Right at this moment Mussolini is about to fool Hitler, England, France and everybody. He is trying to play one part against the other. And in your interest, too. He is a clever gambler."

"He is," Sonia said, dreamily.

"How do *you* know?" I asked. "Did the trees tell you?"

"And do *you* think you know because you live in Rome?"

"No," I said. "Not because I live in Rome. Simply because I *live.* And all I know is that he is a criminal."

"That, too," Father said, putting a finger on his mouth and looking worriedly at Mother. "Statesmen *are* criminals, all of them are. They *have* to be. Does that surprise you at your age? But anyway, whether you are surprised or not, that is none of our business. All we can do is hope that he will keep his head in the present emergency. And that is why *we must not speak to the conductor while the streetcar is in motion.* The wisdom of these great words! The British and the French, spurred by our own national traitors abroad, the various Sforzas and Salveminis, irritate him too much with their scandalous criticism. This is no time for idle talk. This is the time for everyone to mind his own business. Your business is your own family. Leave politics to those whose job it is to govern you."

"I disagree," I said, "and that is why I am leaving."

"If I had ever dared, when I was your age . . . ," he said, then looked in her direction and we all waited for her anger now. She had the right-of-storm. But she surveyed us quietly, from far away, and smiled at me with what appeared in that dim light like a glimpse of approval.

"All right," Father said. "Let's have coffee in the garden. It is nice and cool there."

I ran out first. The glare was such that I crossed the whole garden with closed eyes and seeing red, actually seeing red, but emotionally, too. I was angry at myself for having spoken in that tone. I knew that her "normal" look at lunch had been due to the darkness of the room and to The Pattern in my eyes. I had struck a dead person. And with my father, too, I might have been more patient. Now the situation was the same it had been years before on Sundays, when at dinner I said that I *must* go to the symphony concert in Florence and *must* take the first afternoon train and have the money, and it always came to the point where he said: "Had I ever dared when I was your age . . . ," then put a hand into his pocket and gave me the money with a sad look in his eyes while Mother said that he was weak. I had always felt sorry for him in those years but accepted the money because she was still making me angry.

I reached the oak tree and sat down. But even in its shade the earth and the garden chairs seemed burning. And now the silence, and the flies buzzing in and out of a few beams of sunshine; the chickens cackling sleepily from deep inside the farmhouse, made all my great decisions meaningless. This was a world from which there could be no escape.

I heard the three of them advance through an intricate path of shining, leatherlike magnolia leaves. They were coming to hear more of my "wisdom." Looking up at the trees, I said, to give myself a countenance:

"How they have grown, these trees."

"You have given them time to surprise you," Sonia said. Then she sat down, Mother sat down, Father sat down and sighed. "Aaaah. What peace out here." And he folded his hands behind his neck.

"Doesn't this paradise tempt you, my son?" he asked. "Here it is always cool and breezy, and the water is wonderful. The best spring water in the country. And you want your America. Who wants to go there, anyway? You'll get no thanks from foreigners."

Now Sabina came with the coffee. The noise of those light spoons and those small cups on the tray seemed so huge and so small at the same time. It filled the world, bordering on the distant bangs of freight cars at the station, lazy locomotives, screams of chickens and pigs in their crates, and the rumbling of cars on the highway.

Suddenly the white shepherd dog crashed through the fence and jumped on me, soiling my trousers and shirt. I chased him from me, thinking how long it would take to have trousers and shirt washed, dried and ironed properly. The dog ran to my mother, put a paw on her knee and licked her hand. She smiled and said: "You are a good, nice dog." I had expected her to scream, as she usually did on such occasions, to send away the dog with scathing Russian words, and ask for Eau de Cologne to wipe her hand. "Yes," she went on, "a very nice dog." The animal sighed, as if it had taken him years to obtain that result, then settled down under her chair and sighed again in resignation to the heat.

Now Father snored, Sonia was staring at the ants in the grass, and Mother sniffed the air and looked around, as if she were seeing the place for the first time. I meant to apologize for the way I had spoken at table, but all I found to say was: "Well, and how are all those lawsuits of yours going?"

She shook her head, smiled and dismissed the whole subject with her hand as nonsense. "Now," Father said, awakening, as if his sleep had been a demonstration of something. "Isn't this better and more restful than all the Americas on earth?"

"Decidedly," I said.

"Then leave your politics, your principles, and come here, spend sometime here in peace, and perhaps, who knows, you will want to go back to Rome when things look a little brighter than they do now. I am speaking not for myself, but for your mother, too, who would want you to settle down here." He looked at her and asked: "Am I not right?"

"Beautiful roses," she said, pointing at a tall rosebush. "You can smell them, at night, all through the house."

"Of course," I said, in a last, desperate attempt to make her play the game, "Tuscany is one of the most beautiful countries in the world."

"It has a quiet beauty of its own," she said. "And it takes time to appreciate it."

Sunset pierced the thick foliage of the oak. From faraway the shadows of the poplar trees and cypresses pointed in the direction of the house and slowly covered the windows like quick-rampant weeds. Mother felt chilly. We went in. Supper was silent.

"And how long will you honor us this time?" Father asked before going to bed.

"What is tomorrow, Tuesday?"

"Yes, Tuesday."

"Then," I said, hesitatingly, "I think I had better leave tomorrow."

"Breakfast at seven, wake me up at six," Mother said to Sabina, as if she knew that I was taking the first morning train. I myself had not meant it at all. I would never have dared.

"It seems to me," Father said, "that after a whole year you might consider staying a little longer than twenty-four hours."

"But I will certainly be back," I said, "and anyway, we'll see tomorrow morning."

"And anyway, we'll see tomorrow morning," echoed Sonia's jeering voice from upstairs. She had already gone, without saying goodnight.

Once alone in my room, I found myself surrounded by a familiar fence of thoughts and movements. Every one of my steps had been taken already; *he,* not I, he, the young man out of whose childhood I had grown, was living here. His sleep would be re-slept by me in that old bed. On the shelf near *his* bed, his books of fairy tales with illustrations that had scared him yesterday. Childhood was still next door to manhood and would never move further away. I was hoping to cry, but *he* would cry, for even that was nothing new. But it was not permitted, anyway. My father came into my room twice that night; once to make sure that I was covered up and close the window near my bed, once to re-open it a little bit because the night seemed warm. And both times he left the door wide open, and both times he understood that I was not asleep and told me I must sleep because the sleep of night is the best sleep.

But if I could not cry and could not sleep, neither could I decide what I should do. Staring at the white lines between the shutters, I was feeling so sorry for those people out there, more for the two whose nonsense was still strong, than for the one whose ways were already resembling the proud ways of the dead. Keeping them company seemed now the only task. How could I leave them? The decision to stay, I had often despised in other people who would not leave the country because they had a family, an old mother, a tyrannical father, a lone sister, here it was now, as the only right thing. Why go to America? Why seek a geographical solution to the evils of history?

Across the corridor I heard my father sigh in his bed, and I knew he was *thinking.* There was a click: his lamp and the familiar triangle of yellow light on the floor in the hall. Now he was reading his dear Latin poets and disapproving between verses of that expensive suitcase and that shirt, and that America, and that son who resigned without bargaining. And thinking of that child, due in five months. Wishing he had it there with him, to bring it up in his right way.

Stay with them? Leave them? Stay with them? Will there be war? Will there be peace, and when?

"Are you asleep?" he asked. I gave no answer.

When the day whitened in the room, I had made up my mind that, if she asked me to stay, I would probably stay, or at least think it over very seriously. Thus, at breakfast, I said that I would leave by the evening train. "Good," Father said. "So we'll have time to talk."

We had another heavy dinner with a thorny discussion and the two talked with me. They talked and talked, they said yes, no, then yes again to the same reasons, simply because I was defending the opposite side, and Mother smiled and had a pleasant day and asked me nothing. When the time came to leave, she said: "Good-bye, good luck, and write sometimes."

Father and Sonia walked me to the station, and their nonsense was good, nothing to worry about them. She came just to the gate, waving good-bye. She stood there without crying, then she opened her mouth. I thought it was to speak. It was only to breathe. And her silence came after me like those long shadows that precede the night.

THE EVOLUTION OF KNOWLEDGE

There is something wrong with the floors of our apartment in New York. Not even our superintendent can do anything about it, for the cause of the trouble lies beyond his reach; it may, in fact, be traced back to the incongruities of Progress and to the decay of Western Civilization. Also to my two children, especially my son Vieri, who is seven. Every bounce of Vieri's ball on the floor evokes the spirit of Mr. Feinstein and sets into motion a long line of actions and reactions, which end in Mr. Feinstein's pounding on the radiator pipe or on his ceiling right under our feet. The spirit of Mr. Feinstein grows bigger, bigger, bigger, until *everything* is Mr. Feinstein. Vieri, in fact, is the real Sorcerer's Apprentice with that ball—tum ti, tum ti, tatata, tum ti, tum ti . . .

But there was a time when Mr. Feinstein didn't allow his spirit to reach us through his ceiling. He kept his fuming downstairs. That is why I think the story should be told; it is a highly philosophical story, because it proves that knowledge is not static but instead is constantly in the process of evolution.

Three years ago, when Mr. Feinstein pounded on the radiator, we did not care. Then, one day, I met him in the elevator. Though we had never happened to meet before, each of us knew instinctively who the other was, so, man to man, we had one of those bitter exchanges of words, just off the limits of politeness, that are usually accompanied by acceleration of the heartbeat and heavy breathing. Alas, in our case the exchange was also marked by an uncontrollable relapse into our foreign accents. Though this last hampered the free flow of profanity, it was how I learned that Mr. Feinstein came from Saxony, and how he, who has lived in my country, understood that I came from Tuscany. But what we chiefly managed to convey to each other was that "Man must sleep" (his theory) and "Children must jump" (mine). The next time we met, we realized that we were both haters of hate more than of each other, so we tried to solve the problem by means of diplomatic negotiation. "We exiles," I said, "are always in a state of repressed emotion." He nodded and then explained, with many apologies, that the floor squeaked terribly even when I walked on it barefoot, and I explained, with my own apologies, that I had intended for some time to buy carpets for all the rooms, "but you know . . ." And he said, "Don't I know! You must not misunderstand me, please. It's not your fault. The floors haven't been repaired for the last two years, because of the war. So, you see, it's definitely one of those things that cannot be helped."

I thanked him for the acquittal, and he had an even more encouraging observation for me. Children's noise was also just one of those things that could not be helped, he said. I said, "You're much too kind, and, to tell you the truth, my children should learn how to behave." "Oh, no," he said, and I knew that he was growing political in his thoughts, because his face became quite somber. "We have all suffered too much because of this idea of restraint," he said. "I, who was brought up in the strictest discipline, am now all in favor of the American system. Children here may do just as they please. They grow healthier, freer."

I nodded gratefully and, feeling that I must now repay him for his understanding, began to search my mind for something very bad to say against my children, something that would even make them appear to be unworthy of this blessed American freedom.

But before I could formulate a reply, he made a demand. "All I ask you to do," he said, "is to have the children wear slippers on Saturdays and Sundays until at least ten in the morning, for that's the only time in the week that I can rest a little."

"This is indeed very little to ask," I said, "and I assure you that it will be done."

When I entered my apartment and found my family gathered in plenary session in the kitchen, I announced that I had just had a pleasant talk with the man downstairs. To my wife, I said, by way of comment, "A very civilized, kind person, really," and to the children, by way of injunction, "All he wants from you is that on Saturdays and Sundays, until after ten in the morning, you walk with your slippers on and don't play ball. Can you imagine anything easier than that?" They immediately saw the adventure in a program of this kind; the idea of connecting their slippers with a given period of time seemed full of mystery and charm. Vieri told me that he would watch the clock and the very instant the hand touched the first tiny portion of the figure 10, he would throw his slippers against the ceiling. And Bimba, who is only five, immediately went to her room and came back to the kitchen, where we were sitting, with her slippers and Vieri's, to rehearse the Feast of Liberation.

"No, no!" I shouted, and my wife shouted, "No, no!" But since the slippers were already flying in all directions and landing in the sink, on the gas rings, behind the icebox, and on the breakfast table, I saw that the situation was desperate, and I commanded silence. Then I made an announcement.

"First of all," I said, "when he says ten o'clock, he doesn't mean that at ten sharp we have to start making a lot of noise. Ten o'clock means some time in the middle of the morning. We don't want to impose on his kindness."

"Impose?" Vieri asked. "What does that mean?"

"Now, look," I said. "The idea is this: We don't want to be unkind to this man." And I went on to explain that on Saturday and Sunday mornings we would go to the park if the weather was fine or play quiet games at home if it rained.

In back of our apartment building, above the parkway and the Hudson, there is a wild cliff covered with rocks and trees. This is where all the children of the apartment house play, and in summer or on mild winter days many of the grownups sit there in deck chairs and hate the children while enjoying the view of the boats on the river. My wife sometimes goes to the cliff with the children in the afternoon, and it was there, a few days after our family session, that she first met Mrs. Feinstein. From her, she learned that Mr. Feinstein had been a writer in Germany and that he was now again trying to write, in a new language. He had a quiet office downtown where he worked five days a week, but the shattering experiences of the past in Germany and the difficulty of mastering English had so discouraged him that after a day of writing he could hardly sleep at night, which was why he had to have his rest on Saturdays and Sundays. Mrs. Feinstein also expressed the hope that we would see more of each other and become friends. "You see," said my wife to me later, after recounting all this, "it's really a matter of honor for us to make up for our past sins and show that we are able to bring up our children to be civilized human beings."

"Yes, indeed," I said, "especially as the Feinsteins have asked little enough of us. We won't even try to become real friends with them until after we've given them reason to respect us."

Thus began our ordeal.

The first Saturday morning, both children put on their slippers and climbed on the table in their bedroom to reach for the picture books on the top shelf. I was in my room looking at the paper when I heard the most frightful noise. I rushed into the children's room and saw that all the big books and a box filled with wooden blocks, plus three or four wooden cows, had fallen on the floor. The children were blaming each other for the disaster, and they at once began a battle of shoes, books, and marbles. Needless to say, the reaction from downstairs was none too kind, and we learned later that even though we had gone out for the entire afternoon, Mr. Feinstein had found it impossible to repair the damage done to his sleep that day.

I was lucky enough not to see Mr. Feinstein for a whole week after the incident, but one day my wife met his wife when they were both waiting their turns at the washing machine in the basement. My wife renewed our pledge to keep to the ten-o'clock limit on weekends. This happened on a Friday, so very early the next morning, before the children could wake up, I went into their room and put their slippers in a place where they would be sure to see them. Next to the slippers, I put colored pencils, toys, and other accepted items of pre-breakfast entertainment. Everything went splendidly that one day—so splendidly, in fact, that we often recalled the occasion later and said among ourselves, "Why can't we have another December 17th?" But the fact is that we just didn't; in our family, at least, history does not repeat itself.

A couple of months later, rumors began to reach us from reliable sources, as they say in the papers, to the effect that Mr. Feinstein always spoke of us as "the parents of the two noisy children." Not a friendly word about us. This struck my wife and me painfully, and what disturbed us even more was to learn from one of our neighbors that Mr. Feinstein had received bad news from his family in Europe and was quite depressed.

My wife and I then held a secret meeting to plan a new strategy. It was a Monday morning and we had just got the children off to school.

"I am more worried about ourselves than about Mr. Feinstein," said my wife. "What will become of us in the future when, instead of trying to teach the children not to make noise, we will want to teach them not to wage aggressive wars on their neighbors?"

"The future is not yet," I said, "so don't worry."

The next morning, I stopped in at my children's school and consulted the school psychologist, whom I had come to know and like. He said, "Very simple, my friend. If you want to impress upon your children the notion that Mr. Feinstein is asleep, you must first believe it yourself. It's like the psychology of selling—you can never sell a thing in which you yourself have no faith. And furthermore," he said, "your methods are dictatorial. You can't ask children for exceptional behavior on Saturdays without any previous training. Try to approach Saturday by degrees. Accumulate a capital of habit, act artificially by minor doses, until Saturday comes to them naturally, without a shock."

I thanked him very much for his advice and began that same day to think in terms of Saturday. Mr. Feinstein was away in his office downtown, but I was beginning to prepare a nice silence for him upstairs. It was a wonderful feeling. I almost saw myself as a young bride preparing the first meal for her husband, hours before he comes back from the office. I walked cautiously, even typed cautiously (for I work at home), and when the children returned from school, I said to them, "Let's all work together for a better Saturday."

"Hurrah!" they shouted. "Let's work right away! May we use our shovels?"

"Children!" I whispered in my new velveted, tired voice. "Please, my dear, good, gentle children! Come, let's sit peacefully together and have silent fun!" And while saying this, I caressed their heads and closed my eyes to suggest peace.

I have come to the point at which my critics (among them my wife) accuse me of having brought violence into my advocacy of peace. They may be right; perhaps I am too passionate a character anyway. Well, it was Thursday afternoon and the children were playing in their room while I was writing in the living room. Needless to say, Mr. Feinstein was not at home. Suddenly I heard the sound of hammering. I emerged from the nineteenth century in Rome, in which my work had submerged me, to ask my wife with anguish, "What time is it?" Saturday morning was in my subconscious, so much so that I began to plead with my son to stop hammering. My wife took his side against me; she said he had every right to play with his tool kit. I tried everything, even literature. I said, "If Thursday is here, can Saturday be far behind? Think of that poor man downstairs, who will be asleep in less than two days from now!" Neither Vieri nor my wife was impressed.

That night, I committed my greatest mistake. I went downstairs and asked Mr. Feinstein to help me, and although he said again that those two mornings on the weekend were all he cared for, I insisted so earnestly that he made two more demands: a 1-to-3 P.M. silence on Sundays and a nightly silence after nine. It was a little too much, I felt, but after all I'd asked for it. In fairness to Mr. Feinstein, I must say that he did what he could to help me, pounding his disapproval on the radiator pipe each time we played the victrola or I typed after nine. Since his approval was not shown by any applause but was simply left to our guess, our hopeful guessing, plus those occasional ghostlike rappings on the radiator, seemed to summon up Mr. Feinstein's spirit. The whole family began to flee from it. We withdrew to the kitchen and lived there like fugitives; we talked to our guests in whispers and always told them not to walk too confidently, lest the spirit wake up.

One evening, while we were having guests—Mr. Feinstein was, of course, present in spirit—my wife observed that our lot had not improved much with exile; in Italy the tyrant had been constantly awake over us, here he was asleep under our feet. The joke was such a success that one of our guests, laughing convulsively, drummed on the floor with his heels, and at once—bang, bang—the spirit replied. Before long, the phrase "Mr. Feinstein is asleep" was no longer a phrase; it was a dogma. It was, in fact, the Law. I vaguely recall that this was the period when I could no longer work on my historical research, and while my actions were all devoted to the defense of Mr. Feinstein's sleep, my thoughts centered on hating him. Finally, a friend gave me a key to his apartment, so that I could go there to work in peace. But the fact was that I went there only to be able to hate Mr. Feinstein without interruptions. In the meantime, the children went on making a lot of noise, and they even began taking liberties with Mr. Feinstein such as I would never have dared. One day, my son met him in the elevator. It was the eve of the long Easter holidays, the thought of which was already filling me with dread. Mr. Feinstein said to Vieri, "You are lucky to have such a long vacation." "Yes, I am," answered Vieri with a smile, "but you're not."

At this point, I went to see the school psychologist again. He suggested that I now try the progressive method; namely, teach while playing, in the manner of the modern school. I thanked him for the idea, and the same day I began to make many jokes to the children about Mr. Feinstein, the monster downstairs. I taught them to call him Sleepyhead, and whenever his name was mentioned, we made snoring noises. Then the expression was coined: "As lazy as Mr. Feinstein." This worked pretty well until Mr. Feinstein fell sick and actually had to stay in bed all the time. Vieri had taken up bouncing his ball again, so, to save the day, I at once established a Feinstein Prize for silence.

Unfortunately, one Sunday afternoon not long after, while I was walking through the park with my children, we met a group of friends who were on their way to pay us a visit with their own children, six in all. As it was a beautiful day, we decided to stay outdoors and not go back to our apartment until teatime. When we started on our way home, I noticed that each of my friends' children was armed with a ball and that one of them had iron cleats on his shoes, and I began to warn them of the "monster" that lived under our feet. My children helped me, volunteering the usual epithets and noises, and suddenly, whom did we see passing us but Mr. Feinstein, his face pale and stern. He must have been returning from a Sunday walk in the park and certainly had come up behind us and heard everything. He stared at me and said in a dignified tone that stabbed my heart, "Good afternoon."

I did not sleep that night. One always hates to be caught by an enemy in the act of abusing him behind his back, but what made things worse in my case was that I liked Mr. Feinstein as a person and would have given anything to be forgiven by him. "Horrible!" I thought. "Instead of understanding the delicacy of our motives, he will understand only the indelicacy of our remarks." So, after hours of nightmare, I decided that the only thing to do was face the situation squarely and go to him. But, alas, before I did so bad fortune willed it that I meet him right in front of my door. He wasn't coming to see me, that I knew, but I said, "Mr. Feinstein, I would like to talk to you. Won't you come in?" He hesitated, entered, and sat down without saying a word. Despite my confusion, I immediately noticed that in person he occupied a much smaller portion of the air than did his spirit. I had been unjust. And he looked much kinder than his spirit, too.

"I don't know why you want to see me," he began. "Are you looking for inspiration for more vulgar stunts to teach your children? As a matter of fact," he continued, moving his chair back noisily and preparing to leave, "I don't know what made me accept your offer to come in in the first place."

I was almost speechless, but instinctively said what I now always said to my guests: "Please be careful, we have—" And my finger was pointed toward the floor. He understood, for his face reddened and he said with rage, "Never mind! I'm up here now, not downstairs!" I blushed and sank back on my chair, then stuttered, "Now, Mr. Feinstein, you, who are a philosopher—"

He interrupted me. "I don't see what that has to do with the fact that you teach your children to insult a man who has done you no harm. If that's the way Italian children are brought up, I can almost believe that Italy needs a Mussolini!"

"Please!" I said. "There is no reason why you should insult me! Listen to me, now. I myself never used bad words against you."

"But you laughed when your children used them. You even encouraged them. I heard what you said in the park. So you can hear me 'snore like a pig,' can you?"

"I? We? No, indeed, I never said so."

"You *did* say so. I heard you!"

"I was only joking."

"Only joking! Respect for your neighbor is a joke to you. I knew it all the time, but for a while I thought that you were merely a little casual, like most Italians. But now I know. Respect for others means nothing to you, and you even take pleasure in persecuting others with your jokes. You are a Fascist!"

"Sir!" I cried. "That you should insult me in my own home! I can prove to you that I have fought Fascism, that I have written dozens of articles denouncing all forms of persecution."

"You may have done so, but my experience with you is just the opposite. You have constantly disregarded my very modest demands, and on top of this you make me out a clown to amuse your children. That, sir, is more than I—"

"Please, please!" I said. "All my friends can be witnesses to the fact that your demands for quiet are the only thing I've taken seriously for the last two years. It is, in fact, *I* who may reproach *you* for making me a nervous wreck. Unintentionally, I admit, but still—"

"I?" said he, growing terribly pale. "I? I have made *you* a nervous wreck? All *my* friends are my witnesses, sir, that all I ever asked of you was a few hours of silence a week. Is *that* what makes you a wreck? You and your children have made *me* a wreck! How on earth can you have the nerve to claim that my asking you for those few hours of silence that I never got has made you a wreck! That is indeed Fascist!"

"Sir," I said, "please listen! I admit you never got your rest, and I'm sorry, but you don't know how many sleepless nights I've spent trying to prepare the rest you never got. And let me tell you also that this all came about because I tried to be kind to you. First, I tried to offer you two hours and a quarter of quiet, then three hours, and soon quiet for you became the ruling principle of our existence. Your sleep, Mr. Feinstein, ruled my life! And how could I persuade the children to obey these rules without pretending that I was taking their part against you? If you are to enjoy the sleep of the just, you must allow me to insult you unjustly. If the children know that you are a good man, they will want you to be so good as to cope with their noise, while if they think that you are a monster, they will respect you to avoid trouble."

"But that *is* Fascism! That is horrible! Couldn't you have told them that I was very sick?"

"I did once, when you were, but it didn't help. Besides, though I'm not superstitious, I hate to talk lightly about sickness. To mention it may tempt the Fates."

He looked at me, bit his lip, then said, "Why didn't you just call me a fool?"

"Who was I to do that?" I said. "And you, sir, why did you

always ask with such kindness, and look so pale? That made me act the way I did."

He frowned, looked at me again, and then we both started laughing and my wife came in with a bottle of wine and some wineglasses. The children, too, came running in, and started jumping so hard that this time it was for the protection of the house itself that we had to stop them. "I guess," said Mr. Feinstein now, "this all goes back to the incongruities of Progress."

"Also," I said, "to the decay of Western Civilization."

"Perhaps, too, though only a little, to these darling children here," he said.

"Yes," I said, "or to me, who am silly enough to live in town. Let's drink now and be friends."

So our friendship was sealed, and upon leaving Mr. Feinstein said, "Frankly, I prefer your noise to all that unfair propaganda against me. It's bad enough that the grownups should scare each other with lies. Let's spare these babies if we can."

"This time," I said, "I am *sure* I can keep my promise."

But, alas, this time, too, it was a mistake to make a promise. For now every time I think of my good friend Mr. Feinstein, even late at night, I hope the children will play ball, jump, or do something awful, just to let him know that he has friends upstairs, real friends, and that his name is not being taken in vain. Yet he's so nervous now, so jittery, so sad (and, needless to say, his spirit still sometimes manifests itself by the usual rappings), that I still am afraid to let the children act like children. The result is that I never quite know whether to give rest to his body or to his soul.

THE SCHEMERS

Two summers ago we had decided to stay in town and make the best of the Hudson River that flows right under our windows, of Fort Tryon Park two blocks away from us, and of the black, burning-hot, dusty roof of our apartment house. But, alas, just as we were beginning to be reconciled to this substitute for a real vacation, the mother of a former roommate of mine in college invited us to go and spend five days on her beautiful Long Island estate. Five days are better than nothing, but then they are also worse than nothing. It takes about five days to forget New York and accept the reality of true Heaven around you, and when you have just reached this point, how can you suddenly reverse the process and hope to recover from health and clean air, from the smell of flowers and the gentle shadow of green trees?

Having weighed all these drawbacks of a short vacation in my mind, I put my diplomatic instinct to work and schemed to take along more luggage than we would need for five days, and then hope for something to happen that would result in a prolonged vacation for us. But my wife, who is apt to say good-bye the moment she arrives where she is invited, was very much against it.

"I am not the type to extort invitations from anybody . . . I this and I that . . ."

"Now look here," I said. "First of all, I have known these people for years and they will not be bashful with me if they have to say no. Secondly, you must not think that we intend to impose our presence on them by any devious means. Far from it. We shall just go there and hope. Do you see anything tactless in hoping?"

She did. Hope to her, who comes from a very pessimistic family, was the height of bad manners.

"And now suppose," I said, "just for the sake of argument, suppose that while we are there I fall and break one of my legs?"

"In that case," she said, "we would all come home in an ambulance with you."

Seeing that even destiny was to pattern itself on her decisions, I quietly changed my strategy while she went on with hers, declaring for the first time in our married life that this weekend we would try to leave town with just one suitcase, a wish expressed by me in every tone hundreds of times before. Our weekends had always looked like planned evacuations; after ten pieces of luggage were filled, five more took the overflow, until every bag, basket, box, kerchief, and hand was filled to capacity. It had always come to the point where I was ready to throw myself on the floor and plead, "Now wrap me in tissue paper too and bury me in a suitcase." But with all the memory of those past horrors, this was certainly a strange occasion for her to try to "please" me.

"You always said that we were making ourselves ridiculous with all that luggage and I am determined not to repeat the errors of the past."

"But please," I said, "can't we postpone my being right until next time? May I stay wrong just once more? Won't you persevere in your old errors?"

"No."

I woke up the children and said, "Do you know where we are going tomorrow night? To Duck Island, to the sea, hurray!"

My children had never seen the sea and insisted on calling the Hudson the sea; so after many attempts to teach them the truth, I had given up. Their notions of hydrography were rather limited, but they revealed through them an instinct for classification. The waters of the world had been divided by them into the following categories: (a) drops, (b) glasses, which are made up of many drops, (c) lakes, which are nothing but glasses thrown on the floor, (d) bathtubs, (e) seas, or sea-rivers, also called Hudsons by some people. The idea of a non-Hudson sea excited them very much.

During the morning they behaved like angels. We had a sun bath on the roof and they stayed right on the old square mat without soiling their feet on the black roofing; they remembered not to jump and to run because that is apt to bring the ceiling down on the tenants and the tenants up to the roof and it is so unpleasant. After we had perspired a little, we had our daily tanning treatment: a big cloud of smoke was ejected from the incinerator and curled itself thickly around us, until the ashes had settled on our wet skins. At this point, as usual, we went downstairs to wash and dress up to go to the park. But oh, it was hot downstairs, with the windows tightly closed to keep the heat from coming in (a refinement unknown to those who leave town for the summer), and the books and all the inanimate things had that dry perspiration of theirs; even the ink on the old engravings seemed to wake up and perspire again.

My wife was aging quickly from the untold suffering of deciding what she might not need. In the old days, when she still refused to adopt my point of view, she used to pack her indecision by taking along all the things she would later discard. But this time, oh, this was time for decision indeed. She had emptied all the closets and displayed all our earthly belongings on beds, window sills, tables, chairs, dressers, and the floor. *The* suitcase was there, open, waiting for the miracle, and she was looking at each object, studying it, suffering in front of it all the temptations of the abundant packer. Then she closed her eyes and tried to visualize five days in all their practical details: so many sweaters, so many playsuits, so many handkerchiefs, against a background of the big murmuring trees, the tennis court, the flowers, and the glittering waters of the sea. Indeed it seemed an extremely difficult job to pack on the hypothesis that all those beautiful things existed. Yet I knew they did, and the thought that in six days we would again take our sun bath on the roof under that half-chewed lollipop called the sun, in the hypothesis that the real sun did not exist, confirmed me in my scheme to exploit this invitation to the bitter end.

Before we left for the park, my wife said, "Will you choose from these three piles of shirts which ones you want with you?"

"All of them," I said.

"Impossible."

"All right, then I am going to pack them myself in my suitcase."

She was so horrified at the thought of my packing (she alone knows how), that she agreed with me and I left with the clear conscience of the devil who has done his daily bit of evil.

In the park I tried a little propaganda with the children. "What is this park?" I asked. "Look at it. Smell the bitter asphalt from the road. See these signs forbidding you to play on the grass. Keep Off, Keep Off! Wherever there is a nice spot to lie down, it reads Keep Off on a stupid little sign of black wood. You would think that a man named Keep Off was buried there."

Then to mark the contrast I described the freedom of Long Island, with the cherry trees, the flowers to be picked, the sea, and they promptly repaid me with the same propaganda: they spoke about the ugliness of the park and the signs to Keep Off and they told me what the sea was like; not a Hudson, but bigger than three Hudsons. Then they fought, because each of them felt that this was his or her secret and the other had no right to reveal it to me. At lunch they refused to eat unless their mother promised to pack all their dolls and teddy bears, and Vieri left the table to write on a large sheet of paper: FIFTY YEARS. That was how long he intended to stay. I explained to him that fifty years was too high a claim and not even I would support him. He contended that fifty years passed very quickly and I said:

"That's right, but vacations are not measured in those terms."

Then, while his sister was taking a nap, he and I sat on the window sill near *the* suitcase and I told him he must not soil his clothes, because probably they had no washing machine out in the country. After a brief interruption to help my wife drag another suitcase out of the closet, I resumed my conversation with him.

"And you know what?"

"What?"

"Long Island is a strange place. At times on hot days like this, it turns cold and you have to wear an overcoat."

Second interruption. My wife asked me to call the Weather Bureau, but I said, "What's the use? If we only stay five days it will be sufficient if we take one extra sweater along."

So we decided that a large suitcase with a little extra space would allow us room for things we might forget at the last minute, and thus the familiar procession of suitcases was brought in. Then I went to the grocer to ask for five large cardboard boxes, and they all stood there, gaping, ready to receive thing after thing in careful wrapping and in the slow thoughtful movements of my wife's hands. Teddy bears and dolls descended into their traveling grave, I took along enough papers and books to write three novels, and we left in the usual frenzy ("Close the doors, lock the windows, where are the keys? Should we turn off the ice box? Have we enough toys? Cash this check at the superintendent's"). I had won.

I was hating the family as I usually do on such occasions. It was hard to find a cab; when it came, the children had to go upstairs to the bathroom; then, at last, we got to Pennsylvania Station—redcaps, shrieks, Population of the World with all its suitcases, sunrays through the smoke like illustrations of the Bible, microphones intoning "Newark-Trenton-North-Philadelphia-Philadelphia-30th-Street-Station," in pure Gregorian chant. Then we found that the five-eleven, which doesn't change at Jamaica, did not run on Fridays, so we had to wait an hour under the black stairway between trains. And to amuse the children I had to dance with them and sing nursery rhymes, while my wife stood there with two winter coats on her right arm and a handkerchief in her left hand to wipe her brow.

The station wagon was waiting for us. On our way out to Duck Island we began to believe in the existence of the world again as we sped up on the strip of land between the sound and the bay and saw sailboats and people in shirts and pants as white as sails; then we felt in our stomachs the pleasant skimming sensation of driving over gravel, and finally we got there.

My wife *would* of course greet our hostess with one of those pieces of polite nonsense it takes generations of good upbringing to learn: "Dear Mrs. R., but are you *sure* you want us for a long weekend?"

I pinched her on the arm, Vieri shouted, "She does!" and Bimba began to cry. The nonsense of her politeness became even more apparent as the chauffeur began to unload our luggage.

"You see," I said to our hostess, "all these suitcases and boxes contain bricks we have brought from New York to build ourselves a cottage on your estate."

Vieri took me to task at once: "Oh father, please let's build a cottage here."

"Shut up," I ordered, "and go upstairs."

They ran upstairs and from there shouted at the top of their voices, "Look, but look, please, we are here!" Then came the adventure of the bath, and where did the water go, and was it from the sea, and, if not, where did it come from, and could they see the plumbing all the way to New York, oh please? . . . Tears and shrieks.

Then Vieri inspected all the rooms and counted fourteen beds. There was a bunk room and he wanted to sleep there, but it was at the other end of the house with two squeaky doors to pass, so we said, "No. Tomorrow night if you behave."

Then supper on the porch and Vieri refused to drink his milk, so I whispered something into his ear and he shouted back, "Oh no! You said fifty years and not two weeks! I won't drink my milk if we are only to stay two weeks."

"What nonsense!" I shouted. "Who ever spoke of such things?"

"You," said Vieri and looked at me with indignation.

He was technically right, but I had not quite—that is to say—

anyway, no explanation was possible, and my wife said in her gentle voice, "I think it will be better if we go back Sunday night instead of Tuesday."

"You stay out of this," said Vieri. "This is something between Father and myself. I must have a chance to behave and make no noise, and it will take me much longer than that."

Oh, how good it was to be awakened next morning by the birds, so many of them, near and far away, and they sang clean sunrise and not thick fog and perspiration as they do in town. I woke the children and we ran down barefoot to the beach, where I told them to shout as much as they could so as to use up all their shouting reserves for the day. Then they ran down the slope and Vieri felt that he could run faster than anything on earth.

As we came back and went through the house I went after them from room to room, asking them to tone down, reminding them of our secret plan: "Prudence, prudence. We, the schemers, must be careful if we want to attain our goal." I was making signs with my hands as if I were an orchestra conductor at a rehearsal.

But alas, everything brought out the instinctive generosity of their souls. For example, later on while we were playing on the beach Bimba ran away shouting, "Wait for me here, I am going to tell Mrs. R. that the sea is here."

Vieri of course ran after her to be the first to give the news, and after a fight under the trees, she came back to me crying and he joined us a few minutes later.

"That was very unfair," I began.

But he said, out of breath, "Oh no, you don't know what I have done. I have been very kind. I have shown Mrs. R. the sea and she said thank you."

More shrieks from Bimba who wanted to be kind too. What could I say? Of course he had been kind and I couldn't ask him to be a hypocrite, to be kind the way we grown-ups are. So I began to give up my scheme of staying there any longer.

But when Vieri asked our hostess if it were true that she disliked children who make noise, she reproached me very bitterly and said in his presence, "I think children *should* make noise, even though we grownups are not always in a mood to enjoy it."

"And now," said my son to me in Italian, "now tell her about the fifty years and also about always."

My defeat as a schemer could not have been greater. The only one who triumphed was my wife, but sadly, as befits a civilized person of her type. She discovered that our hostess expected a great number of her grandchildren at the end of the coming week. "And obviously," she said to me, "she invited us only because you must have said something to her the last time you saw her in town. Otherwise," she concluded, "there would be no point in inviting noisy people like ourselves for the only weekend in which she might enjoy a little rest."

"Nonsense," I said. "As a matter of fact, it's you who ruined everything. You made me so self-conscious that I told the children that she did not like their noise. This upsets all my plans now."

Vieri came in and said in a patronizing tone, "Never mind, Father. Mother doesn't know. We can stay even if she has guests. I have counted fourteen beds, and there are couches too, and I can sleep on the floor. And tonight," he added, "I shall sleep in the bunk room, as you promised yesterday. I behaved and was even kind and Mrs. R. liked my noise."

We prepared his bed in the bunk room and all during dinner we ran upstairs in turn to see how well he could climb into bed without the ladder and how well he could come down the same way. His voice resounded like a trumpet all through the house; the doors were continuously swinging back and forth as we passed them in a hurry; and the two doors that led to the bunk room made the strangest whining noises. It was impossible for me to impress upon our hostess the desirability of continuing this sort of vacation much longer.

"Poor child," she said to my wife, "you must be very tired."

"I am not tired," said my wife. "I am anxious to go back to town so you won't hear this awful noise all day long."

"Oh, never mind me," said our hostess. "I think you are very wrong in this. You should leave your children free to make all the noise they want. As I told your husband, I think children *must* be noisy."

In the night, however, her opinion too must have changed, not because the night brings counsel, as they say, but because that night brought noise, a great deal of it. Vieri came to my room at two to tell me a dream; he slammed all the doors, and finally bumped into a wall, so that instead of telling me his dream, he told me his pain, and as soon as that was over he cried even more loudly than before because he had forgotten the dream. I consoled him and we exchanged beds. I went into the bunk room and he slept in my bed. Under my feet the stairs squeaked much more distinctly than they had for him, and also the squeaking of the doors seemed to respond much better to the experienced hand of a grownup. Then, just as I had climbed into his bed, he came again, preceded by the entire sequence of the same noises I had just stopped producing, and he wanted his teddy bear.

"You will not go back," I said.

"Yes, I will," he said.

"No," I said, but he ran away, stumbled twice, and got to the end of his journey crying so loudly that the entire house must have heard him. I wanted to go and frighten him into silence with the most horrible threats, but I did not dare pass the region of horrors again, so I stayed where I was, whispering an uncontrollable "Ssssshhh" in the direction of the door.

The next day, which was Sunday, our hostess was a little tired and said so. It was decided that I would act as an absorbent of whatever noises the children were going to emit that afternoon, but alas, right after lunch, while our hostess was taking a nap, they discovered in the room adjoining hers the strangest collection of drawings made right on the walls and the ceiling by the guests who had come to Duck Island years before.

When I saw their wide-open eyes I realized immediately that the situation required emergency measures; so instead of applying the technique of an orchestra conductor, I said to them:

"Children, the first of you to say that this is beautiful will be punished."

Vieri looked at me for a second, and when he saw that I was trying hard not to laugh, he said to his sister: "Bimba, Father wants us to find everything ugly." And he began to shout: "Uhuuu, what horrible pictures, uhuuuu, what a horrible house, uhuuuu, how disgusting everything is!"

And they laughed so convulsively that my wife emerged from the room where she was blueprinting her next packing job. She grabbed Vieri by the arm and went with him to the end of the corridor. There she stopped in front of the old American clock and said, "See this clock? Look at it. Every minute that goes by on that clock will never come back. We are leaving Tuesday afternoon at three; you still have forty-eight hours to play outside, after which you won't go to the seashore for the rest of the year. Now you know it. Go out and play, and don't come back before supper time."

Vieri disentangled his arm from her grip, looked at the clock and said, "That clock is a dirty swine. Tfu!" He went through the motion of spitting on it.

My wife went through the motion of spanking him and beat the air all around him quite badly. She didn't dare touch him and bring out the noises of which he was so full. Then she dispatched us three downstairs with the gesture of the Angel that banished Adam and Eve from Heaven. I couldn't help laughing. I felt sorry for the clock. It had such a gentle old face with those Roman numbers and the little house and tree painted in the middle. But what does one say when a child insults a clock?

"Nice thing, to laugh," she said. "Those are the words he learns from your political discussions with your friends." So my son had a political thought and said, "That clock is Hitler."

The rest of the afternoon Bimba stayed around her mother to help her pack the dolls, and Vieri tried to bargain with me: "Tell Mother that I will be good. I want you to change every single idea in her head."

"Enough of this, go out and play."

"I will eat all my soup."

"Go out and play."

"I will eat everybody's soup. I will sleep all afternoon."

"It is not a question of that, my son, we *have* to go."

"I'll stay here alone."

"No."

"But I will help."

"No."

"But there are fourteen beds."

"Listen. Do you remember what Mother said about that clock?"

His last question was quite sad: "Does it go all the time?"

"Yes, it goes all the time."

"But I don't want that." This was his protest all during Monday and Tuesday. The weather was beautiful, but he sat in the darkest corner of the porch, with his face in his hands, looking at the cricket balls with which he had played so well the day before, and doing nothing. He didn't want to run faster than anything in the world; he was thinking of his enemy the clock. Before going to bed he asked: "Is tomorrow the last day?" And he fell asleep mumbling: "I don't want that." The last day of his fifty years, of his millions of years. It was quite sad.

Tuesday at three o'clock we left with all our luggage, our regret, our winter coats, and our handkerchiefs to wipe our brows. At seven, with God's help and assistance, we entered the apartment in town, and it smelled like the inside of the Pyramids. I opened all the windows. The tanning cloud was being blown into our house from the neighboring roof now. The sun was there, shaven of all its glorious crown of rays, the same pink lollipop that had nothing to do with shedding light on anything, because the world was all in pencil, dusty and grey as an unframed etching on top of a hot radiator. The tugboats were spitting something white in front of them, and that was water. It was real home again.

At ten, in the dark, while I was on my bed patting my wet knees with my wet hands, the phone rang. From Long Island. Oh, if we could only smell the clean air through the receiver.

There came the voice of our hostess: "Did you get home safely?

Is it hot in town? How are you all? By the way, do you know that my clock stopped today for the first time in years, and that the pendulum is missing?"

"Hold the line," I said, "I'll be right back."

"Vieri, Vieri!" I shook him out of his slumber. He was naked, wet, and suffering. He turned his face to me without opening his eyes. "Vieri," I said, "do you remember that clock?"

He was snoring again, but a voice came, "That clock is Hitler."

"Yes," I said, "but where is the pendulum?"

His hand pointed to the wall, "There."

"Here?"

"No, in Long Island."

"But where in Long Island?"

"Under the dresser." He scratched his eyes with anger as the perspiration was falling into them from his hair and went back to sleep, still mumbling something against his great enemy.

DEATH OF THE PROFESSOR

He looked at the house across the street from Marjorie's apartment and saw that it was moving away from him; it became smaller and smaller, like a railroad station seen from the last car of a train: First the faces become one with the hats and the bodies, then they merge with the platform, then the station itself merges with the trees and the mountains behind it, then there remains but a hole in the horizon, into which are poured telegraph poles, gravel, rails, and bushes shaken by the wind. But for him it was different. These were no new horizons throwing the old one into the caves of time; this was death, darkness that streamed out of his eyes: He kept them open and saw nothing. He woke up on the carpet. There was a man's face above him, with glasses and a bad breath, and the man was asking him, "How are you feeling now?" "You, rather, with that bad breath of yours, how are *you* feeling?" he felt like asking but did not. He contented himself with thinking it, understood that the man was a doctor, and told him right away, in order not to be told by him, "Just a fainting spell, nothing serious." Then he saw Marjorie at a step from him, worried, beautiful as ever; and felt so happy that he did not want her to know he had seen her. This would have been like giving a poor definition of his joy. He kept the notion to himself, thinking that later, with adequate, beautiful, serious words, he would recognize her. "Tell me exactly what happened," said the doctor, and he told him in the most minute details, even using the comparison with the view of the station from an outgoing train, and he did this not to be brilliant but practical, as he would have done with a traffic policeman to avoid a fine. He was hoping to receive from the doctor, as a reward for his presence of mind, a less severe diagnosis. Because he was afraid; he would almost have pleaded with the doctor, "Tell me I am well, I will pay you a bigger fee." As for Marjorie, he knew he had given her a lesson. One does not leave a sick man of seventy. And now Marjorie prepared her bed for him and said to the doctor, "Let's put him here, so he can rest." What a strange, new, and wonderful thing: In the presence of a third person, he was given a right to that bed, the object of so many anguishing discussions and fears. The joy of this gave him such strength that he rose from the carpet by himself, and thought, This I must write; it is a fact of great philosophical importance: Joy as an equivalent of health. . . .

The doctor left, recommending to Marjorie that she keep him very quiet; no emotions. From her bed, with closed eyes, he listened to these words spoken about him and for him in the entrance hall as he would have to great music. How good to have a scientific lawyer to obtain for him what he himself with his best arguments had been unable to obtain for the last several days. He felt a great desire for death, because the mere idea of future discussions with her already proved a strain on his mind, but he felt at the same time an urge to live, which he had not felt for months. Here is another major philosophical fact, he thought: The desire for death coincides with the desire for life. . . . He asked Marjorie for paper and pencil. She at first did not want to give them to him, then yielded when she saw that he was going to be upset. He tried to write and was disappointed; these arguments, on paper, seemed quite childish. He fell asleep, woke up again, and she was still at his bedside, like a wife. "What are we going to do now?" she asked. "You should not move from here." But he jumped out of bed, svelte as ever, for he knew now he could not die. Life was too beautiful. He called his wife, and said, "I have been at the library much longer than I intended to; forgive me. I'll be home right away." And went home.

The next day, he called Marjorie, found her kind and humble, went to her house in a hurry, stayed with her for a few hours, and was pleased to see her anguished. Again he had the feeling that he had made an important philosophical discovery, in the following terms: When the others are afraid of your death, you may be sure that you won't die. If the burden of fear is on you, it will destroy you, and you will die in solitude. But the certainty of other people's love is an equivalent of vital force. . . . He tried again to write this thought and was again disappointed. Then he went to Columbia University by subway, and while crossing Broadway he felt a sudden urge to stay closer to the earth. He did not fall; it was the street that came all toward him, like a good thing. He embraced it and again had a sudden philosophical experience: The earth is cold, but underneath the crust there must be fire. One should study a much deeper geography. . . . Two of his students saw him, picked him up, and he said, "Let me lie for a while. I must first tie my heart to my arms again." And this, too, seemed a discovery to him.

They took him home in a cab, his wife put him to bed, the doctor came. This was another doctor, and with him, too, he tried to give evidence of lucidity by relating the details of the accident. The doctor coldly advised that he go to a hospital for a few days. He seemed so upset by this prospect that his wife did not insist. The next day, he called Marjorie, who knew nothing and seemed worried because he had not called before. This most unusual break in his telephoning was regarded by him as a great personal achievement. "I'm very well," he said. "I was only too busy to call you, and I would like to come now for a moment." Again she consented, without using any of her usual arguments against this. But the moment he tried to leave the house, his wife did not accept his old excuse that he was going to walk in the park for a while. "I'll go with you," she said. "The weather is so fine I feel like taking a short walk." This seemed treason to him. How dare she share with him his philosophical walks? But she seemed quite determined not to let him go out alone. At the corner drugstore, he stopped and called Marjorie to explain the reason for his sudden delay. To his surprise, she seemed pleased; she had always been rather jealous of his wife before.

"I am glad she is going with you," she said. "The weather is so fine today, it will do you a world of good to go to the park."

The park? he thought, and said, "But the park has never existed except as an alibi. Then you don't love me anymore." She answered "Yes," as usual but the tone displeased him; it was clearly the tone of a sick nurse. There was no philosophical discovery, this was an element of fact, and a very painful one. He tried to be resigned, but the company of his wife upset him, so that he felt a new fainting spell coming upon him and was able to avoid it only with great effort. She seemed aware of it, and said, "Let's sit here on this bench. I feel suddenly tired. Let me look for a cab. Will you take me back to the house?" She left, and came back after a minute in a cab to pick him up, and once back home he willingly consented to lie down for a short rest. But the moment he was on his bed, another philosophical thought came to him unexpectedly: The bed is part of our organism, exactly as the earth, except that the bed is in reality an altar on which we sacrifice to all the most important functions in life—birth, reproduction, and death. . . . He instantly wrote down this thought, and again it appeared rather childish in writing. Discouraged, he now tried to think in more technical terms, as he had in his lectures and in the learned articles in the review edited by him. They seemed absurd, incomprehensible. He concluded, I must rest, and again this appeared as a very profound thought, rich in logical consequences and worthy of long discussions. He began to look about him, saw the dresser with the combs and the brushes and cosmetics, and had such a sensation of fatigue that for a while he could not find an explanation for it. Then he understood the reason: There was no chair in front of the dresser. The idea of standing up was in itself a cause of fatigue. He looked at the prints on the wall—reproductions of country houses near Venice by the architect Palladio, and thought, How would it feel to lie down in those villas and enjoy the view of the garden?

He slept awhile and then decided to call Marjorie again. And he had many dreams that he *was* calling her, only to realize each time he had never left his bed. Then the telephone rang several times. He wanted to get up, but before he could move his wife answered it, and he had the impression that she was speaking to Marjorie. This hurt him very much. Perhaps it was not true, but he instinctively felt that there, at a few steps from him, in the corridor, there was Marjorie in that wire. And his wife's tone, circumspect and resigned, made him think of a funeral. They are plotting together to bury me—the only thing on which they can agree. . . . His anger was so violent that he lost consciousness. He had a dream in which he was going to Marjorie's apartment and settling down there in the face of the world; scandal or no scandal, he did not care. This seemed to him the wisest thing to do, and he found enough strength to get up, slip into his clothes, and leave the house without answering his wife's question "Where are you going, dear?" He left the house, ran to Marjorie's place at top speed, found her so affectionate that he could not help bursting into tears, and wiped his tears with his bedsheet. Thus he discovered that he had never left his bed.

Then a strange and new thing happened. An unknown woman came into his room and smiled to him and spoke to him in terms he could hardly understand. He knew he had met her before, but he could not remember where and when. The face seemed extremely familiar, and he felt he must thank her for her kindness, but he was a bit surprised at finding himself in bed in her house, and this caused him embarrassment and anguish. The effort he was making to recognize her was excessive; he fainted again. Then the doctor came. He recognized the doctor, felt like asking him who that woman might be, but did not want to ask him right away. He was too tired to talk. In the meantime, another philosophical discovery dawned upon him: How can a doctor cure you if you lie down and he stands up? . . . He concluded, with gravity: Pain should be understood. He found the strength to reach the pencil on his night table and wrote down this thought with great effort, then reread it and found it too childish again. He cried a bit. The doctor left, and again the strange woman came in, with a towel to wipe his tears. There was in that towel a most beautiful country—an endless beach with much light and red sails in the distance. All of it contained in the clean smell of oxygen that towel had absorbed by hanging on the roof. This, he thought, is a real philosophical fact: Odors are places, and they may be translated into places, as energy into matter, with the help of Einstein's formula. . . . Here is a very important fact: We may travel someday without having to move. . . . He felt like writing it, and looked around for paper and pencil, when a still more important discovery revealed itself to him: There exists gravitation. The earth is profoundly egocentric; she wants us, and then wants us again, all the time. We rise to escape from it. We look at the sky to liberate ourselves. . . . But in the meantime the earth went on pulling his hand, which, finding no support in the bed, after sliding on it for inches, abandoned itself to the earth for a moment. The stream of thought continued, always more philosophical. So much so that he suddenly forgot to breathe and had a coughing spell. He was able to breathe again after a while, and thought, How silly of me. I must make a note of this: I should never stop breathing or how can I go on thinking? . . . He pushed the hand a little farther out and tried to lift it, but the earth, with its old egotism, pulled, and he never reached the pencil.

THE UNDERGROUND SETTLERS

After a ship leaves the land, the light of that land remains attached to it for a while. Days out of Naples, the ship is still a part of Naples. The mountains that have sunk into the waters way behind the horizon still cast invisible shadows on the bridge. The sea road opened up by the ship looks like a country lane, and the water dust looks like the dust that covers the grass along country roads in summertime, and it is quite evident to the exile who stands in the stern of a ship and watches his voyage become part of the past that the water road goes not only all the way back to land but inland as well, that nothing grows in those regions ahead that the ship is exploring but the distance from home, that he is really going nowhere except farther and farther away from all the things he loves.

The last time I went to Italy to attend to some personal business, I came back on a freighter, formerly Italian, and American since the end of the war. The crew, the officers, the food, the passengers—everything but the ship's papers and the flag—were still Italian. The *barba* (beard, or captain, in Venetian sea lingo) was an old friend of mine from the Titoized island of Lussinpiccolo. There were thirty-five or forty passengers, and of these by far the greater number were in their sixties and seventies.

"The latest type of immigrant," the captain said when he saw me watching a group of these old people. "Grandfathers and grandmothers who are going to spend their last days with their immigrant children in America."

As the old people paced the deck in their best black clothes, that allowed none of their familiar working-day movements, they seemed confused and slightly less than themselves. The horizon went up and down in front of them in a slow, blinking movement; the old women tried to keep the wind from whipping their skirts, the old men pressed their hats down on their heads impatiently, and they looked not like passengers (each with his ticket, stateroom number, passport, and place in the dining saloon) but like peasants in a village square on Sunday.

"We never used to have this type of cargo," the captain continued, "though they remind me somewhat of the immigrants in the old days, when there were no quota restrictions. Except, of course, that these aren't bringing their shovels and pickaxes along with them—aren't pioneers. These are underground settlers; they come to fill graves."

The two points of attraction for the old people, their two meeting places, seemd to be bow and stern. There they huddled together trying to get used to the sea. When they stood in the stern, they came away from home; when they were in the bow, they went to America, they *traveled.* I knew this even before I talked with any of them, because that is the law, the basic law, of navigation. The destination end of a ship, the bow, invites people who hope; the stern those who despair. When the old people weren't in either place, they moved about the ship like the souls of the dead in that first stage of the Unbeing, where they are still concerned about the living they have left and cannot recognize among the dead anyone they ever knew.

Because of my friendship with the captain, I had access to the bridge. It was pleasant to watch the sea from farther away than the promenade deck, and at times the wind brought the voices of the old people and even bits of their conversation. Sometimes, after dark, I left the bridge and joined them. They talked, depending on where they were—bow or stern—about their past or their future. And the word that turned up most frequently in their conversation was "America." In colloquial Italian, "America" has come to mean something more than a geographical place. It is, by extension, any deposit of hopes, any tabernacle where all things too big, too difficult, too far beyond one's grasp take shape and become true—so true that all one needs in order to touch them is a ship that will take one there. "America" is, again, something one finds or makes, a stepping stone, a rung in the ladder that allows one to climb a little higher—not, of course, in the country called America but back home. "America" also means the treasure one finds when "America" (the rung in the ladder) is steady under one's feet. Inevitably, the question that the old people asked one another, over and over, was "Is America *America?*"

They also asked the other passengers, particularly former immigrants, of whom there were several on board, naturalized American citizens who had been back to Italy for a visit and were now returning to the United States. One of these, Mr. Esposito, had his wife, mother-in-law, and four children with him. He was a fat, middle-aged man and wore a white linen cap, white trousers, saddle shoes, and bright, impossible neckties. His wife was huge and wore light-colored, flowered cotton dresses. The mother-in-law wore black, but her white hair had been rinsed with bluing. Esposito explained to anyone who would listen to him that they would have taken the Queen Mary, first class, had it not been for the fact that their plans had been changed by circumstances. "Financial circumstances," he would say with a wink. "Matter of dollars and cents." Owing to these financial circumstances, they had been obliged to book passage on this cheap boat, the first one that had available accommodations, from Naples. "Those poor devils there, those immigrants," he would say, pointing with his cigar at some of the old people as they stood in the stern of the ship, in despair at leaving their mountains, "what do they know? They've never been to America. Wait till they see the Empire State Building." Though he affected to despise the old people, I noticed that he wasn't able to leave them alone. Neither could his mother-in-law, who said to a group of them one afternoon, "Listen to me. I am American and I can tell you that America *is* America. Not as much as it was before, but more than Italy, in any case." Then she began to tell them wonders. They all listened to her in awe. By the end of her story, she had twelve toothless old men and women breathing their great amazement in her face, and she did not like it. "And all the people have teeth in America," she said. "They have teeth and they dance. They drive cars. They are cheerful. In Italy, I would be an old woman. In America, I am still young. They call me a girl. All women are called girls."

"But will they let *me* in?" asked a very old woman.

"If you have your papers," Mrs. Esposito said. She and her husband had joined the group.

"And some money," Mr. Esposito said.

"I have a son," said the old woman. "He will take care of everything. He has a car. He will come in his car and drive me home in his car. But if he says I'm not good enough for America, I will go right back to Italy."

Esposito threw a glance at the ship's wake, shook his head, and said, "Italy is all right, but Italy is no good. Imagine that in Condofuri, where I come from, my wife, here, couldn't take a hot bath at home. She is used to a hot bath. We all are, in America. And there was only one place in the whole town where she could have a hot bath—the hotel. All my relatives were against the idea because it was so expensive—too expensive for them, naturally, but not too expensive for me. Even if I'd had to pay a great deal of money, I wouldn't have allowed my wife to give up her hot bath. So every morning in Condofuri we went to the hotel. I walked behind her with a towel and a cake of soap, and everybody knew that this American lady was going to take a hot bath. In America, you have hot water and ice in the house, even if you are poor."

The old people were stunned.

"Italy is beautiful," said Mrs. Esposito, "but you cannot live on beauty."

With the excuse of showing the new settlers what American dollars were like, Esposito exhibited his fat wallet and the hundred-dollar bills in it. The grandmothers were not interested, but the grandfathers were. As they crowded around him, their thin, crooked Tuscan cigars contrasted strangely with the torpedolike cigar in the fat face of the man who had made good, the naturalized American citizen, the inhabitant of Heaven.

An old woman whose name was Ernesta whispered to me, "Are Americans all like that?"

"No," I said, "but you will see."

"And is it true," she asked, "that if a person can't read or write, they will not let her in?"

"If you are old and aren't going there to work, and have someone to look after you, they will certainly let you in," I said. "Can you read and write?"

"Oh, yes," she said. "But if they stop me before we land and ask me to read something—I haven't seen my son for so long. If I know that he and his wife and my grandchildren are there waiting for me, I don't think I will be able to read. And if they ask me to write, that will be even worse."

Ernesta was the only one in the group that I got to know well. Her beautiful brown face was seasoned and lean and traced with lines. She was like an old wooden statue. She came from the village of Piteglio, in the Tuscan mountains, and had been nowhere else in the world, except, a few times, down to Pistoia. The other old people were also mostly from the villages in the Tuscan mountains. Behind them one could imagine a profusion of stones arranged in the shapes of stairs, houses, roofs, streets, without any given order or logic—the streets going right over some of the roofs and the houses built to block the streets at certain levels—and, farther back, the bluish mountain range and a few decorative clouds caught in the picture.

Before Ernesta left Piteglio, she hadn't known any of the other old people. "They are from far away," she told me. "Some from places you couldn't reach unless you walked five hours in the mountains. But now, so far away from home, even those distances seem small. We are all Christians and Tuscans. And that American who talks to us—he is a Neapolitan." To Ernesta, everyone from any region to the south of Tuscany—even a Roman or a Sicilian—was a Neapolitan. She still thought in terms of the Kingdom of Naples, which was brought to an end when Victor Emmanuel became King of Italy, in 1861. Ernesta did not come, really, from Piteglio or any other place; she came directly from the past, and so did the other old women on the ship—a past older than history and still present, rooted in times when Rome was not yet founded, counseling blind obedience and resignation for all women. They were embarrassed in the dining saloon. "It's like a hospital," Ernesta said one day. "They serve you and you can't get out to the kitchen to help. They give you butter, too, and you don't have to pay for it. And lots of bread. This boat is very rich."

"Were you sorry to leave Italy?" I said.

"*Direi!*" she said. "I should say so! But I was all alone there, while in America I will be a grandmother to Americans. So, the night before I left, I went to the cemetery with a letter my oldest son had written to me, and the money he sent me. The custodian unlocked the door and let me in, and I said to my dead, 'Forgive me, but I must go to America. I will be buried out of this cemetery, and I hope you don't mind. You pray for me, and I'll pray for you and see you in Heaven if I can get there.' And here I am, going to find a cemetery in America."

The ship was rolling and pitching, and she took hold of my arm. "America is not Heaven," she explained to me very seriously. "There can only be one such place, and that's the place where we will go if we take everything just as it comes. But if I'd been told that I would travel to America by earthquake, I'd never have believed it."

During the first half of the voyage, Esposito was busy explaining to the new settlers what was waiting for them, looking at their entry papers, and reading aloud, in his best nasal American, the addresses of their immigrant children and grandchildren, so as to teach the settlers where they actually were bound for, "This reads 'Bronx,' not 'Bronk,' " I heard him say. "It is part of New York. Lexington Avenue subway."

"What?" the old people asked with anguish in their voices.

"Subway. Trains under the earth."

"Trains under the earth? And how will they know where they are going?"

"Are there holes for these trains to go through?"

"Holes?" Esposito said. "Tunnels! A whole town under the town. Even shops. Everything."

"Houses, too?"

"Not yet," Esposito said, "but they will build those, too." Then he looked at another old man's papers and said, "Cincinnati. Very far from New York. You'll have to take a train."

"Under the earth?"

"No," Esposito said. "That is, even trains that run across the country start from under the earth. Then they come up." The old people looked at one another and nodded.

Esposito was affected by the basic law of navigation, but in a different manner. When he stood in the stern with the new settlers, he, too, was leaving—he was leaving his triumph and the warm envy of the people in Condofuri. The triumph still continued in his mind, like the excitement of a party that accompanies the guest of honor all the way home, making him smile in the dark and act as if he were still the center of attention. But when Esposito stood in the bow and traveled, he went back to the place where he was a Wop and a nobody. During the second half of the voyage, as America came closer and closer, he became, in his conversation, more and more nostalgic for Europe and less and less boastful about America. This disturbed the new settlers very much. He would say things like "America is not a country for old people; nobody wants them. It used to be for young people, but it isn't even that any more," and "Who is a better pioneer than the Italian? Just think of what the Italians have achieved in America. They built all the railroads. They reclaimed the Sacramento Valley and transformed it into a huge garden. And all that for whose benefit? For the benefit of the English-speaking population."

I remember particularly one bitter conversation that took place between Esposito and the old people on the eve of our arrival. I left the bridge and went to the bow some time before sunset. The old people were fascinated by what was going on in the sky. On the starboard horizon, clouds were coming down to meet the waves in three parallel bands of rain.

"Back in our mountains," said one old man whom I had rarely heard utter a word, "it didn't rain that way, on nobody's head or roof or umbrella. The rain is raining by itself."

"It has always been raining that way," Ernesta said.

"I beg your pardon," the old man said. "It has always been raining on people. That is what makes this rain seem so strange. No one will feel it."

"Yes, that is right," Ernesta agreed solemnly. "No one will feel it."

There was a silence and a change of scenery. Ahead of the boat, a long line of red clouds, evenly spaced, drew together, like actors gathering backstage for their entry. The rain clouds became shapeless and uninteresting. Three, five, ten ribbons of bright sunshine descended to the water on our port side.

"Tomorrow morning, we shall see New York," Ernesta said.

"Yes," said Esposito. "You will see New York, but you won't see anything at all. You will see a beautiful harbor, big towers, the tallest buildings in the world, but all artificial."

"Artificial? Why do you say that?" asked Ernesta. "Are the towers there or are they not there?"

"They are there," Esposito said, "but they are not there. And then everyone is busy. That is artificial, too. All that wealth, and it's not wealth. A glass of wine under a tree in Italy— Why do you go there, anyway? What do you expect to find there?"

Hearing these words, the old people began to gather around in a huddle, as they had so many evenings before.

"I told you," Ernesta said to Esposito. "I am going to America to die, not to live."

"To die?" Esposito repeated. "America is no place to die. Do you know what American cemeteries are like?"

The silence of all the old people spoke for them.

"They have no walls," Esposito said.

"No walls?" shouted Ernesta.

"No," Esposito said. "In America, the cemeteries are open and unguarded. Anywhere along the road, you will find gravestones.

Anyone can go in and walk around, and there are no portraits, no oil lamps—nothing." He took out a cigar, bit the end off, lit it, and said, "I am not going to die in America. I have my place at home in Condofuri."

Not one of the settlers was listening to him. They looked, they searched the horizon, but there was still another night to go; America was still way down under the waters of the world, and nothing would be learned before dark. Yet the new settlers went on looking. The sun was in their worried eyes, and behind their black kerchiefs and hats, from the stern of the ship, from the top of the water road, from Italy, the night was taking over.

THE NEWS

News travels fast. We may learn the most horrible things across three oceans and seven seas while the dead are still warm, the towns still burning, and the eyewitness still too much stunned to realize what has happened. We who receive the news thus swiftly, thanks to the services of progress, may accept our sad fate with resignation, act with the coldest logic, banish a number of people from our lives, change our habits, and revise our thoughts. Yet the things we recall—the memories that form the background of our dreams—will never change until we go back to see for ourselves that they are no longer true. It is only by seeing what has happened that we can put each one of our dear memories to sleep in its own cradle.

And so what good is all that speed if the news that reached us in a matter of minutes is never really received? I wish that the scientists, instead of giving us more speed, would invent a new language, in which words would be stronger than memories. Until they do, it's easier to change the whole face of the earth than the stage setting of a single dream. This is why many emigrants, after learning from the papers and the newsreels that not a stone remains intact of what were once their beloved home towns, will spend all their savings to make a trip to Europe, where nobody awaits them and where no home will shelter them. They go all the same, to correct the geography of their dreams.

I should go with them, for I, too, have unfinished work to do:

essages to understand that I read years ago in a letter or a cable out never really accepted, and dreams to alter—the ones I acquired in my childhood and cannot change. In these dreams, there are not only towns and bridges that exist nowhere else in the world but also people—many friends and three from my immediate family. Of these three, the most stubborn about leaving me is my mother.

She was always stubborn. She used to come into my room on tiptoe while I was doing my lessons, to make sure that I wasn't daydreaming. And today it is still as if she thought she must look after my work, as if she didn't know that *she* is now my lesson instead of history, the mountains of Asia, or the lowest common denominator.

My mother died in the fall of 1939, in a house in Tuscany of which she always said, "I hate this place so much that I will never let myself die here." That summer, she kept writing to me that I must come home for a visit. "Come, just for a few weeks," she wrote again and again. "It will do you good." I was here in New York, living I don't know how, and I wouldn't have gone to Italy even if I had had the money. She knew this. We had talked in 1938 about my reasons for coming to the United States for days before I left home. She had understood everything very clearly. In fact, when my father had offered me, as an alternative to the job in the Italian government that I refused to hold any longer, an idle life at home in the country, she had been against it, and when he had said, "This is no time for anyone to make good in America," she had answered him for me: "There are other reasons besides fortune that may make a young man leave his country." And in my case, too, there simply was no such thing as going back to Italy for a few weeks. It had taken me so long to obtain a temporary leave of absence from the Italian Army and to get a passport from the Italian government and a quota number from the American immigration authorities that it would have been folly to undo all that work, even to answer my mother's call. Besides, I was absolutely certain that once I had reached home, my mother would have said, "This was a great mistake. Why did you come back?"

Yet I could not, in my letters, remind her of my reasons for refusing to come. Italian censorship was heavy; war was near. The only thing to do was to have patience. Still, all those letters of hers were far from pleasant to receive, read, and dismiss. Then, in September, war broke out, and I felt that I would not see her again.

I had just moved into a small cottage in the midst of a beautiful Long Island estate owned by a friend of mine. He had furnished the cottage very nicely for himself, with old Italian furniture and a few pieces of American Colonial, and then had decided to live in the big house and give the cottage to me. It would be a place for me to bring my family when they could join me, for my wife and child were still in Italy. But now, with the war, what was the use? Everything seemed rather fatal. I even resigned myself to the thought that I would never see my son, who had been born in Florence a few months after I had left home.

I wasn't alone in my resignation; it took the whole world only a few days to accept as inevitable the horrible tragedy that had begun. The trembling voice of Neville Chamberlain had told us over the radio that there existed a state of war. Well, but what *is* a state of war? I asked myself. No trace of it was to be found in nature. Outside the windows of my cottage some leaves turned red, as if from a long habit of sunsets; others turned brown and fell, covering the many small ponds of Long Island with a surface of nicely carved leather. The air became a little cooler; all our closest botanical neighbors went on acting as they always do in autumn. The peaceful blades of grass lost their green and the flowers drooped in the frost. And soon, almost as if regretting their poor joke, the nations began to send their boats across the seas again, and everything seemed quiet for a while. But, knowing how men are, I hurriedly borrowed some money, a part of which I spent on a cable to my wife. "HIGHLY PAID JOB HURRAY COME RIGHT AWAY," it read. The highly paid job was a lie; I had no job at all.

When my wife received the cable, there were many things she had to do, such as secure passage on the boat, collect everything a child might need on the journey, get visas, permits, this and that, and so the days passed, and only on the last day before she sailed did she have time to go with the baby to take leave of my parents. She found my mother in bed; she wasn't ill, she was just cold. The child played on her bed and everybody admired him, and before they knew it, it was time to say good-bye. "Well," said my mother, "I was hoping that my son would come back. I don't have to wait now." That same night, she died. My wife was not informed, and my father decided not to let me know until after my wife's arrival in New York.

It was not until three weeks after I had taken my wife and child to the cottage on Long Island that I was told—by a friend of my father's, who summoned me to his office in New York and tried to "prepare" me before he handed me a letter from my father.

I went straight home. I had an assignment and I had to work at it. The first day, I was left alone to concentrate; a blanket was put over the telephone; everyone who came into the house spoke in whispers. But I could not learn my news. All I learned was that people talked in whispers, that I was left alone, that a blanket was put over the telephone. So I went out for a walk, and the walk was enjoyable because I felt so well and so healthy. I looked at all the things that made autumn good and lovable. I walked a long way and found myself in front of a church. Strangely enough, they were having a funeral there that day. Arithmetic, I thought, lowest common denominator—death. I went in and was greeted at the door by an old gentleman in black. I exhibited my serious face as one exhibits the invitation at a private concert, and he showed me to a seat. I noticed that most of the people dressed in black who were passing by me on their way to the front pews didn't seem to know how to behave, and this pleased me, as it used to please me in school, on the days of written examinations, when the faces of my companions betrayed fear and perplexity.

Well, I borrowed the dead from the mourners, but I couldn't transfer the silence, the black coffin, the candles, and the repressed sobs from here—this scene I saw—to the strong memories in which my mother was alive. I just couldn't do it. But I learned a great deal about the efficiency of funeral directors, who have cushions for every fainting spell and dozens of easily applied face-glooms for the different kinds of relatives. I learned how their hired pallbearers march to give the casket that particular swing to right, to left, to right, to left. It was almost like a dance. These things I observed and learned, but who could call them news? On the way home, a farmer spoke to me with sorrow, and I envied him, because his sorrow came from real news. He told me that his entire crop had been ruined by drought and that a piece of land he owned elsewhere had been burned in a forest fire. He was afraid of more forest fires. Perhaps his barn, his home would burn down, too. "It hasn't rained for so long," he said. "We've needed it for months, and even now it doesn't rain." I felt like answering, "With me, too, it doesn't rain. And rain is needed very badly to melt away certain images that are no longer true."

The farmer's drought came to an end with the first winter rains, but mine continued. In the meantime, I thought of my mother and the house in Tuscany without her in it, but I just couldn't picture it. She was always there. I gave up. Bits of sadness passed by, high in the air, like migrating birds. Sometimes they circled lower, all around the house, at night. One night, a storm whipped the windows and they seemed to shiver, and the garbage pail rolled down the back-porch steps toward the trees with a terrible noise. The roof of our small house was almost blown away, but nothing happened in my dreams. Not a leaf shook, not an image was washed away. The news was not received.

So many years have passed since then, it seems almost incredible that even now, when I dream or think of home, my mother is always there. And this is why I must make the trip to Italy and to our home in Tuscany. I shall look at it very well, look into every room. Only then can I *know.*

About the Author

I was born on May 1, 1908, in Lugano, Switzerland, of an Italian father and a Russian mother, and am by nationality a planetarian. From my father I learned the rules of morphology, syntax, logical and grammatical analysis in Italian and Latin; I also learned the names of most flowers in Latin according to the classification of Linnaeus and I learned all about their social standing and gossip (what flowers have pollen relations with what other flowers, whether openly or secretly, that is phanerogamae or cryptogamae, which ones are reliable and which ones venomous, and for this kind of knowledge he used the botanical social register known as the Key of Eulerus); he further taught me to obey all constituted authorities starting with his own and then up all the way to God, and allowed me to get there by any of the given church channels. But what my father really taught me, very much against his intentions, and in spite of the fact that he had taken great precautions not to let me know, was that he himself hardly believed any of the things he wanted me to believe, with due exception for botanical and grammatical knowledge, in both of which he had great faith. From my mother I learned German, French and a bit of Russian, plus a great deal of history, mythology, table manners and formulas of social hypocrisy, written and oral. I also learned that discipline is a sacred thing, especially when it is senseless, and that parents are always right, because they have been wrong too long as children and must take their revenge before it is too late. I further learned that the past is infinitely better than the present, and that the future should reproduce the past; that the feudal system was the only real form of liberty, that people should keep their place, especially those who have none anyway, that people who don't wash their hands are socialists, and that there is, if not God, at least something very mysterious and important which is nobler than us human beings but then also that it takes very little indeed to be nobler than we are so I never knew how flattering this was to God. Later she made a few additions to her knowledge (a thing my father never had to do) and taught me that of course the rain is paid for by the Bolsheviks, but authority is not always a good thing and people who are not born may at times exist just as much as those who are. She taught me that the Jews are as good as the Gentiles, a notion which was inborn in me and strengthened by the teachings of illiterate peasants around me, who were highly civilized people. But alas, she too tried to spare me a certain part of the knowledge she secretly carried in her heart, and that was the only knowledge I really inherited from her and cherish: namely that she thought discipline was foul and ancestors can be as thankless as posterity; that nobody knows anything at all and that the world is a grand place but baffling, very baffling indeed. However, I was also provided with a formal education which enabled me to get some of the most irrefutable nonsense of the world through the living channels of tutors, Kinder-fräuleins and school teachers, and it taught me to think of them exactly what they all knew of themselves and tried to forget and to keep hidden from the others. My education covered several countries and years; I lived through two wars without fighting in any but found myself affected with a strange ailment called War Weariness Without a War, or, to the scientists: W.W.W.W. Which has destroyed whatever faith I had in people and things, and is the main cause of my present and future poverty. This is all. Volumes of lies about me are to be found in the files of the Municipalities of Florence, Italy, Rome, Italy, and in those of the Immigration and Naturalization Division of the Department of Justice in New York City. To complete my life history I must add that my life went through that of one Laura Rusconi of Florence, in the year 1936, with consequences for both of us that may be described as a treaty of mutual aid and assistance, of better understanding between the race of men and that of women, followed by a conspiracy to engage in the production of posterity, so that we may have someone to forget us when we are both gone. We have two specimens of posterity, and time grows in them and around them at terrific speed.

I see that you ask about achievements, too. None. I write stories to describe my failure and my ignorance and the failure and ignorance of many others, always using the present indicative (or if you prefer, the first person) out of politeness.

1946 Niccolò Tucci